CW00420639

DO

DILEMMA

DOUBLE DILEMMA

KAY SILVER

Copyright © 2020 Kay Silver

All rights reserved.

ISBN-13:979-8-69648-607-9

Dedication

I will be forever grateful to:
the amazing Mr Silver, who encouraged and
supported me and shared his technical ability in the
production of this book;
and
my family, who never doubted me.
Thank you.

Special thanks to Adana Gardner who, with unfailing
patience and accuracy, gave freely of her time to copy edit
Double Dilemma. I owe her a debt of gratitude.

Foreword

The characters in this novel are fictional. However, the concentration camps existed, atrocities did happen, the Berlin Wall was real, and Israel as a country did not exist until 1948.

CHAPTER 1

Berlin in 1990. Not long after the fall of the Wall when there was a burgeoning unity between East and West. The deluge of East Berliners had trickled to a steady stream, and Berlin was well able to cope with the newcomers. Hotels and restaurants flourished with new trade, and the lights on the Kurfürstendamm shone even more brightly.

Schönefeld Airport was a fair way from the city centre and Sam's hotel, so he joined the queue for taxis, waiting patiently for his turn. Even though it was midApril, there was a chill in the air, and he turned his coat collar up. It was early afternoon, and he promised himself a brief walk around Berlin once he checked in. It was the first time he'd been to Germany. He corrected himself. It was the first time he'd been to Germany since he left as a baby, after the end of the war. It would be good to acclimatise himself before his all-important interview.

His hotel was set back from the main thoroughfare in a side street near the main shopping area. It was elegantly oldfashioned, with an Eastern European charm. He pushed the revolving door and negotiated his way through, his weekend bag and briefcase banging against his knees. The concierge looked up and smiled briefly.

"Can I help?"

"I have a room reserved. Sam Goldman. Rabbi Sam Goldman."

"Welcome, Rabbi. We have given you a room on the third floor. You have a nice view of the street, but I can promise you it's quiet. We have been renovating the rooms, and you have one of the newly decorated ones." She clicked her fingers, and the uniformed bellboy came over.

"Please take the Rabbi's luggage to room 303." She turned to look at Sam's bags.

"Is this all you have?"

"Yes. I'm only here for a few days, so I don't need much."

"Is there anything else I can get you? Would you like coffee sent up to the room?"

"No, thank you. I'm going to take a brief walk around, and I'll have coffee when I'm out."

The room was large, opulent, almost a suite. Comfortable large settees placed around a coffee table; the heavy, heady smell of late summer roses–their velvety petals drooping a little, one or two gently lying on the polished wood. The bed, high square pillows placed against an upholstered headboard and two fluffy duvets resting gently in tandem, waiting only for the occupants to slide beneath the pristine whiteness, to catch up on much needed sleep.

Sam stood in front of the fireplace, enjoying the warmth, stretching his hands out to the flames. He glanced up, and the mirror above reflected his strong features; light grey hair and beard, just a trace of white at his temples, blue-grey eyes looking a little weary after his tiring journey.

He walked over to the large picture window and moved the drapes aside slightly. He was on the third floor, so low enough to see the street below. There were few people around, but he could see restaurants further down the street, their yellow lights spilling out onto the pavement. He couldn't hear the conversations of the people enjoying a meal or a drink, but he could see the general feeling of relaxation. Waiters with black aprons tied tightly round their waists bustled around, their trays tilting. The brimming glasses of beer were balanced precariously.

He noticed, under a street lamp, a tall figure lighting a cigarette. Further down the road, a car stopped briefly to allow its passengers to get out. A young couple crossed the road, dodging the cars, and ran into the café, laughing at each other. The Berlin of 1990 was a very different city to the one before the Wall came down.

He glanced at the luggage rack, deciding to leave unpacking until later. His weekend case could wait until after he'd had a coffee and a brief rest. He was only in Berlin for a short time, so he needed few clothes. His briefcase was probably the most important bag he had with him. It contained all the paperwork he needed for his interview.

A slight sound caught his attention. Turning round he saw, out of the corner of his eye, a brown envelope sliding under the door. Sighing, he went to pick it up. Work already, and he'd only been in Berlin a couple of hours.

He put the envelope on the table and made a cup of coffee. How wonderful and how unusual to have a kettle in a hotel room. Perhaps work could wait until the morning? He could leave the envelope unopened. Common sense prevailed. It could be important–a message from Helen or the children, something from the synagogue, possibly a note from the Chief Rabbi. Sighing, he ran his finger under the flap, and a small sheet of paper fell out. There were only a few words on it.

"You are me, and I am you. Meet me in the coffee shop in twenty minutes. You will recognise me."

Sam knew no-one in Berlin. He had no idea who the message was from but, wary of danger, he decided to ignore it. It could be some crank, someone who wanted to spook him. Even now, over 45 years after the end of the war, there was AntiSemitism. The Berlin Wall had only been down for a few short months, and all sorts of people had come out of the woodwork. The bed beckoned, and he loosened his tie.

The phone rang, disturbing his thoughts. Wearily he picked up the receiver, expecting it to be one of the conference organisers.

"Have you opened the envelope?" a heavily accented voice asked. "I am waiting for you. I am in the coffee shop, by the window. It is quiet–not many people around so we can talk."

"Who is this?" asked Sam. "I've just arrived, and I'm tired. If this is about the conference, can we talk about it in the morning?"

"No," said the voice. "Tomorrow will not do. It must be now. You must learn the truth before your meeting can go ahead."

"Who are you?" Sam asked again. "It's late, and I really think it would be better if you explained who you are and why you have to meet me now."

There was a silence, then the voice said again,

"You must come now. Or I can come to your room. I know the number."

The fact that the stranger knew his room number was alarming. Thinking rapidly, Sam made a decision.

"I'll be with you in five minutes but we can only talk briefly."

Replacing the receiver firmly on its rest, he picked up his room key and went out of the door. There was something very unsettling about this conversation, and it was better he should meet whoever it was in a public place.

The iron lift groaned and wheezed its way down the floors, coming to an asthmatic stop in the foyer. The concierge barely noticed him as he stepped out of the lift, and his heels clicked on the marble floors as he turned to the right. He saw his reflection in the plate-glass windows of the coffee shop and ran his fingers through his hair to smooth it down. A couple came out, arms linked, and the warm smell of coffee wafted towards him. It reminded him of the cup he'd made and left on the table without drinking.

His caller was right. There were only a few people in the room, and Sam looked around to see if he could locate the mystery person who had said he would be recognised. The tables were spread apart; on each one a menu and a condiment set. He saw on the wall adjacent to the door the wooden rollers holding copies of the day's papers for the customers to read.

Partly screened by a large palm, sat a tallish man, a newspaper held in front of him so that his face was in the shadows. As Sam approached, the man stood up and removed his hat. With a shock, Sam looked into the eyes of the stranger, seeing a mirror image of himself but clean shaven.

"Sit down," said the man. "You've had a shock. Let me get you a drink." He raised his hand and beckoned a waiter.

"Two brandies," he said. "Large, and two coffees."

The two men sat facing each other in silence until the order was put on the table. The waiter bustled about, moving the menu and setting out the cups and saucers, placing the coffee pot precisely in the middle, adding paper napkins until Sam eventually said,

"That's okay. We'll manage now. Thank you."

And then Sam looked straight at the man sitting opposite.

"I don't understand," he said. "What is this all about? Who are you?"

The man smiled, but it was not pleasant. He looked at Sam and shrugged his shoulders.

"In a way you've answered my questions. I always wondered if you knew. If you knew and didn't want to know, or didn't want to accept it. It's obvious that you have no idea who I am and so no idea who you are. But I am you, and you are me."

He picked up his glass of brandy and swallowed it in one gulp.

"I could tell you, but you wouldn't believe me. Talk to your mother. She is the one who should tell you. She is the one who should burst your bubble. Talk to Eva. It's time you knew the facts and, until you know the truth, you should not, must not, proceed with your meeting."

"How did you know about the meeting? In fact, how did you know I would be here?"

"It's not important how I know these things. Just let me tell you that I know all about you and have done for quite a while." The look on his face was threatening, and Sam moved back in his chair.

The stranger stood up and moved towards the door, then stopped and turned and spoke again to Sam.

"There are some things which can change the course of our lives. You need to work out if this is one."

The swing door of the coffee shop clanged shut, and Sam was left alone and shaken. The brandy helped a little, and the coffee cleared his head. He knew that he would have to ask his mother who the man was, and he would have to do it as soon as possible. Before that, though, he needed to sort out the following day. He drained his coffee and left some marks under the saucer to cover the cost. The waiter looked surprised. He had thought Sam's impatience meant he was dissatisfied with the service but, when he counted the money, he saw there was a generous tip.

There was no sign of the mysterious stranger in the foyer and, as Sam waited for the lift to arrive, he thought over the encounter. He definitely felt unsettled–intrigued and worried. His interview tomorrow was perhaps the most important interview of his life. It was the culmination of a series of meetings, interviews and 'heart to hearts' with different rabbis. If he succeeded, he would have reached the pinnacle of his career. Now was not the time for anything to go wrong.

He would phone his mother, but he had a feeling that calling Eva wouldn't solve the problem. He had a choice. He could ignore this whole worrying episode, or he could try and find out what it meant. If Eva was the key, a conversation might be enough but, knowing his mother, Sam rather doubted that she would talk on the phone. If he wanted to make sense of what was happening, he would have to ask Rabbi Langer for a postponement of his interview, and this would not go down well with the old man.

The lift bell clanged, and Sam pressed the button for his floor. There was a faint smell of roses, and he mused that everywhere in this hotel there were flowers, a far cry from the old days he felt, when the communist rule meant austerity.

His key fitted easily in the lock, and he dropped it on the coffee table, glancing around. There was something a little odd –something out of place. Maybe the maid had been in to turn the bed down, but it was still as he'd left it. He glanced at the luggage rack, and it seemed that his bag had moved slightly. He shook his head and reminded himself he wasn't in the middle of a spy movie. He must have caught it as he went out.

He thought over what he would say to his mother. It sounded totally illogical. A strange man came to my room, asked me to meet him in the coffee shop. When I said I was tired, he offered to come to my room, and I was worried he might be a lunatic, so I said I would go to the coffee shop. When I got there, I thought he looked like me, and then he told me to call you. Can you tell me what this is all about? Sam groaned. Maybe he was in the middle of a spy movie.

CHAPTER 2

The time in Berlin was six pm, but it was only five o'clock in England. Sam knew he should call and speak to Eva, assuming she was in and not at one of her bridge afternoons or out to tea with friends. Once the situation was a little clearer, maybe he would be able to continue with the conference with a clear head. He would wait until he'd spoken to his mother in case it wasn't necessary to call Rabbi Langer and re-arrange his meeting on the following day. Maybe he was re-acting too swiftly. Maybe she could tell him all he needed to know on the phone, and he wouldn't have to rush off back to England. He rubbed his temple. So many maybes, he thought.

His room was warm, and he sat on the chair by the bed and picked up the receiver. It wasn't possible to call England direct from the hotel. He had to use the exchange and wait for the international operator. Eventually he heard his mother's voice.

"Hallo," she said, the slight accent giving away her birth. "Hallo. Who is that?"

"Hallo," Sam replied. "It's me, Ma."

"Is everything all right? Why are you calling? Is something wrong?"

Despite his concern, Sam smiled. Typical Eva, always thinking the worst, always worrying, and this trip in particular had been worse than usual. He had tried to explain the importance of it before he left, but Eva was still not convinced he needed to go.

"I was a Berliner," she had said. "I know what it was like during the war for us. Why would you want to go there? You know how I suffered, how your father suffered, how we are lucky to be alive. You, too, are lucky to be alive."

Sam had tried to explain.

"This is a really important interview. A small conference, really. I did tell you, Ma. I have been selected as one of three rabbis on the short list for the next Chief Rabbi. We all have to go to Berlin so we can appear before the panel because Rabbi Brauman is not well enough to travel anywhere. Rabbi Zimmerman is coming from France and Rabbi Langer from Belgium. We will all be interviewed, and the panel will make the decision as to who will be the next Chief Rabbi. This is the last stage in the interview process, and you know, Ma, this is what I want, and I think it is what Pa would have wanted also."

Eva had shaken her head. Chief Rabbi, of course, would be wonderful as long as going to Berlin or anywhere else in Germany was not involved.

"I want what you want, Sam," she said, "but not Germany. Not Berlin. Too many bad memories."

"Without Germany, this will not happen," Sam said, "so I have to go."

"And what about Helen?" asked Eva. "What does she think? Her parents also are Holocaust survivors. How will they feel about you going to a country which was so determined to eliminate all the Jews?"

Sam had looked at Eva.

"That's not fair, Ma," he said. "I have to do this. Helen will support what I do, and her parents will accept the outcome. I may not even be chosen, but at least I have to try."

Sam came back to the present and listened to his mother.

Eva was still talking, asking the reason for the call. Sam found himself in a difficult situation. He wanted to ask Eva questions which he suspected she would find very difficult to answer. And perhaps this was not the right time or place. She could be evasive on the phone. She could refuse to talk with him. She could even hang up. He made a quick decision.

"I'm coming home, Ma. As soon as I can get a flight."

"But what about your interview?"

"I'll ask for it to be postponed. I can get home tomorrow, talk to you, and then be back before the weekend. I think that will work."

He put the phone down, and wondered if he had imagined the catch in Eva's breath. He hadn't given her the opportunity to argue before he'd cut the call short. Time now to call Helen, re-arrange the hotel, and make his apologies to the interview panel. Whoever the man was who had started this chain of events, Sam had no doubt it was a serious problem and one which needed to be resolved before he met the rabbis.

Helen answered the phone after the first ring. She was expecting a 'Goodnight' call, not a worried sounding Sam telling her he was coming back. She was curious about why Sam was coming home.

"You've only just got there, Sam," she said. "And you've had a hard week. Do you really need to do this?"

"I don't know what it's about," Sam said, "but there is something unfathomable about this, and I think my mother is the key." He took a deep breath.

"Helen, this man; it was like looking at myself in the mirror but, again, it wasn't me. I don't know how to describe it but, whatever it is, I have to sort it out. I'll get the first flight out of Berlin and be home as quickly as possible. See you tomorrow."

Helen put the receiver down thoughtfully. She could tell that Sam, usually so calm and measured, was deeply worried by this encounter. And what was it, in fact? A strange man who looked like him, who said he should talk to his mother. With a sigh, she locked the front door and decided an early night would be good.

Rabbi Langer was not impressed when Sam explained he needed to postpone the meeting and was planning to return to England immediately.

"You've only just got here," he said, somewhat petulantly. "You know you are my favourite contender for the job. Don't do this, Sam. It could affect everything you've worked so hard to achieve."

Sam rubbed his head thoughtfully. He knew that Rabbi Langer could be right. To have got so far was nothing short of a miracle, but continuing with the interview might be the worst mistake of his life. He had to go back to England.

"Can you tell me why, Sam?" asked the old rabbi. "Why are you so insistent you need to do this?"

"I can't explain," said Sam, "but something has happened which has made me realise there is something in my past which I need to find out about. I can't go any further with this until I know what it is. I promise I'll tell you as soon as I know myself."

He replaced the receiver and went to his briefcase to get his plane ticket. He would have to cancel and rebook, but he knew there was an early flight from Schönefeld Airport. He only hoped that there would be an available seat.

The travel assistant was efficient and kind but explained that there just weren't any seats on the early flight.

"A lot of people take this flight because they have morning meetings in London," he said. "I'm sorry, sir, there just isn't anything available. Of course, if it's an emergency, we do have a seat in First Class, but that would cost more money." Briefly, Sam weighed up what he wanted to do, but he heard himself saying,

"That's all right. I'll take it." As he gave his credit card number, he wondered what Helen would say once she knew how much the ticket had cost. It was probably the same amount of money as the new settee she wanted. He pushed that thought out of his mind and called Reception.

"It's Rabbi Goldman in room 303. Can you have my bill ready, please? I have to leave very early tomorrow morning." He listened to the voice at the end of the phone.

"Yes, an unexpected problem, but I should be back in a couple of days. Yes, please. An early morning call would be a good idea. Say 5am. Thank you."

His toilet bag was still in the case, so he went to get it out. He was sure it had been right at the top but, when he unzipped the weekend bag fully, he saw it was under a pile of shirts. It must have moved when he lifted the case onto the rack.

He looked at the coffee which was now stone cold, deciding that it wasn't a good idea to make another one. He felt wired enough as it was. Maybe that walk he had promised himself would be a good idea.

The revolving door spun behind him and he hesitated slightly before deciding whether to go right or left. It was still early for people to eat dinner, but the coffee shops were doing good business. The smell of toasted sandwiches was quite tantalising, and his empty stomach reminded him he hadn't eaten since breakfast. That was the trouble with trying to finish work, make phone calls, and catch planes. Helen was forever reminding him to eat.

He turned left and went onto the Kurfürstendamm and stopped in front of a café with tables set on the pavement. The checked cloths fluttered slightly in the light breeze, and that made him feel he would rather be inside. There was a comfortable fug in the room, and the menu looked interesting. There were plenty of vegetarian options, sandwiches and toasties, and his mouth watered at the possibility of a good bowl of potato soup with dumplings and maybe some herring and definitely a cup of good strong coffee.

He let his mind go back to the strange encounter, looking up as a shadow passed the window. The silhouette of a man wearing a hat went by. Sam thought for a moment it was the stranger who had met him in the hotel's coffee shop. He gave himself a shake. He was seeing strangers and mysteries everywhere.

His food arrived, the steam rising from the plate and tempting his taste buds. The waiter brought some dark rye bread and creamy butter and placed a jug of water and a glass at the side of Sam's plate.

"Gut, yah?" he asked, and Sam nodded. "Are you on holiday?" he went on.

"Not exactly. A kind of business trip, but your food is so good I'm glad I came."

The waiter smiled and moved to the next table and, when Sam had finished, he brought him some herring and more of the bread. Sam thought to himself that you can always tell a good restaurant when they replenish the bread basket.

The coffee was just as good as the food, and he took a second cup, briefly wondering if it would keep him awake. He decided that so much had happened during the day that nothing would keep him from his rest. A good night's sleep would refresh him.

The walk back to the hotel was pleasant, although the light was fading. He could see Luna Park in the distance. How the children would have enjoyed that when they were younger, but he didn't think it would be much of an attraction now that twins Daniel and Esther were at university.

He looked briefly into the illuminated shop windows. When he left in the morning, the shops would still be closed, so he wouldn't be able to get a gift for Helen or his mother. Maybe Eva wouldn't accept anything from Germany, he thought. She was so intransigent in her feelings about the country. He decided a gift for Eva could wait until after his next visit. Helen would understand if he went home empty handed. There was always a duty-free shop at the airport for perfume if he had time.

Every now and then as he walked, he had a feeling that someone was behind him. At the corner he stopped and took time looking at the reflections in a shop window, but he couldn't see anything. There wasn't anything concrete, just a strange feeling of being followed. He was glad to see the hotel ahead, spilling bright lights into the street.

CHAPTER 3

Despite the warm bed, Sam couldn't sleep. The coffee? No, he thought, the strange situation in which he found himself. He puzzled over the riddle the strange man had set him. 'I am you and you are me.' He thought about the shock he'd had when he saw the face of the stranger, looking just like his own. In his youth, he'd read books about the similarities between people, doppelgangers they were called, but this seemed more than that. It was almost as if he knew the man. Knew and didn't like him. And the more he thought about it, the more he stayed awake.

At 4.30am, no longer able to lie in his comfortable bed, Sam got up and pulled back the drapes. Rainwater glistened against the window pane and, several floors below, the early morning trams clanged their way along the street. The day held a promise of sunshine, the first feeble rays lightening the darkness of the night.

Swiftly dressing, he picked up his overnight bag and keys and left the room. The night porter looked at him in surprise.

"Leaving already?" he asked. "I thought you were here for a few days."

"Something's cropped up at home," said Sam briefly, "but I expect to be back in a couple of days. I told the desk clerk last night, and so my bill should be ready. Could you call me a taxi to the airport, please? I'm on an early flight." He handed over his credit card then signed the bill. The taxi was already waiting outside, and the driver leaned over to open the passenger door. "Goldman?" he asked. Sam nodded and tossed his weekend bag onto the back seat.

The drive to the airport was smooth, and there were few cars about, but Sam was conscious of a presence behind him. He looked around but could see no-one. A few early morning cyclists on their way to work – a lone man standing under the pale light of a lamppost, and then the taxi picked up speed. And yet he still had an uneasy thought that someone was watching him. The hair on the back of his neck bristled, and he rubbed his hands over it, trying to eradicate the feeling.

He was soon checked in and on the plane. He settled back, waiting for takeoff and a welcome drink, but the sleepless night had taken its toll upon him, and his eyelids drooped. He slept, waking only when the announcement to put the seatbelt on came over the PA system. Smiling wryly, he realised he'd never taken it off and had even missed the breakfast service.

There were no bags to collect, so he was through customs quickly and outside in the damp London air, queuing for a taxi to get home. Everything seemed normal, and the driver was cheerful, asking him if he'd been on holiday. Sam gave his address and answered briefly, saying he'd been away on business.

The driver glanced at him through the mirror, sensing that he had a passenger who didn't want to talk. He left Sam alone, only telling him the cost of the ride as he pulled up outside the house.

Helen was in the kitchen, preparing lunch.

"So what's the mystery, Sam?" she said, putting down the spoon she'd been stirring the soup with and coming over to kiss him.

"I'll tell you what I can, but first some tea. I didn't have breakfast in the hotel, and I slept on the plane."

"OK, Sam, but I want to know what's going on. I can't imagine what could have made you fly home without seeing the panel. I know how much you want this, and I know what it means to you."

"I'm not sure where to start. I had a peculiar encounter with a strange man who told me I shouldn't proceed with the interview and that I needed to talk to my mother."

"And, on the basis of that, you left everything and came home? Sam, I can't believe that you would do something so reckless." She looked carefully at him.

"I know. It's seems totally illogical, but there is something there. Something strange, and I need to find out just what it is. There is no way I can go before a panel if there is something wrong in my life. I have to be totally honest. Totally above board."

"Sam, be logical. What can there be in your life that isn't honest?"

"I don't know, so I need to talk to Eva."

"Are you sure that's a good idea? She's over 70 and not in good health. Maybe this kind of conversation could be bad for her. And, anyway, how could anything Eva might have done affect you becoming the Chief Rabbi?" she asked.

"I know," said Sam thoughtfully, "but this might be my only opportunity, and I need to find out."

"This is so unlike you, Sam. You're such a calm, rational person, and to come back like this just because a strange man said something. To risk everything…"

"I can't explain," Sam interrupted. "I really can't. All I know is that, when I saw this guy, it was like looking at myself in a mirror. Helen, I tell you, it was like looking at my brother, my twin, even. And it wasn't a good feeling."

While Sam had been speaking, Helen had dished up a bowl of soup.

"It's not quite lunch time, Sam," she said, "but you look as if you could do with something hot inside you."

She passed him a spoon and some bread and watched him carefully as he ate. He looked abstracted – worried even. Certainly apprehensive and not at all like the Sam she knew and had been married to for over twenty years.

"So what now?" she asked. "What are you going to do?"

"Well, much as I'm apprehensive about it, I have to talk to Ma. I think she may be the key to all this."

The phone rang, and Helen answered it.

"Yes, he's here," Sam heard her say. "Who's calling?"

Wordlessly she passed the receiver to Sam, shrugging her shoulders.

"Have you spoken to Eva?" asked the voice Sam recognised as belonging to the man from the coffee shop.

"How did you know my number?" Sam asked, shaken.

"You must speak to her before it's too late," the voice continued, and the call was disconnected.

"Darling, what is it?" asked Helen. "You look as if you've seen a ghost."

"It was the guy from Berlin. I recognised his voice, even though I've only heard it once before. I don't know how he knew the number or that I was back." With a shiver, Sam remembered the feeling he'd had of being watched.

"Helen, I must call Ma before this whole thing gets out of hand. I need to find out what's going on." He slowly dialed his mother's number.

"Sam. Is that you? Where are you? Are you all right?"

"Yes, of course it's me. I'm home, and I'm fine." Sam smiled to himself. Forty-six years old, a married man, and a rabbi to boot. And still his mother worried over him.

"Ma, I need to talk to you. Can I come over? I can be with you in twenty minutes."

"Oh Sam, it's not a good time." Eva hesitated. "I have to go out. It's my bridge game this afternoon. Maybe another day."

"Ma, this won't wait. I only have a few hours, then I have to go back to Berlin."

"But it's not convenient," Eva reiterated.

"Convenient or not, I'll be with you in twenty minutes. And, if you go out, I'll just wait until you get home," he added.

Sam replaced the receiver thoughtfully.

"You know, Helen," he said. "This is the first time Ma's ever said not to come. Usually she says I don't see her enough. There is something she's never told me, and I have to know what it is. And even though I only said I wanted to go over and see her, and I didn't give her any idea why, I'm sure she knows what I want to talk about."

21

"Do you want me to come with you?"

"Thank you for offering, but no. I think Eva might speak to me better if I'm on my own." Gathering up his keys and coat, he kissed Helen and shut the front door quietly behind him.

He had time to think during the drive, but he still couldn't imagine what Eva might tell him. He would have to wait until he saw her. Sam knocked at the door of his mother's home. There was no reply, so he let himself into the house.

CHAPTER 4

In Berlin, the three rabbis sat in Rabbi Brauman's book-lined study, drinking tea. The table was spread with papers and the tea glasses were balanced precariously on top of various stacks of books. A plate of cookies nestled in between a pile of newspapers.

"Maybe it's time for something stronger," suggested the frail rabbi.

"A whisky, perhaps?"

"And then we should get down to business. What do you think the problem is with Sam?" asked Rabbi Zimmerman.

"Usually, he's so precise, so methodical. This cancelling...?"

"Postponing," interjected Rabbi Langer swiftly.

"Cancelling, postponing, however you say it, the man's not here. And if this is how he treats the most important interview of his life, I'm not sure he is the right man for the job."

"I can't imagine he would have done this without thinking of the consequences," said Rabbi Langer, "so it must be important."

"Well," said Rabbi Brauman, "I may be old and sick, but I can see who you favour, Isaac."

"Stop, stop. We'll get nowhere like this. We have to decide if we cancel the panel completely, go ahead with the remaining candidates, or wait and see if Sam comes back."

"We'll wait till he comes back," said Rabbi Langer firmly.

"All right, then. Let's have a preliminary look at what we've got. Are we agreed we shouldn't cancel yet?"

The others nodded their heads. The whisky bottle was passed around, glasses filled, and the three old men spread their papers out on the wellworn table.

"Let's begin with Walter Emmanuel. We should do this in alphabetical order."

"He's the right age, over fifty. He has a sensible wife…"

"And she doesn't work," interrupted Rabbi Brauman.

"Hard to work with six kids," added Rabbi Langer. "But I'm not sure it's such a good thing to be a stay-at-home wife."

"Careful, now," Rabbi Brauman continued. "It's Walter we're interviewing, not his wife."

"So it is. So it is," said Rabbi Zimmerman. "But a Chief Rabbi needs a wife who can be with him, support him, and still have interests of her own. Perhaps a wife who doesn't work would be too wrapped up in her own life and family."

"And perhaps a stay-at-home wife would have more time to help her husband with his career. A working wife might not have time to get involved with the community."

Rabbi Langer cleared his throat.

"What of Walter himself? He's been rabbi of his community since he was ordained. Over twenty-five years."

"It's a small community," said the elderly rabbi, "but, when Walter first went there, it was even smaller. He's been able to grow that community, make it stronger."

"And he's dealt with all the little problems," said Rabbi Brauman.

"As well as the not so little ones," added Rabbi Langer.

"True. I remember the problem with the Soloman family. Walter dealt with that very well. I don't know how the community would have coped if Mr. Soloman had continued to refuse his wife a divorce. As it was, he granted her a get, and she moved on."

"Moved away too." All three men smiled at that.

"Moved on, moved away. However you put it, everything worked out in the end, and now they've both remarried. Mr. Soloman is still shul chairman, and the wife he divorced has a new husband and a new family, which wouldn't have been possible without Walter's help."

"Still," said Rabbi Langer, "you can't make a man the Chief Rabbi because he stayed with a community for over twenty-five years and he managed to sort out a 'domestic.' There has to be more than that."

"Well, of course, Walter's an academic. He's already published three books, and he writes for the JC," said Rabbi Brauman.

"Not everyone reads the Jewish Chronicle," said Rabbi Langer jokingly. "I'm not sure that's a good recommendation."

The others laughed with him.

There was a knock at the study door. Rabbi Brauman smiled. "It'll be Miriam. That woman thinks if I haven't eaten for an hour I might die of starvation." The three rabbis waited expectantly for the rebbitzin to come in. "So," said Rabbi Brauman, "what have you brought? I'll take the tray," he said, moving to help his wife.

"Now look," said Miriam. "People here, and such eminent people, too, and no food on the table. Please, take a little. Some chopped herring, maybe. A biscuit?"

She moved the whisky bottle aside and pushed the papers over so the laden tray would find a place on the cluttered table.

"Tsk, tsk," she complained but with a smile. "So untidy. How can you ever find anything in all this mess? Yes, yes, alright, I'll go and leave you to it. But you need food for your body so that you can feed your brain." The door clicked shut, and the three men looked at each other.

"Well, yes. We can eat and talk. Help yourselves. Make yourselves more comfortable. This discussion may take some time. We've looked at Walter; now what do you think about Isidore Goldstein?"

"A good candidate," ventured Rabbi Zimmerman. "Gives a good sermon. Gives good advice too. Follows the rules."

"Maybe a little boring?" countered Rabbi Langer. "Maybe lacking in humour?"

"Maybe both of these things, but a hard, consistent worker," said the old rabbi. "We need strong leadership, someone not afraid to make decisions which sometimes might be a bit unpopular."

"I don't agree," Rabbi Langer interjected. "We need someone who can identify with the communities. Maybe Izzy is a bit too aloof? Would you go to him with a problem?" He pushed his glasses more firmly up the bridge of his nose. "Would you feel comfortable telling him very personal things?"

"And he's not married. I think it's always good for a Chief Rabbi to have a wife. Someone the ladies can go to if they have personal problems – things the ladies wouldn't want to talk to a man about."

Rabbi Brauman and Rabbi Zimmerman nodded at this, imagining a situation where one of the women in their own communities might have a problem, and they would have to deal with it on their own. Each shuddered at such a ghastly thought. They both had comfortable wives, always ready to help in a situation where the rabbi might feel a little out of his depth. Rabbi Langer looked at them over the rim of his glasses.

"That's a good point, but you can't decide that someone doesn't meet the criteria because he's not married. This is a job for a man, after all." Rabbi Langer made his point firmly and then looked surprised as the other two said, almost simultaneously, "It's a job for a partnership…and a solid one at that."

Rabbi Brauman ignored their riposte. He lifted the tea pot and poured the hot liquid into the waiting glasses.

"Take some tea," he urged, proffering the sliced lemon and sugar. "Tea will lubricate our throats."

"But maybe not as well as the whisky, eh?" smiled the others.

"We need to move on to Sam, even though there is some doubt as to whether or not he's still in the running," said Rabbi Zimmerman. "We should at least consider him."

"Do we know what's happening with him? I must say, it's not like him to be so unpredictable. I've always felt that one of his strong points was his steadfastness."

"Mmm," said Rabbi Langer. "You all know that I think he's the best man for the job. I've known Sam almost since he was born. In fact, I did his brit milah." They all smiled.

"Even though he was older than eight days. He was born in a camp and he's lucky to have survived. I met his mother at the end of the war, when Sam was only a few months old. His mother had no idea where her husband was. She thought he had been killed.

"She'd been living in the ruins of Berlin, and I, too, was trying to find anyone left alive. Everywhere there was rubble and destroyed houses, bricks and dust and carnage. People left notes pinned to door frames, asking for information about their loved ones." He stared into space.

"I was lucky. I was in a camp, too, but somehow I managed to survive. There was a great deal of camaraderie in that camp. I was needed, and I was doing good work. God's work, and I think God wanted me to stay alive to continue it."

The other two nodded their heads in agreement. The memories of the war were still fresh enough in their minds for them to remember the hardships.

"And so," he continued, "when I met Eva and Sam it was a kind of miracle. Here was a child, a boy, who had survived the camps, who was still with his mother. It *was* a miracle," he repeated. "And this boy became a symbol of the future for me. In the middle of all the mess, the devastation, we had a brit – a circumcision. Can you imagine what that was like? No sandek or kvatter, no godparents, only Eva and

28

Sam and me, in a bombed-out house. And yet, it was the most spiritual time. Sam just looked at me as if he knew how important it was. I made up my mind that I would keep an eye on him, and I have. I have watched out for him all his life. From near and far."

The other two nodded. They knew of the connection between this old rabbi and Sam but not why.

"That explains a lot," said Rabbi Brauman. "I didn't know why you had such an interest in Sam, but now it's clear."

"But that still doesn't mean he's the right man for the job," Rabbi Zimmerman said softly. "The connection you have is emotional, and we need to be practical. Let's look at what he's been doing over the years."

The whisky bottle was passed around again, the plate of kichel almost emptied.

"Maybe I should ask Miriam for more," Rabbi Brauman said with a smile. "Maybe a few sandwiches?"

"No, maybe later, when we've finished our deliberations."

"You're right. So, how about Sam, then? Married, two children both doing well, an exemplary wife, a good pulpit and a strong academic background. His time teaching students will hold him in good stead…"

"And his last book about problems facing modern orthodoxy was most enlightening," interrupted Rabbi Zimmerman. "Although I can't say I agreed with everything he said."

"Well," interrupted Rabbi Langer, "if you agreed with everything anyone said, it would be a first." They laughed.

Rabbi Zimmerman's argumentative approach to life was well known.

"We need to leave it now," said Rabbi Langer. "I have no doubt that Sam will call me soon, and then we can find out what is going on. We can make a decision as to the way ahead after that."

Miriam Brauman came discreetly into the room, adding some coal to the fire and clearing plates. She glanced at the three men. Rabbi Langer, tall and spare, with a grey beard and a warm smiling face; Rabbi Zimmerman, restless, aesthetic, tapping a pencil on his writing pad; and her own dear husband sitting in his wellloved armchair. His lined face was showing signs of age and worry, but still he kept working.

"I'm sorry to hurry you, gentlemen," she said, "but Nathan has a class in," she looked at her plain simple watch, "twenty minutes. Just enough time for him to find his papers," she added indulgently. "Although, how anyone can find anything in this muddle, I really don't know."

There was a flurry of movement. Coats and umbrellas were reconciled with their owners, hats placed carefully onto grey heads.

Rabbi Langer paused at the doorway. "I will call as soon as I know anything about Sam," he said. "I would really like to get a decision made so we could make an announcement soon."

The door closed softly and the two rabbis went out into the cold Berlin air.

CHAPTER 5

Although only lunchtime, the room was in semidarkness. The blinds were down and the curtains were drawn across the windows. Eva was sitting on the sofa, a newspaper beside her, but she wasn't reading. She constantly touched the string of pearls at her neck.

"You didn't answer the door," said Sam

"No. I knew you had a key. I'm not feeling too well today."

Sam looked at his mother. She did seem pale. Her hands were anxiously twisting a handkerchief.

"What's the matter, Ma?" he asked. "Do you have a cold?"

"No, not a cold," Eva said, "just a cold feeling in my heart. I know, I know, Sam. You have questions. And I will answer them but in my own way. But first, did you eat? Some tea, maybe?"

"Tea would be good, Ma. I had soup a little while ago, so I'm not hungry, but tea is just what I need."

Eva got up slowly from the settee and, as Sam looked at her, he was suddenly aware that she was getting older. He had never thought of Eva as getting old. She was always vigorous, busy with her various interests and with a very full life. He watched her as she straightened her pleated skirt before leaving the room.

The familiar sounds came from the kitchen. The rush of water filling the kettle, the rattle of cups on the tray – the opening of the fridge door for milk and then the hiss of the boiling water going into the teapot. No teabags for Ma. Sam smiled to himself as he listened to the rustle of the biscuit wrappers. No matter what, she would feed him.

He moved the flowers on the coffee table to make room for the tray and waited for the china cup and saucer to be passed to him.

"Ma. We have to talk. I don't know what this is all about, but you have to tell me how you are mixed up in all this."

"So, tell me, Sam. What is it you want to know?"

"Sit down, Ma. I'll explain to you what's happened, even though I don't understand." He patted the settee. Sit beside me. "You know I had to go to Berlin, and I know you didn't want me to, but it was, it is, necessary. This opportunity is so important to me. Even if I'm not appointed Chief Rabbi, I will know I was good enough to be considered.

"I was in my hotel room, when a letter slid under the door. I thought it was about the meeting but, when I opened it, it was an invitation to meet someone in the coffee bar. It was strange, unnerving, and I wasn't going to do anything about it. There are still a lot of cranks out there." He laughed, and Eva sat watching him carefully.

"Go on, Sam," she said.

"So then the phone rang. This voice speaking in English but with an accent, told me to meet him in the coffee shop. I wasn't going to. I told him, 'No,' but then he said he would come up to the room, and there was something even more scary about that. I decided I didn't want to meet a strange man alone in the room.

"I took the lift and I went to the coffee shop and there, in the corner, a man was sitting – a man I had never met before. When he got up, I got such a shock. It was like looking at myself in the mirror. Ma, I tell you, it was like looking at my brother. He told me to talk to you, and then he left."

Eva sat very still, only her twisting hands giving away her anxiety.

He went on,

"What is this all about? If it concerns me, I think I have the right to know. And from what this chap said, it will affect my standing with the interview board. I don't want to be dramatic, Ma, but I think it could affect the rest of my life."

Eva got up and stood by the door. She pulled her blue cardigan closely to her.

"I can't do this. This is something I never thought I would have to tell you. I just don't know where to start."

"So, do as you always told me when I was a child. Start at the beginning." Sam sipped at his tea, watching Eva from lowered eyes. He saw how she shook and how she made a conscious effort to control herself.

"Come on, Ma", he cajoled. "It'll get easier once you get going."

"I don't think so. I really don't think so," said Eva. "But it's time. You need to know. And afterwards…well, we'll just have to deal with it."

She took a deep breath and sat down again. "I need to tell you about my life in Germany before the war so you can understand what happened later."

"I think that's a good place to start," Sam interrupted. "You've never really spoken about it. Rachel and I have often wondered but we always thought it was too painful for you to remember. When we were kids, Rachel and I used to make up stories about you and Grandma and Grandpa, but we never really knew if that's what it was like when you were little. We never knew, never met our grandparents."

"I know," said Eva. "They were lost; I would say murdered, in one of the camps. I don't have photographs or anything to remember them by. I don't have a grave to visit, to put a stone on. I have only my memories and, as I get older, they seem so distant. It was all such a long time ago, but we shouldn't forget." She wiped her eyes with the handkerchief.

Sam took her hand. "Go on, Ma. Go on."

"So, I was born…you know this already…but I will start at the beginning. I was born in 1913, just before the first world war. 'The war to end all wars,' they said, only it didn't. My father, your grandfather, was a doctor, and he went to serve in the German Army as a medic. He never spoke about his experiences, but I know they affected him and never left him.

"I grew up in a little village in the mountains, and my Papa was the village doctor. There were few Jews there – a couple of families only, but it didn't matter. Everyone knew everyone, and we all got on well together. I was a bright child, studious and hard working. I enjoyed school, I played tennis, I had piano lessons. I went for walks with my two sisters and my brother. It was a very normal childhood."

Sam interrupted. "You had piano lessons. Ma, I've never heard you play the piano. The only time I've ever seen you go near it was when you polished it. It was always Dad who played. I didn't even know you could play."

"I had my reasons, Sam. And, besides, there was no need to play when other people in the house were so musical." She reminisced, "I remember you and Rachel playing, then fighting over the piano. I was sad when you gave up but glad that Rachel carried on. And," she smiled, "she's not bad."

"Anyway, when I was eighteen, I went to study in Berlin. I wanted to be a doctor like my father, and he was quite enlightened. Unusually for a Jewish Papa, he was happy for me to go to university a long way off. I had two years in medical school before Hitler began his regime in 1933. I was twenty, idealistic, and couldn't possibly have seen the future. I had met a boy – he was two years older than me, so ahead in his studies. He just had his last year to complete before he started in the hospital.

"That summer of 1933 was in many ways idyllic. I took Friedrich home to meet my parents. They liked him and had no objection to us getting married, just not so soon. I was only twenty, and they wanted me to wait. I also wanted to finish my studies and become a qualified doctor. We planned to join my father in his practice. At some time, he would retire, and we would continue his work.

"In January 1933, there had been problems in attending schools and colleges if you were Jewish." Her lips twisted as she remembered. "Only five percent of the students could be

Jewish, and at the time, it was boys…men…who were enrolled. The girls lost out. I wasn't able to go back to school, my permit was revoked, and so I had to wave Friedrich off to start his new term. I watched him walk down the mountain to get to the road until I couldn't see him anymore. He was just a distant dark speck against the green of the meadow.

"It's strange, because, as he walked off, I could still see the flowers in the hedges, pink and blue. I could still smell their delicate perfume. The birds carried on singing, but I thought that my world had come to an end. I was devastated that I could no longer study, and I was frightened I might never see Friedrich again.

"Friedrich resumed his studies, and he wrote, of course. I needn't have worried about whether or not our love was strong enough to stand the separation. I treasured those letters, Sam. I can still remember what he wrote but, of course, they were lost in the war. They were so important to me in a world which was constantly changing.

"The restrictions against Jews got harsher, but in our mountain home I suppose we were a little naive. Papa was kept busy with the usual ailments, and he encouraged me to help him. He didn't have a practice nurse, so he was glad that I had some knowledge, and he taught me as we worked together.

"Friedrich graduated, but Jews were not allowed to attend graduation ceremonies. There was no actual refusal for me because, in fact, I didn't apply to go. I knew there were restrictions on the movement of Jews. I felt safe in the mountains, and I saw the wisdom of Papa's decision that we should stay home and keep a low profile.

"Friedrich understood and sent photographs of himself wearing the black gown of a newly qualified doctor. He was lucky, actually, to be able to finish his studies and qualify. A couple of years later and that wouldn't have been possible.

"On my dressing table there was a picture of me as a child, and I took it out of the frame and replaced it with the picture Friedrich had sent. Every night I kissed that picture. Oh yes, Sam, I was a romantic. I never doubted for one minute that Friedrich would get home and we would be able to marry.

"Time passed and, suddenly, it was 1938, and still I hadn't seen Friedrich. There had been phone calls, and Papa would tell him over and over again that he should not draw attention to himself. But, you know, even when I spoke to Friedrich and I could hear his voice, nothing could replace the feel of his arms about me." She gazed into the distance, re-living those years.

"And so the time passed. Papa said he was sure if I had completed my studies I would have made a very good doctor. As it was, I wasn't qualified, but people seemed to accept that it was okay to come to me if Papa wasn't available.

"In the spring time, we had an unexpected visitor. It was Friedrich. Remember, I hadn't seen him for nearly five years, but the moment he stepped through the door it was if we had only just said goodbye the night before. Our letters had kept our relationship alive and we decided to marry. There was only one problem. There was no rabbi nearby.

"As far as Mama was concerned, we needed a rabbi; otherwise, the marriage wouldn't be kosher. Friedrich and I sat outside on the swing seat, listening to them talking.

'They could get married in the town hall,' said Papa.

'Pshaw,' I heard Mama say. 'What kind of a marriage would that be?'

'A legal one,' said Papa. 'Later, when things have calmed down, they could have a proper chuppah but in the meantime, well you've seen how they are. Let's do at least part of it.'

"Reluctantly, Mama agreed. She had been making things for my bottom drawer, probably since the day after I was born. She managed to make me a dress out of some of the fabric she'd put away. She still had her veil from when she and Papa had married, and I was thrilled she would let me wear it. Friedrich only had a week's leave from the hospital, so we had to get a move on.

"The whole village came out to see us. It really was the happiest day of my life. We walked from our house to the town hall and made a civil pledge in front of the mayor. He was delighted – there hadn't been a lot of weddings recently, and this was quite prestigious. The daughter of the doctor and a handsome young medic from Berlin. No mention was made of the fact that we were Jews. Maybe no-one remembered. We hoped that no-one remembered. We walked out from the town hall through two lines of people who threw some of their precious rice ration at us to wish us luck.

"Of course, there was no time for a proper honeymoon and, anyway, there was nowhere we could go, but my sisters and brother had fixed up the barn. They had made it look beautiful, with flowers and a lamp, and had donated some of their food ration for us to eat for our first meal together as man and wife.

"The next morning, Friedrich went back to the hospital. I returned to Papa's clinic and life went on. But gradually, we were beginning to see that, actually, life was very different. Papa was in touch with colleagues in Berlin. They told him what was happening and how they were planning their escape from Hitler's Germany. Sometimes Papa would call them and there was no answer or the line would be dead. We never knew what happened to those people. Had they managed to get out or had they been arrested?

"Remember, Sam, there was no television for us then. We couldn't see what was happening and the radio news was heavily censored. The Jews were 'becoming a problem' Hitler said and needed to be resettled. A euphemism for murdered, we all found out later.

"We felt we would be safe because we were already in a remote part of the country and because people didn't know or remember we were Jewish. Maybe they just didn't care.

"Friedrich's visits became fewer and further apart. When he did come, we were both fearful that he would be arrested for travelling without a warrant and, if he didn't come, I was distraught because I didn't know where he was or how he was. His letters were beautiful, but they didn't compensate for us being apart. We had spent such little time together, but I told myself that the wives of soldiers had to suffer similar separations.

"Things came to a head in November of 1938, with Kristallnacht. Jewish premises were desecrated, synagogues burned, and Jews of all ages herded up and taken to camps. It was the first time I had ever seen Papa cry, when he heard of some of the awful things that were happening. He learned of the death of his closest friend who was out in the street when the Brown Shirts were rampaging around.

"After that night, so many people were lost – either murdered or rounded up and taken away. Papa and Mama began to plan the family's escape. They would arrange for us all to leave Germany and travel to America where Papa had relatives. For this, everyone needed papers and permits, and they realised this would only draw attention to the fact we were Jews. So far, we didn't have J on our passports, but this might be picked up if we had to apply for any movement papers.

"Mama and I cried together when I told her I couldn't leave without Friedrich, but she understood.

'I wouldn't leave Papa,' she said, wiping her eyes on a corner of her apron.

"They were worried about me and my sisters and brother. My brother, your Uncle Reuben, decided he would go further up into the mountains and link up with a group of other Jews who were hiding there. In December we spent our last Chanukah together as a family, although we didn't know that would be the case. We lit the candles and we sang Mao Tzur, the Song of Freedom, little realising that soon our wings would be clipped and we would not have any freedom at all.

"For the last time together, we ate Mama's doughnuts and latkes, and then Reuben took his rucksack and left. He was eighteen and we never saw him again. Even after all this time, I don't know where he's buried. I can't go to a cemetery and put a stone on his grave."

Sam reached his arm out to his mother, taking on board some of her grief, and listening to her gentle sobbing.

"Reuben never had the opportunity to grow up, to get married, to have a family. We lost a whole generation when we lost Reuben." She took a deep breath. "Sam, I have to stop a moment. I need to rest. I'll make some coffee, and we can have a sandwich, and then I'll carry on."

Sam looked at his watch. Only two o'clock, and yet it seemed as if hours had passed while Eva was telling her story. And this was only the beginning, he felt, the tip of the iceberg. It was going to be a long day.

Eva passed him a plate.

"Some chopped liver and crackers. I don't seem to have the energy to do more."

They sat quietly for a while, wrapped up in their own thoughts. Sam could sense that Eva was back in the war days, re-living a time in her life which was full of angst. He waited for her to begin again.

CHAPTER 6

"In 1939, war was declared. The restrictions against Jews became even harsher. I hadn't heard from Friedrich for such a long time, and we didn't know where Reuben was. My sisters became almost recluses. They didn't want to go out. They were frightened they would be asked questions they couldn't answer.

"Papa and I kept on working. Even in war, there are the common ailments – chickenpox and tonsillitis and childbirth. Papa had to remember his surgical training, as people were reluctant to go to hospital. They preferred Papa to operate. I helped out by passing instruments and administering anaesthesia.

"Our village was quite secluded and a long way from the front line and any bombing, but this didn't mean that we avoided the rationing. Food supplies began to get shorter, and we depended on the generosity of local farmers to just survive. Money was in short supply, so people often paid for their treatment with a few eggs or a chicken or didn't pay at all. Papa would never have refused treatment because a patient couldn't pay so it was also hard for us to manage. We were often short of food.

"By the summer of 1941, things changed dramatically. The German government decided that the mountain air would be good for recovering soldiers. The village hall was requisitioned as a base, and a staff officer visited everyone to see who had spare rooms. Mama met him on our doorstep and invited him in with a smile, although I knew how terrified she was.

"She explained that Papa was the village doctor and that we needed our spare rooms so that we could care for postoperative patients. He demanded her papers and the papers of everyone living in the house. They were kept in the drawer of the big dresser in the kitchen, and he followed her in. Mama was well over forty, but she was still an attractive woman. She felt his eyes on her as she bent to open the drawer.

"Suddenly, he was behind her, his arms going around her waist. She could feel his breath on the back of her neck, and she stood stock still, frightened to move, frightened in case he attacked her. He caught her by her pearl necklace, and the string snapped. Pearls bounced all over the floor, and we stood horrified.

"Just then, there was the sound of a key in the lock and Papa came into the kitchen. The soldier jumped away from Mama, but not before Papa noticed. He moved towards the man, shoving a chair aside, arm raised, ready to strike. And this from Papa who was the mildest man you could ever meet." Eva relived the moment, her eyes showing the shock she had felt when she saw her father about to attack the German soldier. She pulled herself together and went on, shakily.

"Mama moved to stand in between them.

'It's all right,' she said. 'No harm done. He was just going.' And she held the door open for the soldier, who made sure he knocked a cup off the table as he went past. It shattered into pieces as it hit the stone floor.

'Let that be a lesson to you,' he said. 'Life is fragile.'

"My sisters were in the next room listening. They rushed in, and Anna went to get a dust pan and brush to sweep the broken china up. Leah had tears in her eyes, and she just stood there, trembling. It was becoming increasingly obvious that our time on the mountain was limited. My sisters begged Papa to find a way to get us out of Germany and to safety.

"The soldiers seemed to invade the village. They were either recovering from wounds or on leave, and they were all a nuisance. Even the staunch supporters of Hitler, and there were some in the village who agreed with everything he said, resented the way they bought everything in the shops and the way they looked at and talked to the village girls.

"The commanding officer organised dances, and all the village women were forced to attend. I went with my sisters and watched them carefully as the young men put sweaty hands over their pretty frocks. At the end of each dance, they clicked their heels together and saluted their partners. We came to hate the noise of those heels meeting, but we kept smiles plastered tightly on our faces.

"The one advantage of those dances was the food the soldiers brought for a buffet. For people on rationing, without even basic bread and butter, the temptation was too great. Everyone who could went to those dances and enjoyed the food, if not the close association. Of course, there were always a few who became, shall we say, friendly with those soldiers, but we sisters kept away as much as possible.

"Papa's workload increased, and he was grateful for my help. The commanding officer asked if I was qualified, and Papa had to tell him, 'No.'

'Why not?' he demanded. 'If she hasn't qualified, is she safe enough to help you?'

"Papa, of course, couldn't tell him the real reason why I hadn't completed my studies. He told the officer it was because he wanted me at home to help Mama who had been ill, and then I decided not to return to my studies because I had lost too much ground. It seemed to satisfy Commander Horst, but Papa and I knew it was only a question of time before we had to move on.

"The winter passed and we waited for spring. The snow melted and the daffodils poked their yellow heads through the earth. We had survived. Clothes rationing meant we had little to wear. Mama became adept at fashioning clothes out of blankets and curtains – anything to keep us warm and clothed. Food rationing meant we had little to eat, and we didn't even have our traditions, our rituals, to keep us safe.

"Papa decided that all references to Judaism should be hidden. He and Mama collected up the candlesticks and the menorah, our prayer books, anything written in Hebrew, even the challah cloth for the bread. Papa's kippah went into the metal box. Everything was carefully wrapped. Even the snowy white Shabbat tablecloth. From now on we would only use the rough linen ones that most villagers had.

"We had one last Friday night dinner, enjoying the chicken soup and the challah and making the blessings over the wine and bread.

'From now on' Papa said, 'we will not do this again.' He lifted his hand to silence Mama. I knew what she was about to say. She was going to tell him she didn't need a prayer book or a candle to say the prayers. She could do it from memory. Papa just looked at her and said,

'From today we forget we are Jewish. The most important commandment we have is to save life. And if we have to become another religion, or no religion at all, so be it. We will stay alive.'

"The following morning, on Shabbat, a day when no work was ever done, Papa went out into the garden to dig a trench. Whilst pretending to 'plant potatoes,' he carefully buried everything that could identify us as Jews. He had wrapped them in oiled cloth and put them into tin boxesand, in reality, there didn't seem such a lot.

'I will get them back after this war,' he said. 'They will not stay there. Mark carefully where we put them so you know where to dig in case I forget.' We knew what that meant. It was his way of saying he might not live to the end of the war. We marked the spot with some bulbs. Every year they would grow and every year we would know where to look for our treasures. We paced out the steps from the old apple tree, and we knew we would always remember that day.

"I was so worried about Friedrich. I hadn't heard from him for such a long time. By then I knew about the camps. I knew that the Jewish Resettlement Plan suggested by Hitler's government was actually a way to annihilate all the

Jews. I knew that the distant rumble of lorries was probably the transportation of Jews to these camps.

"It all came to an end in the autumn of 1943. We had no opportunity to pack, to gather up any valuables like jewellery, or even a crust of bread. We were sleeping for once with the windows open because the September air was warm. The blackout curtains were pulled across the glass but the breeze still managed to find its way into the hot bedrooms. I heard the coughing of heavy engines as they rumbled up the lane, and then I heard the banging on the front door. Sam, I can't tell you what that was like. Even now, it makes me shudder to remember."

Sam put his arm round Eva's shoulder. "It's ok, Ma," he murmured. "It's ok. It's all over."

"No, Sam, it's not," she said. "Wait until you hear the whole story before you say that.

"The soldiers burst into my bedroom, shouting and banging. The noise was deafening. I couldn't take on board what they were saying, and they shouted again. They didn't give us time to pack, just pushed us down the stairs. I looked at my room for what I knew would be the last time. I saw my dressing table with the picture of Friedrich on it; a half empty bottle of perfume, and a tin of talcum powder lying on its side. My warm cardigan was lying over the chair back, and I grabbed it as I was hustled past.

"My mother was outside in her nightgown, shivering, despite the warm air. Papa had his arm around her trying to comfort her. They weren't allowed to go back indoors to get dressed. The soldiers were laughing at the sight of my parents in their night clothes. They pushed them into the back of the wagon with my sisters, and one of the soldiers roughly shoved me in after them. They locked the tailgate, and the engine revved. There was no-one else in the truck, just us. No-one to ask about what was happening; no-one to reassure us. We could only imagine and worry.

"At the town hall, we were pushed into one of the committee rooms and left alone. There was a soldier outside, so we knew there was no point in trying to escape. There was no heating in the room, and I tried to wrap my cardigan around Mama, but she wouldn't let me. We were all cold and shivering, when the commandant came in with the town mayor.

'So,' he barked. 'All this time we have had Jews in our midst. And not just Jews but medical Jews. Who knows how many of our soldiers you have killed while pretending to cure them.'

"Papa tried to speak, but the mayor said to him,

'It's no good Herr Doktor. I know you are a Jew. We have tried to keep quiet about it because you are a good man and we needed you, but they have my wife. They said, if I didn't tell them about all the Jews in the region, they would shoot her. I had to tell them about you.'

"Even after this admission, Papa was gracious.

'It's all right, Ernst,' he said. 'You did what you had to do. This war can't last much longer, and then we'll be friends again.'

CHAPTER 7

"I don't remember much about the journey to the camp. I've seen a lot of tv documentaries about the cattle trucks and so on, but we travelled in style." She smiled wryly. "We were taken on our own in a truck and handed in through the wire gates. But the routine inside was the same.

"My parents were separated from us and we never saw them again. Can you imagine, Sam? To be shoved and pushed, not to be able to say goodbye. No last kiss or embrace. My mother was still shivering from cold or fright, and Papa still had his arms around her. They looked back for one last time, and then they were gone. I knew what would happen to them.

"My sisters and I were taken to a shower block, and you've seen the programmes, too, but we were lucky. They really were showers – cold water, of course but nonetheless it was water and not gas. You know, Sam, at that time I wasn't frightened of the showers, only of the cold. How that changed when I got to talking to the other women.

"We huddled together, trying to cover our nakedness, sadly grateful for the clothes that were eventually thrown at us. We didn't get tattooed; only Auschwitz prisoners were tattooed, and the camp we were in was supposed to be a work camp, not a death camp.

"Our names were entered into the camp register, once we were 'processed,' and we were given camp numbers. This was one way of taking our identities by removing our names. And woe betide anyone who forgot their number. It was a flogging offence." Sam looked shocked.

"Efficient German bureaucracy," she added with a wry smile.

"You know, Sam, all of this was a way of de – humanising us. The way our heads were shaved, our clothes taken away, and our 'uniform' issued. And the first day in that camp, new inmates didn't get any food. We arrived hungry, we went to bed hungry, and we woke up hungry."

Sam leaned forward. This was the first time he had ever heard his mother talk about her time in the camp. Whenever he'd asked, she'd always refused to give him any information. So, why now? The mysterious man obviously had something to do with it.

"Sam. I'm so tired. Can we stop and pick this up again tomorrow?"

"Could you go on for a bit longer?" Sam asked gently. "I have to get back to Berlin as soon as I can, and I don't think I can go till I've heard all your story and solved the mystery." He hugged Eva.

"Have a glass of wine, Ma," he said. "Maybe that'll relax you a bit."

"No, not now, Sam. I need to keep my mind sharp. So, where was I? Yes, hungry."

"Maybe that's why you always want to feed people," Sam smiled, trying to lighten Eva's mood.

"Maybe," she shrugged. "But I think it's more of a Jewish tradition than something left over from my past.

"So, ok. We are woken early in the morning. I don't know what time because, of course, my watch has been taken away. We are herded out into the barrack ground. We are lined up, cold and shivering in our thin clothes, and a count of us made. As if anyone could have escaped in the night. Because, of course, no-one escaped except through death.

"The Camp Commandant is there. He looks over the new arrivals and pulls my sisters out of the lines. Anna and Leah are such pretty girls. They are crying and I step forward too. I want to be with them, but he points to where a group of officers are waiting, and the girls are dragged away.

"I am pushed back into line but not before the Commandant tells me that my turn will come. I don't understand what he means, but the women in the barracks tell me later. The prettiest girls are picked out and sent to a room for the pleasure of the officers. I never find Anna or Leah again. So much loss, Sam. So much loss." She wiped her eyes with the back of her hand before continuing.

"The fittest are marched away to work and the others – well, I don't have to tell you what happens to the others. And more people are arriving. More frightened women and children. More screams and more separations, and now I can have my first meal. I don't know what it is, but I don't care. I will eat it, and I will stay strong."

Sam noticed that Eva was speaking in the present tense and her accent was getting stronger. She was reliving her experiences. She was still there in that camp.

"And then, Ma?" he encouraged. "What then?"

51

"We go to our barracks. We sleep, we get up the next morning, we work, and that is our life."

"You worked?"

"Yes, in the socalled hospital. With no drugs, with not even an aspirin, where people came to die, but perhaps more peacefully than they would in their barracks. The Germans don't know I am a medic, of course. If they had, I don't know what would have happened to me. I am working as an orderly, trying to make people more comfortable, and I am left alone.

"There is a men's camp next to ours, separated only by a wire fence. It is the kind of fence that people throw themselves on when they can no longer face life and dream only of dying. I will never forget the smell of burning and seeing the way in which the bodies were left hanging on the fence as a warning to everyone.

"I am so worried about Friedrich, and I try to get near that fence every day. Of course, I know he won't be there. I don't want him to be there, but maybe I will see someone who knows what has happened to him. And then I see him. I can't believe it. Sam, I can't tell you how I feel when I see him. I see Friedrich through the wires. He is thin, dirty, dressed in the camp uniform, but it is him, my Friedrich. It is a real miracle. It is the best day of my life, but it is also the worst day of my life. I had hoped and prayed that he was still free, and so when I see him, I can only cry.

"I try to catch his attention, but I am afraid I will be seen by the guards. And then I remember the songs we used to sing in happier days. I begin to hum the music and the melody drifts over the wires. Friedrich looks up and sees me. I am sure that his face is a reflection of mine; sadness, incredulity and misery.

"He blinks rapidly, and I understand. He knows it is me, but I must not acknowledge him or look in his direction. He will somehow find me. I don't know whether to be happy I can see him or miserable because he, too, has been captured and held in a camp. Every day for a week I just wander casually past that fence, and every day for a week he is there, sweeping the stones up, nearer and nearer until we can see into each other's eyes.

'The cook house,' he whispers. 'Tomorrow at six am,' and then he moves away, still sweeping.

"I can't sleep that night. I toss and turn in my bunk until my sleeping partners shout at me to be still. There is no room for restless sleepers and we are four to a bunk. I try so hard to lie straight, but eventually I crawl out. I have no idea what time it is but dawn is breaking. I creep out into the early morning light as if I am going to the latrine, and I work my way round the camp until I am behind the cookhouse itself. And there is Friedrich.

'My God, Eva,' he breathes, 'you're so beautiful.'

"You know, Sam, only a man as romantic as my Friedrich could see beauty in the emaciated scarecrow which stood before him. I was dirty, my head was shaved with only a little stubble coming through, and there was the smell of death about me."

"Oh, Ma," said Sam brokenly. "Why have you never spoken about this?"

"Some things are too private to speak about, Sam," Eva answered. "And too painful. Friedrich and I had only an hour before he had to get back to his hut. One of the other

53

men is covering for him and, of course, he doesn't want to get his friend into trouble." Eva came back into the present with a slight shudder. "This hour with my husband was the biggest gift I could have had in the world, and Sam, he said we could meet again. He would blink at me through the wire and, if I counted the number of times he shut his eyes, it would tell me what time to be there the following day.

"I suppose we were in a kind of honeymoon daze. Remember, we had spent only one night together after our wedding day and only brief times after that, so we made up for lost time as best as we could. The other women in my barracks covered for me when they could. They were enjoying this romance almost as much as us."

Sam flushed, embarrassed to hear his mother talk like this but glad she had had some comfort at the most terrible time of her life.

"And then the worst happened. I realised I was pregnant. I didn't think I could get pregnant because I was malnourished, had no regular periods." Eva looked at Sam. "Excuse me for being so personal, but you should know this. I told Friedrich and we didn't know what to do. He was a doctor and I also had a lot of medical experience, so we tried to think if we could somehow abort the baby. But there was no way we could do this. This child was our hope for the future. We still thought we might succeed in surviving the war…"

"And we did, Ma. We did."

"Sam, please, let me finish. There's more to this than you think." She coughed and cleared her throat. "In the beginning, I could hide my swelling stomach. Lots of women had big stomachs because of malnutrition, but there came the time when our barrack leader asked me if I was expecting. I know there were some kapos who were unkind, but this woman was an angel. She had seen me creep out of the barracks every now and then and just kept her eyes shut. She could have informed on me and been given extra rations, but she didn't. She did her best to shield the women who were ill, giving them the lightest jobs she could to save them from the gas chamber. When she asked me, I could only tell the truth.

'You know what will happen to you if they find out,' she whispered in the small hours of the night. 'We have to find a way of keeping you safe. You need to be out of that hospital and somewhere warm.'

"We looked at each other and actually laughed, as if there was a choice of work and a coal fire to sit beside.

'I'll organise a private room for you in the maternity hospital,' she added, 'with room service,' and we laughed even harder, until there was a shout from one of the bunks telling us to be quiet.

'Let me think,' she said. 'I'll see what I can do.'

"But I really didn't expect a solution. Here, in the camp, we were expendable. When we got too sick to work – well, the gas chamber, of course, but not before every bit of us could be used to help the German war effort. Not just the gold teeth but hair and skin." Sam looked horrified. He lifted his hand in despair but Eva waved him away.

"I want to go on," she said. "I need to go on now.

"Friedrich wasn't at our meeting place the next day. I was so anxious, Sam, but I couldn't do anything about it. He didn't come the next day, or the day after that and then, after a week, an emaciated figure came near the fence and whispered to me,

'They came for Friedrich in the night and took him away. We have no idea where he is. Maybe the punishment block. We must hope for the best.'

"I was distraught. I knew I might never find out what happened to him. I asked if the guards had hurt Friedrich, and then was a silence before I heard the reply.

'When they came into the barracks, they hit him with big wooden sticks on the soles of his feet. He couldn't stand, and they dragged him away. I'm so sorry, Eva. We couldn't help. We just had to lie as quiet as possible. We could see the trail of blood he left behind.'

"I appreciated this man coming to tell me. I knew he was risking his life, but I also knew that he was really telling me there was no hope that Friedrich would have survived. I don't know how I got back to the barracks, where I didn't even have the luxury of being able to cry privately."

CHAPTER 8

"Two days later, my friend Mina was thrown roughly into my hut. Her face was bloody and her arms and hands were bruised. The women crowded round her, clamouring to find out what had happened.

'They will hang me tomorrow,' she said.

'Hang you? Why? What did you do?'

'I stole.'

'What do you mean, you stole?'

'I've been working for the Commandant's wife, looking after the children. I ate the scraps off their plates. The Commandant said I was stealing, and I am to be hanged as a lesson to everyone. But I'm so tired that I think it will be a relief.'

"We all moved to her, hugging her and stroking her hair. We knew there was no appeal, and we sat with her all night. In the morning, at first light, they came for her but not before she whispered in my ear.

'You can sew. You can care for children. You know how to cook. The Commandant will want to replace me, and his house is warm. Just don't even think of taking even a crust, and you will be ok.'

"And then she took off her shoes and gave them to me. Mine were worn out, and my feet were constantly wet and covered in mud. 'I won't need these where I'm going,' she said.

"Mina walked out barefoot, across the stony barrack ground to where the gibbet was standing. She climbed the steps on her own, shrugging off the hands of the guards. We were all outside watching, and I tried to give her strength with warm looks and smiles, but my eyes were filled with tears.

"I heard the sound of the trapdoor opening, then the noise of her body banging against the wooden frame. I just hoped it had been quick and her neck had broken at once. Sometimes this didn't happen, and the bodies were left to swing in agony.

"Mina and I had been to school together. We had played tennis together, and she had married before me, but I wasn't allowed to grieve. I needed to give her death meaning, and so life had to go on.

"Our barrack kapo came over to speak to me.

'I have told the Commandant about you.' My face must have paled because she reassured me. 'No, not about your condition, about how you could help with the children. He wants to talk to you. Do your best.'

"I had never been in the Commandant's house before, so I was amazed at what it was like. The outside was as grim and unattractive as the rest of the camp, but the inside. Oh, Sam, the inside was like the houses I had known as a child. I felt as if I was in a fairy tale.

"The soldiers pushed me through that heavy front door into another world. There was carpet on the floor and a chandelier with at least eight lamps on it. I could smell something warm and fragrant coming from the kitchen, and I was conscious of my own looks and my own smell.

"Ernst Hoffman was the Camp Commandant. Tall and thin, with a moustache like Hitler's, he ruled with an iron rod. Everyone was afraid of him. I had met him when I first arrived at the camp, and he had looked at me, but I didn't expect him to remember. I didn't want him to remember. I didn't want to stand out among all the other women. I just wanted to fade into the background, but I remembered that he had pointed his ferrule at my sisters and watched with a smile as they were dragged off.

"I didn't dare raise my eyes, and he came to inspect me. 'Can you sew?' he asked abruptly. 'My wife needs someone to make baby clothes and do the mending for the other children.'

'I can sew,' I answered, and quite boldly, 'I can also embroider, and I can cook, and I am good with little ones.'

"He beckoned to his wife who was standing in the shadow of a large potted plant. She was dressed so elegantly, wearing a pale blue costume with sparkling jewels at her ears, but she looked weary. Her hand was supporting the small of her back.

'Yes, Ernst,' she said. 'She might do. Let's give her a try.'

"The Commandant looked over at the soldier.

'Take her downstairs to her quarters and show her where to shower.' By then I knew what going to the showers meant. I was trembling – was this going to be the end? Was this just some cruel joke, to bring me into this house and give me some hope and then to extinguish that hope in a gas chamber?

"He looked at his wife. 'She will need clean clothes. A uniform of some kind. Can you see to this liebchen?'

"I felt sick listening to him speaking these words of endearment to his wife when I knew how he behaved towards the prisoners, but I didn't let it show on my face. I just went down the stairs to a cellar where there was a makeshift shower – a bucket with holes in the bottom, attached to a pipe. The water was warm, almost hot, and there was real soap and a scratchy sack to dry myself on. It was a luxury.

"I got dressed in the clothes that were thrown at me – a dress owned by another inmate before she came into the camp, I assumed, and a clean, verywhite apron to cover it. I waited to see what would happen next.

"There was a camp bed in the corner. A whole bed to myself, Sam. Even though I was in the middle of the most appalling time, or maybe *because* I was in the middle of an appalling time, I felt as if suddenly I was a millionaire. A whole bed, with a blanket. And the cellar was fairly warm because of the central heating pipes which ran around the walls. They heated the house, of course, but they made the temperature in the cellar comfortable. When you have nothing, a small something means the world, and that bed and blanket became the world to me.

"I had tried to comb my hair as best as I could by running my fingers through it. Of course, when I had gone into the camp my head had been shaved but now my hair had grown in a bit. Without the attentions of a hairdresser, though, I looked like a scarecrow. I wondered what the Commandant's wife would say about that.

"The soldier who had taken me to the cellar came back and pushed me up the stairs and back into the world of warmth and delicious smells. Frau Hoffman came out of the drawing room to talk to me. She was very explicit in her demands.

'You will look after the children when I tell you. You will clear up after them. You will feed them. You will mend their clothes.' She looked straight at me. 'You said you could embroider. I am expecting another baby in a few weeks, and there has been no opportunity to get baby clothes. You will be able to sew these?' There was a question mark in her voice, and I hastily said, 'Yes. Yes, I can. I will.'

'All right,' she went on. 'I will give you a trial. But I must warn you that neither the Commandant nor I will tolerate any insubordination. You will do as you are told *when* you are told. Neither will we tolerate any thieving. You will get food, and we expect you to eat it all. But, under no circumstances are you to finish the children's food or eat kitchen scraps. If we are not happy with your work, you will be sent back to the barracks. Do you understand?'

"I understood all right. I had seen what happened to Mina, and I was sure I didn't want to go that way myself. Neither me nor the child I was carrying.

"Frau Hoffman went on,

'Every evening you will go to the camp kitchen for our supplies. You will bring them back and give them to our cook. You will not touch them or eat them. Only give them to Hilde, our cook.'

"I had kept my eyes lowered and my hands behind my back. I was so relieved that I wasn't to be kept in the cellar all the time I wasn't working. I had worried about giving birth, and now I realised I would have to make sure it happened on my evening walk to the kitchens.

'Go now,' said Frau Hoffman. 'Go to the children, but first cover your hair. I don't want them to be frightened by your appearance.' She tossed a kerchief at me, and I wrapped it round my head. 'Now go.'

"I looked around anxiously.

'They are in their bedrooms. It is time for their baths and bed. You will see to that. Quickly, now. They are waiting. Up the stairs.'

"The staircase was covered with soft carpet. I felt as if my feet would just sink down into it. There were paintings on the wall. I was no connoisseur of art, but I could see they were originals. At the top was a portrait of Hitler, gazing down. A shudder went through my spine as I passed it, not daring to look up, or look down or look anywhere. I had the feeling that wherever I went in that house, and whatever I did, Hitler would be able to see me.

"The children were waiting; a fairhaired boy of about five and a blonde pigtailed girl of three. They looked at me solemnly.

'Are you going to look after us now?' asked the girl. 'Mina went away. Mama said she was naughty and she wasn't coming back.'

'Do you know where she went?' asked the boy. 'She was going to play with us today. She said we could draw pictures, but she went away after supper one day, and she hasn't come back.'

"I tried to keep my voice steady as I told the children I didn't know where Mina was. 'Perhaps she's gone on a holiday,' I said, and with that they seemed to be content.

"They each took one of my hands and led me to their bathroom. It was like something out of a magazine, Sam, all chrome and tiles and soft white towels. Bottles of bath salts were arranged on the window sills, blue and pink and lemon yellow.

"I put the plug in the bath and turned the taps on, shaking some bath salts under the running water. Clouds of fragrant steam rose into the air, and when I turned round I could see that the children had taken off their clothes. Before I let them get in, I tested the water with my elbow, and they giggled.

'Mina always did that too,' they chorused.

"I used the time they were playing in the water to get to know them a bit. Dietrich enjoyed being the older brother and telling Giselle what to do. She was at the age where she looked up to her older sibling, so she was happy to do as she was told. She would repeat what he said with a cheeky smile on her face. By the time they were washed and wrapped in those fluffy towels, they were relaxed with me."

"It sounds as if you liked the children, Ma," said Sam.

"Yes, I did. They were just innocent children. They didn't know how evil Hitler and his world were.

"I sang to them, quietly at first, until they joined in, and then they said their prayers, making sure that they said something special for 'Uncle Adolf,' and I put the light out.

"Frau Hoffman was waiting at the bottom of the stairs.

'A good start,' she said. 'You can go to your room, now. There is some food for you on a tray.'

"I was surprised that no-one locked me into the cellar. But, of course, there was no way I could escape. The only window was high up on the wall, and the cellar itself was largely under the ground level of the house. I'm sure I could have got out if I wanted to, but there was nowhere to go.

"On the floor by my bed was a tin tray and on it some rough bread, a cup of something – I couldn't work out if it was coffee or watery soup." Eva laughed at this, surprising herself. "And there was a piece of apple." She repeated that. "A piece of apple. My God, It was the best meal I'd ever had.

"There was a light in the ceiling – a naked light bulb just hanging there but, when I pressed the switch, it didn't work. I wasn't really surprised. Why would my jailers provide me with a light when there was nothing for me to do? I lay down on that bed and stretched full length. It was a luxury to be able to do that. There was no-one to share my space. In the barracks there were sometimes four of us to one bunk, and we slept like sardines, top to toe, each turning at the same time. In my cellar, I was even warm, the rough blanket wrapped cocoonlike round me. I slept.

"Each day was the same. I got up early and ate my bread. I woke the children and gave them breakfast, trying hard not to salivate when I saw they had milk and meat and even oranges sometimes. How I wanted those things for my baby, but I knew better than to take even a pip. I would have eaten the orange peel if I could, but I made sure every scrap was left for the kitchen staff to check.

"I played with the children, I gave them lunch and tea, I bathed them, and I told them stories and sang. The days passed.

"Frau Hoffman was pleased with me, I could tell. One morning she brought me a navy blue cardigan.

'I can see you are cold sometimes,' she said. 'Wear this.' I was amazed. The cardigan was long and loose and covered my belly. I saw her looking at me, but I was grateful, and stammered my thanks.

"The following morning, she was not there. She had gone to the hospital in the nearby town to have her baby. How I envied her the clean sheets and the gentle nurses, the words of encouragement I knew they would say to her. I even envied her, but only for a moment," Eva laughed bitterly, "the company of the Commandant who no doubt would be proud when his child was born. Another child for Hitler's dream.

"I told the children they would soon have a new brother or sister, and they spent time talking about names. Dietrich liked Otto for a boy and Trudi for a girl, and of course little Giselle piped up,

'They are my favourites too.' They were lovely children. Eva rubbed her eyes and paused for a moment.

"The Commandant came home smiling. All had gone well. Frau Hoffman was recovering nicely and would soon be back. He beckoned to me,

'Is everything ready for when my wife returns? You will have extra work, of course, but I am sure you will manage. Anyway, you know the alternative if you do not.'

"He turned on his heel and went into the drawing room, closing the door behind him. I could hear him talking to the excited children and suggesting names. Dietrich was shouting happily,

'Otto, Papa. We must call our new brother Otto. It is a strong name, and I think Uncle Adolf would like it.'

CHAPTER 9

"That morning I had woken up with a toothache. My face was swollen and my jaw was stiff. I was in agony, and I knew there would be no relief from the pain. I paused for a moment, my hand to my mouth, just as the Commandant came out of the drawing room.

'What's the matter with you?' he barked. 'Why are you still standing there? Don't you have any work to do?' He looked closely at me. 'What's the matter with your face? Did someone hit you? Have you been fighting?' Fighting in the camp was an offence punishable by death, so I was quick to tell him I had a toothache.

"I waited to see what would happen. The Commandant spoke.

'Frau Hoffman seems to think you are the best girl we've had, so I will take you to the dentist. I am going into town myself.' He gave me a coat to cover my camp uniform, and I put it on quickly.

"I couldn't believe this. The Commandant was going to take me to the dentist. Frau Hoffman giving birth must have softened his attitude, I thought.

"The staff car was parked at the back of the house, and we went out through the kitchen door. He gestured for me to get in. I didn't know what to do. Was it all a trick? Would he shoot me for trying to steal the car or trying to escape?

'Get in,' he shouted. 'Now!'

"I didn't have a choice. I got into the back and sat motionless, trying not to moan with pain.

'Keep your head down when we go through the gates. I don't want the guard to see I am taking you out,' he said, and I was so scared that I did.

"The dentist's office was a half hour drive away. It was the first time I had been out of the camp since I arrived– the only time I had seen outside the wire fence that kept me confined. On the way, I saw trees with leaves drifting down onto the road. I could smell the flowers growing in the verge. I could even hear birds singing. It was a different world.

"In the town, Hoffman stopped the car at the kerbside and told me to get out. I scrambled as quickly as I could out of the back seat onto the pavement.

"I looked around, and I could see people in the streets doing their shopping. There were overweight fraus with shopping bags, children riding their bicycles, delivery vans, and postmen pushing letters through letter boxes. Everything looked normal but, of course, it wasn't normal. Germany was at war, not just with Britain and Europe but with its own Jewish citizens.

"The smell of the surgery was clean and antiseptic, and I felt completely out of place. The patients sitting on chairs around the walls obviously thought so, too, as they looked away from me. It was pretty obvious I wasn't the usual kind of patient.

"I didn't have to wait my turn. The Commandant pushed his way into the surgery, pulling me with him.

'She has a toothache, Doctor,' he said. 'My wife has just given birth, and we have two other children. We need this person to help with the children, so you can see what the problem is. I have no time to wait for her to get over a toothache, which might stop her working.'

"The dentist pointed to the chair. 'Sit down,' he said, 'And I will see what I can do.'

"Even his gentle probing hurt, but I stayed as still as I could because I needed him to fix my tooth.

'So?' asked the Commandant.

'She needs to have it filled,' the dentist replied. 'It won't take long. But this could be a recurring problem as there are signs of decay. Ideally, I would like to–'

"The Commandant interrupted him.

'There is no time for that. Take them all out.'

'What?' exclaimed the dentist. 'I can't do that. There are healthy teeth there as well as decayed ones, and it could all be corrected.'

'I have told you what to do. I want to avoid any more visits here. If you remove all the teeth, there will be no problem.'

"Again, the dentist tried to argue.

'Did you not understand me? Do it now. And I will watch to make sure you do it properly.'

"I was still in the chair listening with horror. The dentist looked at me and whispered, 'I don't have a choice. I have to do it, otherwise, he will have me shot for disobeying him, even though I am a loyal German citizen. I have a wife and family to consider.' He started to prepare the anaesthetic.

'No anaesthetic,' said the Commandant, taking the hypodermic from him. 'It is not necessary. We cannot waste precious drugs on Jews.'

"I could see the pity in the dentist's eyes.

'I will need to strap you in the chair so you will stay still,' he said. And I sat rigid whilst he fixed leather straps over my hands. I knew there was no point in arguing.

'Open wide,' he said and came towards me with the pliers. The agony of that first tooth coming out was more than I could bear, and I passed out mercifully. When I came round, I was still sitting in the chair, and he was pressing a bloody cloth to my mouth.

'You must rinse your mouth out with salt water a few times a day. Your mouth will soon heal, and the pain will go away.'

"The Commandant took me out of the surgery the back way and pushed me into the car.

'Don't get any blood on the leather,' he said, and I sat there in shock for the drive back. I kept pressing the cloth to my mouth to stop the bleeding, and I can't describe what the pain was like. I was frightened I might faint again and stain the seats.

'You can take the rest of the day off and stay in your room. Get some salt from Hilde, and tell her I gave you permission,' he said. 'It would be better for the children not to see you. But tomorrow you will be doing your normal duties.'

"I lay on my bed for the rest of the day, too weak to even cry. The pain was almost unbearable, and every time I

70

rinsed my mouth with the salt water, I was spitting blood. I was only a young woman, and I still had some remnants of vanity. Can you understand that?" She looked at Sam. "I couldn't imagine what I might look like but, if the Commandant thought I would frighten the children, it was obviously not good."

Sam looked at his mother in horror.

"You had all your teeth out without an anaesthetic?" he said.

"Yes, darling" she replied. "Now you know why I always took such good care of yours and Rachel's."

Sam did remember. And, now, he had a mouth of perfect teeth, with not even a filling. He could understand his mother's obsession after what she had experienced.

Eva started to speak again.

"That evening, my food arrived; dry bread as usual, with the same poor soup. I soaked the bread in the soup and ate it with my fingers, despite the pain. I was determined to keep my strength up, even if I could only swallow. I was determined to survive.

"In the morning, my face was swollen, but I cleaned it as best as I could, managed to eat my meagre breakfast, and went to attend to the children.

"You know, Sam, it's amazing how accepting children are. Of course I knew they were excited about having a new baby brother. They hardly noticed the swelling on my face and the fact I could barely speak. And the dentist was right. In time, the pain lessened, and my gums healed.

"Frau Hoffman arrived home, and the children were allowed into the drawing room. I could hear them making baby noises and cooing away, and I could hear the little cries of infant lungs. I waited in the hall for them to come out, imagining how wonderful it would be to have my baby in such clean surroundings. I knew that I would be giving birth alone.

"Of course, I wasn't exactly sure when my baby would arrive. I had a rough idea when Friedrich had come to the camp, and I felt that it would be perhaps at the end of November. I had seen enough babies born, so I knew what to expect. First labours can be long, and I was weak and malnourished, and I would have no help.

"There was so much I would need; a blanket for the baby, clean water, scissors, a piece of string. All of these things seemed unobtainable. I couldn't imagine that I would be able to find anything sharp. There might be a few weeks before I gave birth, but I felt I had to start now to gather them together.

"I decided I couldn't risk stealing things from the Commandant's house. Someone would notice, and I knew what the penalty would be. The only other place was the camp kitchen, but every item was carefully checked by the kapo in command. Often I couldn't sleep because I was worrying about how I would get what I needed.

"The walk from the Commandant's house to the kitchen took only a few minutes. It had been an irrational thought that I could deliver a child in the time it took to get there. I would have to think of something else. That evening, the kapo from my old barracks was collecting the soup, and I confided in her.

'The only thing I can think of is that, when the time comes, you should tell Frau Hoffman you are needed in your old barracks because a friend is dying, and she has asked for you. Frau Hoffman might let you go. If not, I think it will be the end for you.'

"I knew that there would be no rehearsal for this. I would have only one opportunity, and I would have to choose the right time. In the meantime, I would keep a sharp look out for a knife. I could only hope that I would have a straightforward delivery.

"When I looked down, I thought my belly looked huge, but in reality I knew it wasn't. In a way, I hoped I wouldn't go to full term. This wouldn't be good for the baby's health, but it might be our only way of surviving.

"I was very careful not to take any food, but there were other things I had to have; something clean to wrap the baby in, for example. I managed to tuck a tea towel beneath my cardigan and smuggle it into my room. I put it under the mattress and just hoped it wouldn't be missed. It was just a small linen towel."

CHAPTER 10

"I woke the next morning to the crash of drawers being dragged out, people shouting, and the sound of Hilde crying. My heart sank. I hoped it was because she had burned the porridge," Eva shrugged, "but I knew that wasn't the case. And I knew the soldiers would come to my room. I sat on my bed and waited.

"The noise of their boots on the concrete stairs was like a death knell to me. They burst into the room and asked me if I had the missing tea towel. I was terrified. I couldn't speak. My tongue was stuck to the roof of my mouth. There was little to search in the room, only the bed and, when the mattress was thrown on the floor, my crime was visible for all to see.

"This was it, then. The death penalty. Maybe, like Mina, I would be relieved, but then I thought of the unborn baby. Two lives were going to be lost, and all because I had taken a tea towel – only a tea towel.

"The soldiers had to half carry me up the stairs, and they threw me onto the floor in the kitchen. I could see my face in the polish of the Commandant's boots.

'I told you,' he said. 'I told you what would happen if you stole anything. It's a shame because Frau Hoffman was pleased with you. However, I will make no exceptions.' He turned to the soldiers.

'Take her away. Put her back in the barracks, and we will hang her in the morning. She will be one more example to the other women of what happens if you take things which do not belong to you.'

"Frau Hoffman came into the kitchen.

'What's going on?' she asked. 'The children can hear all this noise, and they want to know what's happening.'

"The Commandant explained.

'And so, I have to do my duty. She will be hanged in the morning.'

'Is there nothing you can do?' She looked at him, and his face softened. For such a strict disciplinarian in the camp, he could deny her nothing.

'She didn't take food, and it might just have been an accident that she took the towel.' She looked at me, and I nodded.

"I must have forgotten it when I was in the kitchen," I croaked. "I didn't mean to take it."

'So why was it under the mattress?' the Commandant barked.

"I thought rapidly.

'It must have been when I made the bed. I must have accidentally tucked it in.'

'No,' he said. 'You took something which was not yours, and you must be punished.'

'Anything,' I sobbed on my knees. 'Just don't hang me.'

"The Commandant moved towards me. 'I understand in some countries a thief is punished by having their hand chopped off. How do you feel about that?'

'Ernst,' said Frau Hoffman. 'You wouldn't. She would die anyway from loss of blood.'

'Maybe not her hand, then. Just a finger.' He walked over to the kitchen table and selected a knife. 'You choose which finger,' he said, 'and think yourself lucky.'

"I had no time to think. Remember, Sam, I loved to play the piano. I tried to work out which finger I used least, and the Commandant shouted again.

'Choose one, or I'll take your whole hand.'

"The whole kitchen was silent. Even Frau Hoffman stood still, her hand pressed to her mouth.

"Wordlessly, I held out the little finger of my left hand and watched as the knife swooped down and my finger lay disconnected on the floor. I grabbed hold of the table edge, swaying as the Commandant threw the tea towel at me.

'You can have this now,' he said laughing. 'To staunch the blood.'

"I took it and wrapped it round my hand. There was surprisingly little blood and no pain. That would come later."

Sam looked at his mother. This was the real reason, he thought, that Eva didn't play the piano.

"The barbarian," he said through clenched teeth. "You've kept this to yourself all these years."

"Well, yes, but my life was saved. And I still have nine fingers."

How could Eva say such a thing? How could she be so accepting of what had happened?

Telling the story so far had taken it out of Eva, and it had taken it out of Sam too.

"Let's stop now, Ma," he murmured. "I'll stay over. I'm not going to leave you now. Helen won't mind – she'll understand, so I'll give her a quick ring."

Eva started to protest, but seeing the look on Sam's face, she sat down, glad that she wouldn't be alone. Sam went into the hall to make his call, and she could hear him talking to Helen.

"Hello, darling," he said. "I think it would be a good idea for me to stay with Ma tonight." There was a pause; obviously Helen was speaking. "No, she's ok but exhausted. Helen, she's been talking about the war years and her time in the camp. Something she's never spoken about before. In fact, whenever Rachel and I asked her, she refused to speak. We just thought it was too traumatic, and we never pushed it." Another pause. "No, I'll find something to eat. Will you mind if I stay over? Okay, I'll call later and let you know what's happening."

Sam replaced the receiver thoughtfully and went back into the sitting room. Eva was leaning back in the chair, her eyes closed and her face as white as parchment. Sam looked at his watch and saw it was almost six o'clock. During the telling of her story, time had passed swiftly. He could see that Eva was sleeping, and he thought it was probably the best thing. She had talked for so long that she must be exhausted. He would leave her while he had a look in the cupboards to see what kind of meal he could rustle up. His culinary skills were not his strong point, but maybe he could manage cheese on toast.

There was a wool rug over the arm of the settee, and he gently covered Eva up and then sat himself in an easy chair to think over what she had said.

Talking about her time in the camp was obviously important to her, but was it important to what was happening now? Could it have any relevance to what was going on? Try as he might, Sam couldn't come up with any answers. He would have to wait until Eva was awake and composed enough to continue her story. But first, they should eat. He let her sleep for an hour then woke her carefully, with a tray of food.

"No, Sam," she said, brushing it aside. "I can't face anything."

"But, Ma, you have to eat. It's what you always say to us. Now it's time to follow your own advice."

Reluctantly, Eva picked up her knife and fork.

"Just to please you," she said with a weak smile, but she managed most of what was on her plate.

"I've poured you a glass of wine, Ma," said Sam. "It'll give you strength to continue."

"Really? I don't think so," but obediently she took a swallow of the red liquid and felt its fiery bite as it reached her stomach.

"Before you go on, Ma, I just want to say I wish you'd shared this before. Maybe it would have helped?"

"No, I don't think so, Sam. There's more to come. The worst part. Just let me speak."

Sam took the tray from her and sat down on the settee, putting his arm around her shoulders.

"No, don't be kind. I won't be able to cope if you are kind." She settled back in the chair and picked up the story where she had left off.

"So, I carried on with my duties, grateful to Frau Hoffman for her intervention. I couldn't understand why she had done this, except she said I was a good worker, but there were plenty of other 'good' girls, I thought."

"But the pain of your finger, Ma."

"Yes, by now I could feel the pain. The adrenalin had worn off and every movement of my hand hurt, but at least I'd had the presence of mind to hold out my left hand so I could continue to use my right one. I don't know how I would have managed if my right hand had been damaged.

"And you know, pain is just relative, Sam." Eva continued "The real pain was in my heart. Losing my Friedrich, worrying about my baby. The loss of a finger is nothing in comparison to the loss of a husband and child.

"I started my labour at midnight. That was a worry because I couldn't ask for permission to go to the barracks to 'help' my friend. I was awake all night, struggling with the pains, trying to keep quiet because, although my room was in the basement, I was worried in case someone might hear me. Certainly, they would hear if I started to moan or scream, so I walked around and rubbed my stomach and then my back. Honestly, Sam, I didn't know where to put myself, but somehow I found the strength I needed.

"The following morning the children asked me if I was all right, because I doubled over at one point when I was putting their milk on the table. I tried to smile, and just said I had a 'tummy ache'." She looked sideways at Sam and added, "Sort of true, don't you think?"

"Mmmm," responded Sam wryly. "Some tummy ache."

"Frau Hoffman came into the room when I was clearing the table. She also asked if I was all right. I suppose I looked pale. I was certainly concentrating on keeping a smile on my face and trying to ignore the contractions.

"Frau Hoffman never used my name. I didn't think she even knew what it was, but she looked closely at me then said,

'I'm taking the children out today. There is plenty for you to do. There is some sewing, the children's laundry and some of my ironing. After you've finished you can go to your room.'

"This was my opportunity.

'Frau Hoffman,' I started. 'I have a friend in the barracks I used to be in. She is very ill. Might I please go and see her when I've finished my work?'

'Ill? What is wrong with her? Is it infectious?'

"I hadn't thought of that but I said quickly,

'No, I think she fell and banged her head. She's unconscious a lot of the time, but sometimes she wakes up, and the barracks kapo said she won't live long. I was at school with her…'

"I knew I was babbling, and so I waited while Frau Hoffman raised an elegant hand.

'If that's the case, you may go. We should be back by eight pm, and I expect you to be here and to put the children to bed. I will give you a letter saying you have permission to visit your friend.'

"I raced through those chores, stopping every now and then to catch my breath when a pain ripped through me. I did the washing and the ironing and put the sewing in a clean pillow case to take with me. I hoped someone else would be able to do it because I definitely didn't feel I would manage.

"Nobody stopped me as I crossed the parade ground, so I didn't even have to show my paper to anyone. The guards were all having their midday meal, and the whole camp was quiet. It was Sunday, and not a work day, and the prisoners took the opportunity to rest."

CHAPTER 11

"The barracks were quiet. Most of the women were lying on their bunks, either sleeping or just staying there with their eyes closed. As I went through the door, a couple of them sat up in surprise. It was very unusual for anyone who did not belong to the barracks to be allowed in.

"The kapo was there. She motioned to one of the women to move and settled me onto a lower bunk. She asked how far apart my pains were. I told her a couple of minutes, and she nodded her head.

'Not long, then,' she said. 'That's good.' She placed her hand on my belly. 'Yes, pretty soon I think you will have your baby.'

"I gave her the pillow case with the sewing in.

'I need for this to be finished before Frau Hoffman comes back, otherwise I will be in serious trouble.'

"She beckoned to one of the women.

'Take this,' she said. 'Do your best. Eva's life will depend on it.'

"I waited for a contraction to pass. By now I was pretty good at holding in cries of pain. I knew if someone overheard me moaning I could be taken away and gassed. It made me hold the noise in." There was that look in Eva's eyes again. A lost, far away expression.

Sam prompted her. "So I was born?"

"Yes, my baby was born quite quickly," Eva murmured. "I had no idea it would happen so soon. The kapo held my hand and told me to push. Push, Sam. You know what that's like. You were there when your kids were born.

"Even though Helen is quite disciplined, I have no doubt she made some noise during her delivery. Can you imagine giving birth and having to keep quiet? At one point the kapo stuffed a rag in my mouth so I could bite on it, and it would muffle my cries. The other women could see I was struggling and, in order to cover any noise I was making, they started to sing. This was not so unusual. If there was a woman dying, the others might sing quietly to comfort her.

"I was exhausted pretty soon, so how fortunate I was that it was over quickly. Of course there was no pretty blanket to wrap the child in. No adoring husband to put his arms round me and kiss away my tears. Instead, I had a smelly, rough cloth and no pain killers. I didn't even have any water to clean the baby and myself afterwards. And then next, the afterbirth.

"I hadn't managed to steal a knife or scissors, but I remembered reading somewhere, perhaps when I was studying medicine, that in some parts of the world native women cut the umbilical cord with their teeth. The kapo pulled some thread from the sack so that we could tie the cord, and I bit my way through it. Then she wrapped the baby in the cloth and gave him to me.

'What are you going to do now?' she asked. 'You can't take the baby back to your room. He would be discovered. You would both be killed.'

"I hadn't thought that far. I had only been thinking of the birth, not what I could do afterwards. I remember shaking. The birth itself had been a shock and I was weak, but the realisation that we might both lose our lives after all I'd been through was even more of a shock.

"I don't know what I can do," I said. "What *can* I do? If I take the baby back to the Commandant's house, someone will find out and we will be killed and if I stay here, someone will come for me and we will lose our lives."

'There is one thing you could do,' said the kapo slowly. 'Marianna has lost her baby, but she still has milk. You could leave him here…'

'No, no,' I protested,'I can't leave him.'

"The kapo went on,

'It's the best chance he has. It's the best chance you *both* have. And when you go to the kitchen, you can see him. You can walk back to the Commandant's house, past the barracks, and Marianne will hold him up for you to see when it is safe to do. It's not ideal but it's the best I can think of.' She looked kindly at me. Her hands were rough, but they soothed my brow.

'We all want this baby to survive. In the middle of all this death and destruction, this child is a beacon of hope.'

"She made it sound so easy. Sometimes, when your life is all horror, the simplest of suggestions is enough to lift you out of the pit of despair. Of course I wanted my child to live, and I realised that if I took him with me, it wasn't going to happen.

'How long have you got before you need to go back?' asked the kapo.

'I have to be back by eight o'clock,' I answered.

'So, you have time for a rest. Try and sleep for a bit. I'll wake you up when it's time to go back.' She helped me lie down and tucked the baby in beside me.

'Make the most of this time,' she said. 'Make the memories which will keep you strong when you and your child are apart.'

"At first I couldn't sleep. I unwrapped the cloth and looked at every inch of my child. I stroked his cheeks and I counted his fingers and toes as women all over the world who have given birth do. I wrapped my arms round this new life and held my precious boy close. And then I slept. Even in the middle of all the anxiety and worry, I slept, and I woke only when I felt my shoulder being shaken.

'Can you walk?' asked the kapo.

'I know I have to,' I answered, and slowly I got up from the bunk.

"It was the hardest thing I had ever done in my life, handing over my child to Marianne.

'Please be careful,' I begged her. I started to give her instructions about keeping the cord clean and she smiled at me.

'It's all right,' she said. 'I will take care. He will be ok with me.' My last sight of them both was that Marianne was unbuttoning her dress so she could feed the little one.

"The walk back to the Commandant's house seemed like five miles. I was exhausted, I was bleeding and I was aching with the effort of the delivery. Somehow I managed to get to my room and use the bucket shower. Both Frau Hoffman and the Commandant were sticklers for cleanliness, so I knew I had to look as normal as possible. I had just finished, when I could hear the children coming in the front door. They were singing and laughing, and I went to greet them with a smile on my face.

'Did you have a nice time?' I asked.

"They looked at me in surprise.

'Of course we had a nice time. We had tea with Mama and Papa at the café in town, and then we went to the cinema.'

"I was surprised. There had been a lot of Allied bombing, so I wasn't sure the cinema would even be standing.

'But it was very untidy in the town,' Dietrich said. 'There were bricks everywhere and some fallen down houses.'

'And there was lots of smoke too,' added Giselle. 'And lots and lots of soldiers. I saw a truck with a lot of soldiers in it. They all looked very miserable.'

"I didn't know whether to be happy or not. It seemed as if the war was getting closer, and I couldn't work out what effect this might have on the camp and everyone in it.

'Time for your bath and bed,' I said and followed the children up the stairs. Every step was like climbing Everest. How I longed to sink into a warm bath and ease away my aches and pains, but it wasn't possible.

'Milk and biscuits,' I suggested, 'and then a story and then bed.' The children were tired and didn't argue. When I had finished cleaning the bathroom and tidying up after them, I was able to go to my room and lie down. I slept in my clothes that night, too weary to change and too sad to even think of the new baby I had left, alone in the barracks. Alone and without a mother.

"Life went on. I recovered from the birth. Things seemed to be in order, and I didn't have any infection or problems. I was lucky to have my bucket shower, and I made sure I washed regularly and kept clean. Every afternoon, I detoured back from collecting the food ration and managed to walk back past my old barracks. Some days I was able to see the baby. Some days the kapo wasn't there, and when I got back to the Commandant's house, I worried and shed tears alone in my cellar. I couldn't understand why the baby remained undetected in the barracks, but I could only say a prayer for his continuing safety.

"It began to be obvious that the tide of the war was turning. I overheard the Commandant making plans to move all the prisoners out of the camp. After the war they called these evacuations 'Death Marches' because so many prisoners died. The sick and elderly and the children would be 'disposed of'. We didn't know what happened on these marches, just that people were transferred to other camps.

There was often a lot of movement of prisoners, and we were so malnourished that we just took everything that was happening as normal. Can you imagine, Sam, we thought this kind of life was normal. It's amazing how people can accept what is happening to them.

"Now I had something else to worry about. What would happen if I was separated from my child because we went in different groups? Of course, no-one told me anything. I was just a Jew – the lowest of the low. I had to wait and see what would happen. Even my friend, the kapo, couldn't tell me anything but she promised to somehow re-unite me with my baby, and for that I had to be content.

"The air raids happened more frequently and the noise of the bombs reverberated round the camp. A guard was killed by an explosion, and after that there were reprisals. The Commandant walked about, indiscriminately selecting people to go before the firing squad. There were always screams and shouts and people being dragged away to the punishment block. The camp smelt of burning, and there was a low blanket of smoke over everything. I kept a low profile in the house, trying to become as invisible as possible.

"Frau Hoffman was scared of the bombs. The noise and smoke and crashing upset her, and she worried about the children. She made me sit with them in case they woke, but actually, the children seem to be quite resilient and they slept through most of it.

"And then, there was a night of constant bombardment. Frau Hoffman came to where I was sitting and told me to get dressed. 'You are one of the lucky ones. You are leaving,' she said.

CHAPTER 12

"I couldn't believe this. Was I to leave my baby behind and join one of the Death Marches?

'The Commandant will take you to Berlin,' she said. 'Get your things together.'

'Berlin,' I stammered. 'Why?'

'Because the war is coming to an end, and I can see what will happen. You have been a good worker, so I want you to have a chance.'

"I couldn't believe this. She wanted me to have a chance. Only I knew I couldn't leave without my child. There was no way *I* could have a chance without him, too, having a chance.

"There was only one thing to do. I would have to tell Frau Hoffman about the baby.

'Frau Hoffman,' I began, but she took the wind out of my sails.

'Ah,' she said. 'I expect you want your baby too.'

"I couldn't believe what I was hearing. She knew that I'd had a baby?

'Did you think I was stupid?' she asked. 'It was obvious that you were expecting, although my husband never knew till I told him.'

"My heart sank. She had told the Commandant who, no doubt, would just shoot us both.

'No,' she said. 'We are not going to shoot you. You can take the baby with you. Now hurry. Take these clothes and change. You certainly can't go in what you are wearing.'

"The windows shook and so did I. I could hear crashes and bangs and the sounding of the alarm as the guards rushed to put out several of the fires started by falling bombs.

"She gave me a warm coat and hat. 'Put these on, get into the car and wait for the Commandant.'

"Could I believe her? Was this some warped plan to kill me and my child? I didn't know. Nevertheless, I did as I was told and slipped down the stairs. She followed me.

'Here,' she said, giving me an envelope. 'There is a passport, some papers and some money. You'll need it to buy food. Now, hurry. Go. Get into the car. I'll bring the baby.'

"I sat in the back, shaking and trembling until I heard the firm step of the Commandant, who proceeded to open the boot and load it with various things. Last of all was a bundle, which he placed carefully on top of some blankets.

"He adjusted the mirror and started the engine.

"I saw Frau Hoffman standing by the open door, tears running down her cheeks. I couldn't understand why she was crying.

'The baby? Where is my baby?' I begged the Commandant.

'He's in the boot,' he said unsmilingly. 'I have given him something to make him sleep so he won't cry, and when we get to Berlin you shall have him.'

"There was no sound from the boot. No whimpers, nothing so that when we passed through the various checkpoints there would be no need to explain why he was driving with a woman and child at that time of night.

"The broken buildings of Berlin approached, and he slowed the car.

'Not long now,' he said and pulled up beside a half demolished block of flats. The top half had gone completely, but there seemed to be some windows intact on the bottom few floors.

'Sit there,' he said forcefully. 'Sit.'

"I was too scared to move. I waited till the boot was emptied and moved towards the car door.

'Sit,' he barked again and I sat, terrified.

"Finally, he pointed to the pavement and gestured to me to get out. There was quite a bit of stuff piled on the ground, including a small pushchair and several suitcases.

'These are for you. I wish you luck,' he said, 'and if we meet again when all this over, I will claim back what is mine.' I didn't know what he meant, but I thought perhaps he would come back for some payment after the war. Somehow that seemed very threatening.

"I still couldn't understand why he was helping me, other than he might have thought I came from a rich Jewish family and he would get some reward. And, you know, Sam," Eva looked directly at her son, "sometimes the most bestial people can do a good deed. I wasn't going to question him or argue. I was one of the lucky ones. I was out of the camp, and I had my son, and we were going to survive. I was still very, very frightened, so I stood on the pavement waiting for him to drive off.

"He got back into the car and I heard the engine fading into the distance. It was dark, past curfew time, and if there were any soldiers about, I would be arrested for being out so late. I needed to get off the street as soon as possible.

"The baby stirred and whimpered. I was bewildered, of course. I couldn't understand why I had been taken out of the camp and left in a suburb of Berlin. The baby cried again, and I picked him up, peeling back his blanket. I hadn't seen my child for a while, and I was trembling with excitement that he and I were together again, albeit it in awful circumstances. I had only seen him from a distance, and that had been torture for me. I was grateful to Marianne for caring for him, for feeding him, but I was jealous too.

"Two bright eyes looked up at me, the sobbing stilled as he nestled into my arms. A thumb dislodged itself from his blanket and was put firmly in his mouth. But the little face that looked up at me was a replica of the Commandant's." Eva paused, shaking with emotion.

"What are you saying?" cried Sam. "You mean that the Commandant is…was…my father? He raped you?" Sam put his head in his hands as he tried to process what Eva was saying. A look of horror crossed his face. "You told me about the brothel your sisters went to. Did you go there as well?"

"No, he didn't rape me. The officers' brothel was where Anna and Leah went. I was spared that."

Sam interrupted.

"You mean…you mean…" he stuttered. "I can't bear to think of it." His words ran one into the other, and he didn't let Eva speak.

"You went with the man who had all your teeth ripped out, who chopped off your finger, who kept you in a cellar. Ma…I can't believe it. I don't want to believe it. You said you and Dad…"

He stopped, unable to continue, and his shoulders shook with emotion.

"Tell me it's not true, Ma, tell me it's not true."

"Sam, Sam, listen to me. Calm down." Eva tried to look into his eyes, but he kept his face turned away from her. "I did *not* sleep with the Commandant. I would rather have died than let him put his hands on me."

"Then, if that's the case…"

"That *is* the case, my darling. These are words I never thought I would say to you. Words I never thought you would have to hear. Sam, Sam, look at me. You know how much I love you. You have to believe that."

"Then what, Ma? What is the missing bit of this puzzle?"

"The missing bit, as you put it, is that I did not give birth to you but, Sam, in all other ways I am your mother." Grasping his hands, she looked directly at Sam.

"Sam, look at me. Talk to me."

"So if you aren't my mother, then who is?"

"Can't you guess, Sam?"

"There was a dawning reality in Sam's eyes. "Frau Hoffman," he said slowly. "Frau Hoffman."

"Yes, Frau Hoffman."

"All these years, Ma, all these years. You've never said anything."

"How could I, Sam? You are my son and I love you. There was no need. I thought the Hoffmans were all dead, so what was there to tell?"

Sam got up and went to the door.

"I have to go out, Ma," he said. "I have to clear my head. I can't take all this in. I need to talk to Helen. I need to think things over."

"But it's late. It's dark. Wait until morning. Stay over like you said you would. We can talk some more, and I can tell you the rest of my story."

"I know there's more to tell but not now. I need to be on my own, but I will come back. I have my key, so don't wait up."

The front door shut quietly behind him. Even in moments of great stress, Sam was controlled and careful. His mind was racing as he paced down the empty street. Eva was right, it was late and there was a chill in the air and a fine rain just starting. He turned his coat collar up and headed for the main road.

Behind him he could hear footsteps. Another late walker, or maybe not. Something made him stop and turn round. There was the man from the coffee shop in Berlin, smiling strangely at him.

"Did she tell you?" he asked. "Do you know everything now?"

Sam was stunned. "How did you know I was here?" he asked. "How did you know where to find me?"

"You would be surprised at what I know about you, Sam," the man leered at him. "What did Eva tell you?"

Sam had an unexplained feeling that he should tell this man everything Eva had told him, but he fought down the urge. There was no way he should confide in this sinister stranger.

"What my mother told me is nothing to do with you," he shouted and walked off quickly.

"That's what you think now," the stranger screamed back. You obviously don't know it all. But you will. Wait till you hear the rest of the story. We'll meet again, Sam. Oh yes, we'll meet again."

CHAPTER 13

Sam's brain was overactive, trying to absorb everything he had heard. He took no notice of the rain, which was getting heavier and soaking through his coat. Rivulets ran down his face and suddenly he realised how wet he was.

The open door of a pub beckoned, and he went into the smoky warmth. There was no curiosity on the face of the man behind the counter. He'd seen it all before. He thought he could recognise in Sam the demeanour of a man who had rowed with his wife and when Sam asked for whisky he passed it over the counter without a word. Sam dug into his pockets for change to pay for his drink.

He took it to a table in the window. Condensation was running down the glass, and the table had ring marks on its top. There was a comforting dense atmosphere, and the sound of the juke box playing in the background wasn't loud enough to interrupt his thoughts.

He wasn't who he thought he was. This thought kept churning over and over in his mind. He wasn't who he thought he was. Realisation struck him. What about Rachel – was she his sister or not? Had Friedrich known he wasn't Sam's real father? There were so many questions circulating in Sam's mind and he knew that, once again, Eva was the key.

There would have to be further explanations of how he came to be here, in London, forty-six years old and just finding out about his parentage. Even though he wanted, no needed, to know, he wasn't ready to process the information. He didn't want to go back to Eva's house, so he sat, as the warmth of the pub dried out his coat. The smell of damp wool mingled with pipe tobacco and cigarette smoke. He crossed to the bar and asked for another drink, conscious that he hadn't eaten much and that he probably shouldn't have any more.

He realised he was lightheaded when he thought of possible news headlines. 'Dedicated rabbi drunk in the pub.'

He groaned. He needed to clear his head, ready for further revelations. He checked his watch and, with a shock, realised he'd been out for over two hours. Eva would be worried, so he should get back. He tossed back the last of his drink and pushed through the door. The rain had stopped, but drips fell on his head from the shop awnings. Shivering, he speeded up to get back to the house. He looked over his shoulder, but there was no sign of the stranger.

Eva was pacing the floor. She had never seen Sam so distressed. He was usually so calm and collected, and she worried about where he was. He'd been away for over two hours, and she decided she would have to call Helen to see if he'd gone home. Obviously, she didn't want to worry her daughter-in-law, but she knew that Helen also would be wondering what was going on. She was just about to pick up the receiver to call her when she heard the quiet closing of the front door.

"Oh Sam," she breathed. "I was so worried about you. Are you alright?"

"Yes, I'm alright." Sam stopped. "Actually, no. I'm not alright. I've just had the worst shock of my life and you ask me if I'm alright. Of course I'm not alright. How could I be alright? You owe it to me to tell me the rest of the story."

"It's midnight…"

"I don't care if it's midnight or two o'clock in the morning. You have to tell me. I'm torturing myself, and I need to know."

He took his coat off, shook it, and hung it on the coat hook.

"Now, Ma…" and saying that word made him break down completely. "Everything I took for granted has just gone up in smoke. My parents, my life, even my religion. No wonder that man in Berlin wanted me to talk to you before I go before the panel, although how he knew about all this beats me."

Eva took his arm.

"Sit, sit. I'll get you a hot drink. You're shivering, Sam. You don't want to get ill."

Sam allowed himself to be guided into the sitting room, where he collapsed into an armchair. With a start, he remembered Helen. "Ma, I need to call Helen…I need to tell her."

"It's ok, I'll call. I'll tell her you're staying over. We can tell her the rest when we see her. Now is not the time."

"What did she say?" Sam asked as Eva came back into the room.

"You know Helen. She knew you and I were going to talk, so she didn't expect you back early. She said to sleep well and she'll see you tomorrow. Now, I really think we should go to bed. You know where everything is."

Sam sat upright.

"I have no intention of going to sleep while this, this…news, is going round and round in my head. I want you to tell me the rest of the story."

"I don't know if I can."

Sam looked at her sternly.

"Well, okay, Sam. But it's a long story."

"So what happened after you realised that the baby wasn't your own son. What did you do?"

"What could I do? I wanted my own child, of course, but this little face peering up at me would have melted a heart of stone. I didn't know where I was, and most of all, I didn't know where the Commandant and Frau Hoffman were or what might happen to them. I didn't know how to give you back.

"Somehow, I managed to haul all the cases to the door of the flats. I thought maybe someone would take me in. I had a child to feed and no place to sleep. There were railings along the side of the pavement, and I could see that there was a flight of stairs down to a basement. The door was half open, so I left all the stuff outside and went to investigate. The creak of the door sounded so loud in the still night air. I was so frightened that soldiers would come and drag me away.

"There was a small room behind the door, probably for the caretaker, but it was obvious no-one had lived there for a while. There was a table and a couple of chairs and, in the corner, a bed. On the other wall was a sink, and that made me aware of how thirsty I was. The water that came from that tap was better than any glass of wine I had before or since. There was a narrow alcove at the back of the room and inside a toilet. There was no door, just a tattered curtain hanging limply from a wire.

"I decided that I would have to take a chance, so I pushed and pulled until everything was with me in that room. I put you on the bed, Sam, and you just lay there and watched me, as if you knew that you had to be quiet. Once everything was in, I was able to turn my attention to you. You needed food, but where on earth could I find food at that time of night, especially as I didn't know where I was and where the shops were.

"I remembered the packet of papers Frau Hoffman had given me. I opened the envelope and tipped everything out onto the table. There was a large amount of money, identity papers, ration card, passports and a letter with my name on. I will get it for you and you can read for yourself."

She crossed to the sideboard and pulled open a drawer, rummaging around for the important document. Wordlessly she passed it to Sam.

"It's in German, of course but you can manage that, can't you?"

Absently, Sam nodded.

"As long as it's not too complicated. Anyway, you could read it."

"No, Sam. I want you to read what it says for yourself. I'll go and make some sandwiches while you do."

Sam opened the envelope and withdrew the closely written sheets of paper. He realised that he would be able to understand it quite easily.

My dear Eva,

Of course you will be surprised that I know your name. I have always known your name, ever since you came into our household. I knew from the first time I saw you that you would be the perfect person to help me if the war took a wrong direction for Germany. I knew you came from a good family, that you might have been a doctor if you had finished your studies and that you were pregnant. Of course, I knew that you were a Jew but I decided that you might be the only way out so I would have to ignore that. I didn't have a plan at that time, no ideas about how to keep my children safe but, somehow, I knew that you would be part of it.

I was pregnant with my third child. Hitler wanted us all to have lots of children so I was doing my bit. My life was easy compared to yours but I suffered the agony of uncertainty of whether or not we would live, just as you were doing.

I knew the war wasn't going well and I had listened to some of the other wives. They were all such devotees of Hitler and said that if anything were to happen to him, they and all their family, their children would die. They would see to it.

I didn't want my children to die. I wanted them to live but as the days and weeks drew on I could see that timewas getting short. And then I went into hospital to have my baby. I don't know who was more surprised when I gave birth to twins. There had been no indication that I was expecting two babies, and it was at that time that my plan began to formulate. I had to persuade Ernst but you have seen how he is with me. He would give me anything I asked for. I wanted, so much, for all my children to live but I knew when the time came that wouldn't happen. Ernst had cyanide capsules for us both and poison to put in the chocolate milk for the children.

I begged him to let one of the babies live. I told him we could keep the second baby a secret and we would give him to you and help you escape. I told him you were expecting but I knew that your baby couldn't survive. The rest of us would have to take our chances. He was shocked and angry but eventually he agreed. He said that if things turned out differently we would claim the baby back as our own.

My husband made sure that the nurse who attended me wouldn't speak. One day she had an 'accident' on the way to work. Things were so disorganised at the hospital that we knew no-one would remember we had left with two babies, not one.

We only registered one baby and when we came home we made sure that no-one ever saw both of them at the same time. Of course, they are identical so that was the easy bit. I had been trying to do my bit for Hitler's Germany so I was sad that I couldn't claim the

Mutterkreuz, the award given for having 4 children. On the positive side, I was hoping that one of my children, at least, would live. The worst decision I had to make in my life was which one I would give to you because I loved them both. I had to decide that the stronger of the two would be given the chance of life.

Did you think I didn't know you were pregnant? Did you think I didn't know when you went into labour? I made it easier for you by taking the children out for the day. And when you came back from visiting your 'friend' I made it easy for you to manage your chores.

All this was my idea but I needed to convince Ernst it would work. He was happy to die for the Fuhrer and in the beginning he wanted all of us to die together. I tried so hard to persuade him that one child, at least, should live to carry on the Hoffman name. We talked far into the night to see how we could achieve this. Ernst, at first, was not happy to entrust a child to you.

You are a Jew and there was no reason why you would do this. There were so many imponderables and we knew that if we were caught, trying to smuggle a prisoner and an Aryan child out of the camp, it would be the end for us all. He didn't know if he could trust you with his child. You might decide to take your revenge for the ill treatment in the camp and kill the baby. I told him over and over again that you wouldn't do that and I hope so much that I am right.

There were some positives. No-one would question the Commandant leaving the camp. No-one would know what was in the boot of the car and as long as the baby didn't cry, his hiding place would be a secret.

We knew we couldn't ask you to help. Somehow, we would have to convince you that you were leaving with your own child and the best way to do this would be to just spring it on you. There would be no time for you to think.

So why did we choose this time to carry out our plan? Well, Eva, you will be wondering now what happened to your own child. I have to tell you that your baby died yesterday. He was just too weak and frail to survive. I know you have been seeing him every day at your old barracks. If we waited any longer we knew you would find out your child had died and you would not agree to this escape plan.

In preparation for your departure, I had put some clothes together – some for my son and some for you. There is food in another of the bags, the small baby carriage so you can go out and some other things I thought you might find useful.

I don't know what the future holds for any of us but this is the only chance my son has. Please care for him as if he was your own. I know that you will do your best and, when this war is over, if we can, we will find you and reclaim our child. If we do not survive, I leave him in your care.

The letter was signed Greta Hoffman.

CHAPTER 14

Sam had been so very still while reading it. Eva sat opposite watching his face and waited for him to speak.

Finally, he looked up. There were tears running down Eva's face and, faced with her grief, his tears also fell. Wordlessly he held out his arms, and they clung on to each other.

"I can't take all this in. To find out in one night that you are not who you think you are is something I am having great difficulty in assimilating."

"I know, Sam, but all this is true. And when I read the letter, I realised what the Commandant had meant when he said he would come back for what was rightly his. I could understand why Frau Hoffman was crying silent tears as I got into the car. She hadn't even been able to hug you before the Commandant put you in the basket.

"You need to understand that I was in shock. I had learned that my own child, my darling baby, had died. And at the same time I was given another child. You know, some people replace a dog with a puppy if the older dog dies. They think it will help with the healing process. I've never understood this but I found myself in that position. My child had died. No time to grieve, to sit shiva, and then I was given another child."

"I can understand your shock, but you need to tell me why you didn't try to hand me back. Why didn't you try and trace the Hoffman family after the war?"

"Oh Sam, it's not as easy as that. I want you to try and think what Berlin was like at that time, and how I was in constant danger of my life. The war was still raging when I got out of the camp, and I was a Jewish woman now in hiding and with a German child. That would have been instant death. There is much more to tell Sam, and I don't think either of us will sleep until you hear it all." She passed him the plate of sandwiches.

"No, I can't eat. I need to hear the rest."

"Alright, I will go on. There was some baby formula in the bag and bottles. Somehow I had to find a way of mixing the two together and feeding you. I said before there was water but there was no cooker. No way of heating any food, but there was a fireplace and a lot of broken bits of wood on the floor. Surprisingly, there were matches in the bag and I managed to make a fire. It made the room warmer while I investigated the cupboards.

"I suspected there had been looters in because there was little left. I found an enamel basin, and I filled it with water and put it on the fire. I know, very primitive, not hygienic, but it was the best I could do. You watched me from the bed, as if you knew you had to be patient, but when I put the bottle in your mouth, you drank it straight down and snuggled against me. You were not a replacement for my child, Sam, but you were easing my heartache."

"Frau Hoffman had really thought about what to put together. There were candles, some tins of food, even some soap. I emptied the larger suitcase of clothes and the smaller bag of nappies and blankets. I made a bed for you in the suitcase – it was the best I could do, and when you were warm and clean and fed, you put your thumb back in your mouth and went to sleep.

"By the light of one of the candles, I examined the paperwork. According to the identity card and passport I was Eva Hoffman. The passport looked authentic. The picture was certainly of me, and I remembered that when I first went into the camp there was a photographer taking photos. The Commandant must have used one of those.

"There was a travel pass and two ration books; as a German mother, I was entitled to extra food and could get this at any shop, once I had the necessary stamps in the books. All this depended on whether or not I would have the confidence to go out into the street and make my way to the town hall to register. It would mean going to the heart of the Nazi command in Berlin. I would have to brave any questions that would be asked.

"I didn't think I would sleep that night, even though I was exhausted. My thoughts were going round and round in my head. I was out of the camp, and I knew my child was dead. Yet, here beside me, was another child, and I knew I had to protect him. I lay on the bed, my hand touching you in the suitcase crib I had made for you, expecting to lie awake all night.

"I was so surprised when the early morning light came in through the cracks in the door and woke me. The dirty windows had black paper taped over them so the room was very dark, but those shreds of light were enough. I had no idea of the time, but I was hungry and amazed that you hadn't woken during the night. You seemed to have an in built sensor which kept you sleeping. That had allowed me to have some proper rest, because I did feel rested. I knew there was a hard job ahead but I felt more able to cope.

"The fire was still alight and I heated more water. I was able to wash and I sponged you down. You enjoyed another bottle, clutching on to my hands. In retrospect, I'm not sure how you survived, you know. Now we place such emphasis on keeping everything clean, and I can tell you that the sanitary arrangements in that room were very primitive. I think what saved our lives was that I could keep a fire going and that there was still water.

"The first task was to register at the town hall. Without a Berlin stamp on my ration books, I would not be allowed to buy food. I had to appear clean and tidy and confident when I presented myself so I searched through the clothes Frau Hoffman had put together to find something to wear. I found a blue costume and a small hat, some clean clothes for you and wrapped you carefully in a blanket ready to go into the baby carriage. I pulled the door carefully behind me and just hoped that when I returned everything would be as I had left it.

"Outside, the street was another world. It was difficult to get between the piles of rubble and broken bricks. Whole houses had collapsed, and people were climbing through the ruins trying to find the bodies of their relatives or trying to salvage anything which might be of use. Women, with their hair wrapped in headscarves, pulled at huge lumps of masonry and, occasionally, there was a shout as something

109

was found. I hurried past. I didn't want to be challenged. I thought that my tidy dress made me stand out a bit. I realised I should have been more thoughtful about what to wear so that I would fit in. I made up my mind that I wouldn't make that mistake again.

"The town hall was still standing, the red and black flags fluttering in the breeze. There were soldiers flanking the great wooden door, and they asked me what I wanted. I told them I had come to register, and they indicated the second floor. One of them came over to help me with the baby carriage and I smiled my thanks. Inside, I was like a jelly. I thought that any minute I would be stopped and challenged, but nothing happened.

"Inside the Registration Office I was asked why I wanted to register in Berlin. I told the officer that I had come from Cologne, where I had been staying with my parents after the baby was born. My whole family had been killed in an air raid, and so I came back to Berlin to be with my husband who was stationed here.

"They believed me, and I was amazed at how easy it was for me to tell this story. The issuing officer looked at you, asleep in the baby carriage, and smiled. I don't suppose it crossed their minds that a Jew would have the confidence…the chutzpah to do what I was doing. Actually, Inever thought I would be strong enough, but there was no alternative if I wanted to live.

"They stamped my papers and told me where the nearest shops were. Two soldiers helped me down the stairs again, and I breathed a sigh of relief as I turned my back and set off to reconnoitre the area. I thought that the shopkeepers might be suspicious of me but you know, Sam, there is a saying that we should hide things in plain view, and it was certainly working for me. I was a Jew, walking around where anyone could see me. It was obvious though, that no-one would ever have thought that a Jew would be so bold as to register at the town hall.

"There was little food in the shops, and it seemed to take a lot of coupons to get what I needed. I bought carefully because I had no idea how long the money would last and no idea where I could get more.

"I walked back to my little room. I could see that outside there was a large truck, soldiers shouting and people being hustled on. I realised this was another round up, and my heart bled for those poor souls who were being taken away. I felt helpless. I knew there was nothing I could do, but my instincts made me want to shout and scream and yell. Instead I walked briskly to the flat.

"The whole country was in chaos. The Death Marches were taking prisoners from one camp to another, but the soldiers were still obeying orders to round up more people. I turned to go into the flat and an officer came over.

'Papers?' he asked, and I handed them over. I thought he looked carefully at them and that the inspection seemed to take an age, but eventually he handed them back and waved me on.

"The little room already seemed like home. I lived there for three months, Sam. Three long months, worrying all the time that I would be stopped and arrested when I went out; worrying that there wouldn't be any food, or wood for the fire or anything else we might need. I worried that I might run out of money, that you might fall ill – so many worries and no-one I could confide in – no-one I could trust.

"Like the other women, I scavenged as much as I could, feeling elated when I found something which could be of use; a bucket with only a small hole in it, a kettle without a lid. Once there was some tinned food from the kitchen of a demolished house. One day I found an alarm clock with broken feet. It was a great find. All of these things went back to my new home.

"And you thrived. You were about six months old and so very, very bright. You said your first word in that little room. As you can imagine, I spent all day talking to you, so no wonder you were able to talk back.

You said, 'Mama,' and I cried. I cried for my loss and for what might have been. I was resigned to the fact that Friedrich and my own child were dead, but I knew that in you I had the opportunity for rebirth."

"So what you're saying is that you had no intention of giving me back." Eva shook her head. "That's not true, Sam. You must know I love you."

"You wanted me to replace your dead child. Did this child have a name? Please don't tell me you called me 'Sam' after him. That would be too much to bear." Sam went on angrily.

"No, of course not. I couldn't do that. I called my child 'Reuben' after my brother, but there was no way I would give you the same name. You know our tradition to name a child after someone who had died."

"Because people would have worked out you were Jewish, if you had a child with a Jewish name?" asked Sam bitterly. Eva shivered.

"No. You already had a name, but I didn't know what it was. Remember I didn't know that Frau Hoffman had twins.

I knew she had a baby called Hans, but I didn't know there was another one. Sam, you have to believe me. So I didn't know if your name was Hans or if that was the name of your brother."

Sam rolled the word 'brother' round on his tongue. It was a strange feeling to think he had a brother – actually, a twin brother.

"So, why call me Sam?"

"Well, Hans means 'Gift from God.' I knew that. And Samuel has two meanings, Sam. You should know this. It means either 'God's name' or 'God heard.' I knew this also. I felt that the two meanings just fitted my situation and the situation of Frau Hoffman. God had heard both of our prayers – I had the opportunity to love another child, and she had the opportunity to ensure her baby's safety.

"And then there was 'Reuben'. My brother was the only son my parents had. Reuben means 'behold a son', so how strange that all these names should be interlinked. And every day, when I looked at you, I thanked God for leaving you in my charge. I didn't really look to the future, although I knew that one day I would have to give you back, even if I didn't know how."

Sam raised an eyebrow in disbelief.

"I made friends with some of the other women, and soon the rumours started that the Red Army was coming. It was spring time, April, and Berlin had suffered heavy bombardment. The damage to property got worse and hordes of soldiers were sweeping the streets for any Jews they might have missed.

"Every night I lay in bed praying that we would survive. I didn't know whether I should try and find another place to

113

live, but the other women urged me to stay. They, too, were without men, and there was a camaraderie between us, a bit like the friendship with the villagers I had enjoyed before the war." Eva stopped to think about that, then nodded.

"Were you never worried that people would discover you were Jewish?" Sam asked thoughtfully.

"Of course I was worried. I worried from the moment I woke up each morning till I went to sleep again at night. But what could I do?

"I had to be extremely watchful all the time. I constantly reminded myself that if they did find out I was Jewish, my time on earth would be shortened. And that meant you, too, would die. You have to realise that most people hated the Jews. No matter how irrational it was, Hitler had spread the seeds of hatred in Germany, and they had certainly grown shoots and sprouted in Berlin."

CHAPTER 15

"I stayed in that little flat, holding on to you night after night while bombs rained down upon the city. Afterwards, I knew that this was the Fall of Berlin but, at the time, I only knew that our lives were in danger. The city was reduced to rubble during this bombardment. Somehow, I don't know how, we women learned that Hitler had obviously realised he wouldn't win this war and he had taken his own life.

"There was total chaos. Water pipes were severed, gas mains were on fire and I felt as if I was living in hell. It *was* hell, make no bones about it. And over the city there was a pall of smoke and a stink of," Eva paused to catch her breath, "a stink of death. And then there was the sound of tanks, crunching over the bricks, stopping only when they found a woman. I knew what was happening. I heard the screams. It was the Russians, the Red Army.

"I had survived the early years of the war. I had lived through being in a camp. I had somehow managed to stay alive in a war torn city and now my greatest fear was that I would be raped before I was killed. Again, I thought of you. You were my life and I had to protect you.

"I barricaded the flat. I pushed everything I could against the front door, and I stayed hidden for days. I couldn't put a fire on, I couldn't heat water, and I had to use the bucket with a hole in after the toilet became blocked. My meagre supply of food was dwindling, and I thought there was a real possibility we would die from starvation.

"I could hear the Russians outside, coming nearer. They were systematic in their search, and when they came to the door, I put my hand over your mouth in case you cried. There was banging and pushing, but in the end they stopped and moved away. I thanked God again for saving us.

"I welcomed the thin rays of sunlight coming through the cracks in the door and when I heard a faint cry outside, I made up my mind to see what or who it was. I took my barricade down very carefully and looked through the crack to see what it was. The emaciated figure of a man lay on the steps, and I thought he was dead. There was nothing I could do but retreat back into my hiding place and I turned to do just that. Then I heard a voice saying,

'Help me,' and I realised that he was still alive.

"I couldn't leave him on the step. I could see he wasn't a Russian soldier. He was too old and still dressed in camp clothes. I knew he was a Jew like me. It was my duty to help, so somehow I found the strength to drag him in and heave him on to the bed. I made sure the door was boarded up again before I went to him. Safety was still my first thought.

"He was filthy, dressed in the stripy uniform of a concentration camp. I knew those clothes well for I had worn them myself. His finger nails were cracked and his feet were bare, but when I took a closer look at him, I realised he was not an old man. In fact, he was probably around the same age as me.

"I held a cup of water to his lips and he drank gratefully. Then he asked for more. He was exhausted – too exhausted to eat, so I left him to sleep while I tried to get some food together for him. There was little left in my store cupboard and no way to cook anything, but I had a couple of carrots and a potato. When he woke up, I offered them to him. He hadn't eaten in days and gnawed at that raw potato as if it were the finest steak.

"He told me his story. He had been an inmate of Sachsenhausen concentration camp." Eva's voice shook. "If you don't know what that was, Sam, it was a death camp. People who were imprisoned there worked until they died. He had been fortunate that other inmates had protected him because he was a rabbi. Can you imagine, a rabbi had survived? It truly was a miracle.

"The Russian Army, the same one that had been terrorising the women of Germany, had liberated the camp on the day that Hitler had killed himself. But with liberation came the realisation that he had nowhere to go. Like many of the other released prisoners, he could only go home. But there was no home for him.

"The Berlin he knew, where he had been a young rabbi before the war, no longer existed. By the time he got to my flat, he was nearly at death's door. And so, you see, Sam, it was bershert that he should find himself outside my flat."

Sam was so still listening to this. He had been holding his breath and he exhaled slowly, imagining himself in that situation. Eva coughed and went on,

"It was amazing how he managed to pull himself together. I really thought he would die, but after two days he was well enough to talk more. He wanted to know how I had managed to survive, especially with a baby.

"I had to be economical with the truth. I couldn't tell him that you were a German baby; I couldn't tell him what the Commandant and Frau Hoffman had done. I only told him that you had been born in the camp, which of course was true, and that we had escaped, which was also true. He had no reason to disbelieve me and he accepted my story.

"I told him about Friedrich and we said kaddish together, and then he asked if you had been circumcised. My heart sank, as this was something I'd never thought about. I could only tell him that there was no-one in the camp who could have done it and his eyes twinkled at me.

'We can soon put that right,' he said. 'In Sachsenhausen I made sure any boys born had a brit milah. It was the greatest mitzvah I could do. I kept everything I need in a hidden pocket on the inside of my jacket. 'He showed me. 'We can make sure this precious boy becomes a part of our community.'

"Oh Sam, what could I do? I knew you weren't Jewish. You were German born, and the son of a commandant to boot." Sam groaned at this. His whole life, he realised, had been a sham, and yet he felt Jewish. He was a rabbi, he couldn't be more Jewish.

"So there in that dirty cellar, Rabbi Langer circumcised you, while I watched terrified that you might scream and draw attention to us. I worried that you might get an infection. You did neither. You took everything in your stride, just as you do now, and you healed quickly.

"And then we knew the war was over. Well, it might have been over officially, but Berlin wasn't suddenly resurrected. There were still piles of bricks and fallen masonry and demolished properties. There was still nowhere to live and little food. Now we were at risk from the Russians; there were looters everywhere, even though there was little to steal and we were desperately hungry.

"And for me, the worst sound of all was the noise of the tanks as they heaved their way over everything in front of them. I will never forget that noise as they crushed buildings which had been razed to the ground and surged down what was left of the streets. They were like evil armadillos.

"Rabbi Langer and I talked endlessly about what to do. We needed food; you needed food. The choice was simple; starve to death in this little flat or risk our lives by going out. Rabbi Langer wanted to go on his own. He thought it would be safer if I stayed behind. I, on the other hand, felt there was safety in numbers and eventually he gave in. I suspected that he was weaker than he was saying, so an arm to lean on might be useful.

"When we emerged into the street, it was a whole different world. A nightmare world. There were bodies lying where they had fallen, and we had to step carefully over them in order to get to where we thought the town hall might be. We needed official papers from the Russian Army to get food.

"We rounded a corner and, surprisingly, the Reichstag was still standing. The hated German flag was down, only to be replaced by the Russian one. There was nothing for it. We had to go and brave the soldiers and ask for help. I shuddered but I had done this before, so I knew I could do it again.

"I had forgotten that I had German papers. They had worked well for me when Germany was still in control, but now they would only hinder me. Hurriedly, I pushed them in between some loose bricks at the bottom of the stairs, and we walked up those steps, even though we were both shaking inside.

"Rabbi Langer had no papers at all but, dressed in his camp rags, he was obviously a Jewish refugee. I, on the other hand, was dressed relatively well and did not look at all like someone who had just been liberated from a camp and you, Sam, looked like a typical German child.

"I couldn't speak Russian so I wasn't able to answer the soldier's questions, but Rabbi Langer managed to communicate with him. He seemed reluctant to believe him, but eventually, after a lot of persuasion, he gave us a folder of papers and allowed us to leave.

"Of course I couldn't understand the conversation, but I was relieved we were able to walk back down the steps. I could hardly keep quiet till we were back on the street and I could ask Rabbi Langer what had happened.

"He explained that he had told the soldier he had been in Sachsenhausen Camp which was liberated by the Russians. He was liberated but he had nowhere to go, so he had travelled back to Berlin, hoping to find some family left. Miraculously, he said, he had found his sister.

"Rabbi Langer smiled at me, pleased with himself. 'You didn't know I was your brother,' he said, laughing. 'I told the soldier you had been helped by local people because you had a child, even though you are Jewish. They had hidden you and Sam in that basement room.

'And then I said we both needed somewhere to live and food, and the soldier had given us a warrant to use any accommodation we could find and a chitty for some food.

'I think having Sam with us helped,' added the good rabbi, rubbing his face. Berlin was full of dust and grit which seemed to get everywhere, and our eyes were constantly red and sore.

Sam interrupted Eva again.

"Did you try and find any relatives, any of the Hoffmans, anyone at all?"

"Sam, please. This was 1945, when cities were in ruins, train lines were down, phones didn't work. People couldn't move around easily. Of course, there was a procedure for people like us to *try* and find relatives, but there was no way I could have traced the commandant of a concentration camp and told the authorities I had his child.

"The Germans, with characteristic efficiency, had made countless lists of people who had been sent to camps, those who had been exterminated and so on. However, once they could see the beginning of the end, they had tried to destroy everything.

"We went to the records office, but we couldn't find out any information about Friedrich or my family or Rabbi Langer's family. They told us to register our names and said they would contact us if they found out anything. They asked us what we wanted to do now, and we couldn't answer. We were bewildered. Deep in my heart I knew Friedrich was dead, but this seemed to confirm it. It was so final.

"The Jewish Agency had set up an office in the building. It's amazing how quickly they had organised themselves, and for that I will be eternally grateful. The advice they offered was for us to apply to go to Palestine.

"This was something neither Rabbi Langer nor I had thought about, but it seemed entirely logical. It was obvious that we didn't have any family left, and neither of us wanted to stay in a country which held such awful memories. The sooner we could leave Germany the better.

"In the meantime, we had to live as best as we could. I was worried that you would get typhus or cholera because of the dead bodies lying around and the lack of clean water. I couldn't get away soon enough. We decided to stay in the little flat, rather than look for somewhere else.

"I began to be very frightened of what was happening in the streets. I could hear the noise of shouting constantly, and one day when I looked out of the window, I could see a group of young boys – teenagers, stumbling down the road. They were wearing German Army uniforms, but they were only children, Sam. They were the remnants of the Hitler Youth, enlisted by Hitler to fight his war. I felt so sorry for them."

Sam interrupted incredulously.

"You felt sorry for them when they were programmed to kill you. They were German. Didn't you think of that?"

"Yes of course I knew they were German but so was I. I was a German Jew, don't forget, and these were just children. How could I do anything but pity them?"

Sam shook his head in disbelief.

"After all that had happened to you, you still had the capacity to forgive." His tears began to flow again, as he tried to digest everything Eva was saying.

"So how did we get to Palestine?"

"A woman from the Jewish Agency came to see me. She, too, was anxious for us to get away. She said they were making sure the children got out as soon as possible, and with their relatives too. Rabbi Langer said he wasn't a relative, and she smiled rather sadly at him and said he would have to wait a little longer. There was a ship leaving in two days and I was to make sure I was ready to go.

"Rabbi Langer came with me to the docks at Warnemünde. Somehow, the Jewish Agency had managed to find a ship to agree to sail to Haifa. There were crowds of people there; families, unaccompanied children, dazed looking teenagers and just a few men, looking gaunt and ill.

"Everyone was clutching pitifully small amounts of luggage. Most people seemed to have very little, only the clothes they were wearing and maybe a brown paper parcel. The unaccompanied children looked pale and wan, and it was clear that they had been liberated from camps. They were quiet, and it struck me as unusual and sad, that small children were waiting patiently, not asking for anything and not crying.

"The families seemed stunned. The docks were noisy and confusing, and the people from the Jewish Agency were trying to organise a smooth transition from dry land to the ship. I think there was huge anxiety around whether or not we could trust what was going on.

"You know, after the war, I learned that 1,700 Jews had been hiding in Berlin – another example of what I said before, Sam. If you want to hide it, put it in plain view. These were men, women and children who had been assimilated into German life because they looked Aryan. Blond and blue eyed, and with forged papers which looked absolutely real. They had lived in full view of the Nazis and the soldiers – a few had even worked in German families or for Army officers.

"Some of them were amongst the crowd getting on the ship. The one thing they all had in common was their survival. Their anxious faces as they looked at the freedom the ship offered, just showed how much stress they had been under.

"Rabbi Langer stood awkwardly at the gang plank, waiting for us to take our first steps to Palestine. We had helped each other so much and I felt such a sense of loss that I was leaving this good man behind. My life so far had been a series of losses and I wished so much that the Rabbi could have travelled with us.

'Make sure you leave your new address at the office in Haifa,' he said, 'and I will come to see you when I arrive.'

"It wasn't acceptable for us to touch. I wanted to put my arms around him but I had to content myself with a wave, but you – you he embraced warmly.

'We will meet again,' he said, 'In happier days. Maybe next year in Jerusalem.'

CHAPTER 16

"After that I just walked straight up that gang plank and I didn't look back. I had said too many goodbyes and this was particularly painful. Rabbi Langer and I had shared so much and now I was on my own again.

"There was a huge difference in the way people were behaving. Some stood stock still, stopping others from moving on, and others were moving swiftly but directionless. It was all chaos and confusion. At the end of the gangplank was a desk and a young woman was checking names off lists. I had given my name as Goldman; I wanted to leave the false Hoffman behind and now was as good a time as any. She put a tick against my name and gave me a blue folder.

'This is all the information you need for your journey. Please take it and read it. There will be a meeting in the Ballroom at eight pm tonight and we expect everyone to be there. We will go through what will happen when we arrive in Haifa and we will talk about all the options you have. Do you speak Hebrew?'

"A little," I responded. "The prayer book, that's about all."

'You will find it a bit different because modern Hebrew is a new language, but there will be some words you recognise.'

"I shifted you to my other hip. You were getting heavy, and the young woman smiled.

'It's nice to see a happy baby,' she said. 'So many of the children are damaged by what has happened to them. Your little boy looks okay, though.'

"I looked at you. She was right. You were looking around with intense curiosity at your new surroundings. The ship was wonderful. It had probably been a cruise ship before the Agency had commandeered it and everywhere was understated luxury.

"The walls were decorated with pictures of exotic scenes. The woodwork was highly polished mahogany and the lifts were endlessly moving silently up and down, transporting the passengers to their staterooms.

'So,' she said, 'you have a small cabin just for you and,' she looked at her list, 'Sam. There will be a crib for him and a bunk for you. We have a lot of people on this ship, so I'm sorry we couldn't give you a bigger cabin. We've kept those for couples with children and I can see from my list it's just you and Sam…' her voice tailed off as she saw a tear appearing in my eye.

"She rushed on, 'I think it was originally crew quarters but it is comfortable and clean and you have your own bathroom. Take your luggage with you and settle in. We know that many passengers have been liberated from camps, so I expect you will be glad to have a shower.' She watched my reaction carefully.

'Yes,' I told her. 'I was in a camp but I managed to get away with Sam. I am not frightened of showers but I know many will be after their experiences.'

"She smiled sadly.

'From what I've seen so far, the word 'shower' strikes terror into many, but I can assure that here the water is hot and there is soap and clean towels. Enjoy!' And with that she handed over the folder and moved on to the next person in the line.

"She had said the cabin was small and I suppose it was, but the bed was soft and welcoming. There was a chair and desk and I sat you down on the floor. You were crawling by now so this was new territory to explore. I looked at the papers. There were all sorts of instructions, but the one at the top of the page just leaped out at me.

'If you need clothing, please go to the meeting room between four pm and six pm where you will find a selection of items.'

"I had no idea of the time but thought perhaps it would be better to go before we showered. I couldn't remember the last time I had showered properly and had a change of clothes and my skin tingled in anticipation.

"I was in the meeting room early. The big mahogany clock on the wall said it was only three o'clock, but already there were people setting up long tables. Some of them were piled high with brown paper packages. A redhaired woman beckoned me over and gave me one.

'To make things easier, we have made up individual parcels of clothing for each person,' she said looking at me. 'Of course, we have to estimate sizes, etc, but I think what's in here will fit, even if you don't like the styles.' She smiled

127

at me. 'There will be an opportunity for shopping when we get to Haifa. The markets are wonderful. Here is another parcel for your little one; some nappies, some rompers, and you can get baby formula if you need it when you go into dinner.'

"Her kindness was overwhelming and for the first time I could feel tears in my eyes.

'Now come along,' she said gently. 'We can't have that. You're safe now and soon you will be in Palestine and starting a new life.' She put a comforting hand around my shoulder and this made the tears flow even faster. It was the first time I had felt the warmth of another person's protective arm around me. I can't tell you what that meant. I think it was the beginning of normality again for me.

"Until now, I had washed only briefly in my little room in Berlin. The joy of standing under a steady stream of water was indescribable. I held you in my arms and we stood together until, finally, the water ran clear and we were squeaky clean. You put your little fist out and tried to catch the droplets of water and you giggled as the spray hit your chest. There were big, soft clean towels, and I wrapped you in one and I had the other.

"You looked gravely at me, as much as to say, 'Well what now?' That spotlessly clean thumb went into your mouth and I could read your mind. 'Will it be dinner time soon?'

"I threw away the dirty clothes we had been wearing and undid the string around the parcel. The things inside smelt sweet and clean. I guessed they had been collected from German women, but I didn't care because for the first time in a long time I felt feminine and young.

"Of course, when I looked in the mirror, my face was pale and my hair, though newly washed, was a cloud of curls, falling to my ears. I twisted it into a bun on the top of my head and smiled at my reflection. I rubbed my cheeks to get a bit of colour in them, but nothing could improve where they had sunken in because I had no teeth. The thought crossed my mind that I might be able to remedy that at a dentist in Palestine. Maybe.

"The ship's horn sounded and there was a sudden surge towards the doorways. We were about to sail, and so many of the passengers crowded onto the railings. They waved to people on the docks; small antlike men and women, who were scurrying around, moving the gangplank and picking up rubbish. Very few of us had anyone to wave to and, although I looked for Rabbi Langer, I couldn't see him.

"I had no regrets leaving Germany. As far as I was concerned, I had lost everything apart from you. I never wanted to see Germany again and I had no intentions of ever going back.

"I held you up as high as I could and you waved your chubby arms at no-one in particular. You were just copying everyone else and your giggle was contagious. People around us turned to look and smiled back at you. There was a general movement back inside the ship as we realised we were hungry.

"The dining room was magnificent. The round tables were covered in blue tablecloths and the napkins were all standing to attention in the wine glasses. The lights were sparkling and there were beautifully illustrated menus. Waiters bustled around, taking orders.

"There was a choice of food but for many, this was all too much. They couldn't decide what to have and many ordered several dishes. It was obvious that, despite being refugees, we were going to be treated as special guests. I chose a simple meal; soup with bread, chicken and vegetables and an orange for pudding.

"That meal was so good but I did worry about eating too much. I knew that my stomach would only tolerate a small amount so I started with the soup – so different from the watery offerings I had in the camp and the basic rations I'd eaten in the flat. I could only manage a little chicken but the waiter understood when I explained to him.

"He was a young chap, American or Canadian I think, and he told me that I was being very sensible. He had done this trip a few times already, and one of the biggest problems was the difficulties people had eating a proper meal. He told me to take the orange and have it later.

"I know I was wise because so many passengers were ill that night. I could hear them vomiting and retching and the sea was calm so I don't think it was sea sickness. The next morning at breakfast, there were a few gaps at the tables.

"It took us about a week to get to Haifa and there was a very busy programme for us. Every day there were language lessons in the morning, gentle exercise classes and information about Palestine in the afternoon. In the evening we had free time and there were films to watch or board games to play.

"The children were supervised by willing volunteers and, although I didn't want to leave you in someone else's care, I knew that it was essential for me to learn as much as I could. You came back to me every day at five o'clock, waving your hands at me and shouting 'Mama.' It seemed to me that all the carers wanted to feed the children up because you always had something in your hand when you came back – a piece of apple or a biscuit. Once you were even chewing on a banana. I was amazed that you took to all these new tastes because in Berlin your diet had been very bland.

"I preferred to spend the time in the evening with you. I missed you so much and I loved to smell your baby smell and listen to you giggling in the shower, which never seemed to lose its appeal.

"Midway through the voyage it was Friday. One of the men decided he would organise an erev Shabbat service. There were many who participated but there were also those who refused, saying that God had deserted them. I went along with you because I wanted to make my peace with God.

"Sam, I loved you…and I will love you forever, but I knew that what I was doing was wrong in the eyes of the law. I hoped I would get strength and absolution from God because I would take great care of you. I wanted to tell someone, but I knew I had to keep this secret for ever. And it never crossed my mind that any of your birth family would have survived. The intention of the Hoffman's had been all too clear from Frau Hoffman's letter. They would follow Hitler's example and die together. I think *I* would have died if anyone had taken you away.

"The night before we docked in Haifa, groups of us sat together chatting and exchanging addresses. I was pleased that some of the women who had been friendly towards me wanted to keep in touch. We promised to meet up once we were settled. We were excited and I don't think many people slept that night. Most of us were on deck as the ship sailed into Haifa.

"I was disappointed. I thought it would have been beautiful, with sandy beaches and elegant houses but, in reality, it was industrial and the houses looked shabby and run down. I wondered what kind of place I had come to. Later, I realised that there were indeed beautiful beaches, not visible from the docks, but I didn't know that as I carried you on to dry land. My heart sank when I thought what lay ahead.

"One of the volunteers had given me a shopping bag and I packed everything we had been given into it. There wasn't a lot there – a few clothes and baby bottles and those all important documents which said I had the right to go to Palestine.

"My new friend pressed a piece of paper into my hand.

'It's my address,' she said, 'Just in case you want to contact me.'

"I had become very attached to this woman over the week. She was about my age, tall and slim, and with a strong London accent I found difficult to understand. I had thought my English was reasonably good but obviously not. She was from the East End of London and had answered an appeal from the Jewish Agency to go to Berlin to help with the huge number of displaced persons. 'One day,' she told me, 'I will make aliyah so I might even visit you first, but please keep in touch. I have enjoyed being with you and Sam this week.' She tickled you under your chin and you gave your customary giggle. Nothing seemed to upset or bother you.

"We had been alone when we embarked on the ship and we were alone when we left. There was no-one to meet us, and once again we found ourselves in a line of people, but this time I hoped we had a future."

CHAPTER 17

"You were an immediate success with all the kibbutzniks, who smiled at you and gave you fruit or chocolate. This was a new taste and you soon developed an obsession for it. I don't think it's ever left you, has it Sam?" Eva added with a half smile.

"There was a large tented reception area and tables with signs on in Hebrew. I was so glad of those lessons on board the ship because I was able to make out some of the words. They were the names of various kibbutzes. All the thousand or so passengers on the ship were given the opportunity of deciding which kibbutz to go to, unless of course they already had family there. Sadly, this group was very small.

"I knew what a kibbutz was, of course, but I hadn't realised there were so many different types. I thought they were all religious, ultra orthodox in fact, and undoubtedly some were. But many were secular and all had different purposes. I couldn't decide which I preferred so I stood in the middle of that large tent clutching my papers, the bags and you, until eventually someone came over to see if I wanted any help.

"I knew that this decision would impact on the rest of my life as I couldn't see any way I could leave the confines of a kibbutz. I had no money, no job, nothing but I knew whichever kibbutz I ended up at would offer me a safe haven.

"A young man wearing khaki shorts and jacket spoke gently to me. 'Do you know where you want to go?' he asked gently.

'I can't decide, I can't even think. And I have the baby to consider.'

'So, okay,' he continued. 'I live about 100 kilometres from here on an agricultural kibbutz. We grow avocado pears and potatoes. Stuff like that.'

"I tried to look interested but I didn't know what an avocado was.

'You grow pears?' I questioned.

'Avocado pears. They're not like the usual pears. You have them in salads and they're very good for you. You would be planting and picking and we're a young group. Not too many prayers, actually, but enough. We have a small shul and we have Friday night dinners. You look as if you would enjoy that.'

"I could only nod. Sometimes decisions are made for us and I felt that this was happening now.

'So. Before you get on the bus, you need to go to the medical tent and have a check up. Many of our new arrivals have health problems and if we find out what they are before they come to us, it helps us to organise treatment.'

"He manoeuvred me to the small shedlike building and I stepped anxiously over the threshold. People in white coats made me feel very anxious because I knew that in the camps the doctors would select inmates for experiments. I was surprised to find that no-one inside was wearing a white coat, though, just the same kind of khaki outfit my new friend was wearing, and I was so relieved.

"I couldn't work out which were the doctors and which were the nurses but it didn't matter. They were all kind and gentle and thorough.

"They checked both of us over. You were pronounced fit and healthy.

'Although some sunshine wouldn't go amiss,' said one of the pretty girls.

"I was told I was very underweight. Yes, yes, I know, Sam, not now," Eva said looking down at her ample figure. "My need for food has never left me after nearly starving for so long. And at first it was so difficult for me to eat. I could only really manage soft foods and they were in short supply I can tell you.

"The doctor asked me to open my mouth so he could check my teeth. I had been careful to half cover my mouth with my hand when I spoke. I was very conscious that my face was sunken in and all my teeth were missing.

'You are very young to have lost all your teeth. How did this happen?' he asked kindly, looking at me over his round, rimless glasses. When I explained, I could see tears glistening in the corner of his eyes.

'The mamzer,' he said. 'How could anyone do this to a beautiful young woman? In fact, how could anyone do this to another person? Don't worry. We have dentists who can help. I will give you a letter to take with you so you won't have to tell your story again. There will be a dentist at the kibbutz and he will work wonders. You'll soon be eating hard candy again,' he said laughing. I couldn't fail to be carried along with his enthusiasm. I stood there, smiling, while he wrote and then I took the letter and tucked it carefully into my bag.

"There was a lot of shouting going on outside, and the nurse told me to hurry. The bus would be leaving and I should get on it as quickly as possible. My young friend was there and he held out his arms for you so I could get up the steps. Once I was settled, he passed you back to me and then went down the length of the bus giving out packets of sandwiches, oranges and bottles of water.

"In those days the roads in Palestine were not good and there was a lot of bumping and rocking as the bus picked up speed. Nowadays we can travel 100 kilometres in a short time, but in 1945 it seemed to take forever. It was warm and you dozed against me and only woke occasionally to have a drink.

"I didn't want to nod off. I kept looking around at my new surroundings. The roads were dry and dusty and either side there were pale, flatroofed houses.

"We drove through the gates of the kibbutz and along a long drive, with white stones either side of the roadway. There was a welcome committee waiting in front of long low buildings. I could see a tennis court and winding pathways, red blossom on the trees and the all pervasive smell of roses. It brought back memories of my childhood and Papa coming home on Friday nights with a bunch of flowers for Mama. Grief overcame me. I could see other people, too, were crying. We had been given the gift of freedom when so many of our family had not.

'My name is Avram,' said a deep voice. 'Welcome to your new home. We have food waiting so come, let us get acquainted.' It was obvious that the kibbutz had welcomed other refugees before because as we disembarked the bus there were people waiting to help us. Each one of us was escorted by a kibbutznik into the dining hall. I felt warm and safe and happier than I had been for a long time. I felt a strange shiver down my spine. It was a sense of homecoming.

"The food was delicious. There was a large buffet table where we could go and help ourselves. I noticed that people were not rushing to get food, the way they had done on the ship. They were beginning to realise that there would be more food at the next meal, although I did notice that the bread rolls disappeared into pockets and bags before we left the table." Eva laughed, remembering what it was like.

"And they still do, Ma," Sam said, joining in her laughter. "You always seem to come home from a meal out with a bread roll in your bag." Eva shrugged. It was true she suffered from what people called 'siege mentality' and couldn't bear to see food wasted, even after all these years. "Okay, Sam, enough. Let me tell you about our time in Palestine.

"After we'd eaten, one of the young women came over to me.

'Come, I will show you your new home,' said my guide. It was a small prefabricated building with a corrugated iron roof. There was a large window at the front and the door was open, beckoning me in. I looked around at my new surroundings.

"The little house I was allocated was austere, almost nun like in its simplicity, but there was everything I needed. There was a bed and a crib for you, a couple of armchairs and a small table. On a shelf in the corner, there was a little sink and a gas ring with a kettle placed sturdily on it. There were little jars of tea and coffee, some sugar in a bowl and a packet of biscuits. On the table was a bowl of fruit.

"The small bathroom had a toilet and shower, soap, and toothbrush and paste. I smiled at that. That was something I didn't need. There was a pile of linen on the bed and some clothes.

'You will need this,' said Natasha, handing me a hat. 'The sun gets very strong here, and you should cover your head when you go out so you don't get sunstroke. You're fair skinned,' she added, 'so I'll get you some cream from our pharmacy and some for the baby, and then you won't get sun burned.'

"My tears seemed to fall easily now. For so long I had kept all my feelings tightly locked inside but now that I had started the healing process, they flowed like a waterfall whenever something affected me.

'How do I pay for all this?' I asked hesitantly, pointing at the food and the clothes. 'I don't have any money and nothing I can sell.'

'You don't need to sell anything,' Natasha said and I could see she was moved. 'Here everything is shared and we all work so that makes it all right.' This worried me a bit because I had you to consider. How could I work when I had a baby to care for? Maybe I would be allowed to keep you with me. My thoughts were all over the place. If I kept you with me, I wouldn't be able to work and then what would I do?

'I'll leave you now. Take a rest and when you feel like it, come over to the hall and we can sort out what job you would like.' She gave me a hug and as before, the warmth of someone's arms moved me. The tears started to flow again. Natasha looked at me.

'I think we need a change of plan,' she said gently. 'Come, let's go now. I don't want to leave you while you're upset. I'll walk with you to the hall and you'll be able to get the best job.' There was laughter in her voice and I couldn't fail to like this happy young woman.

'Oh, I nearly forgot, I think you have a letter for the doctor?' There was a question in her voice. I coloured. It was still embarrassing for me to speak. 'Not the doctor,' I replied. 'The dentist.'

'So, ok. Give it to me and we'll arrange a time for you to go and see him.'

"All this was very new and different and I was scared, and when I looked around in the hall I saw many other worried faces.

We sat in rows, waiting for Avram to speak.

'Welcome again and please don't be worried. We are here to help and we are all Jews. Many of us are refugees from the camps. Others are refugees from other countries where Jews were persecuted. Some, a very few, were born here. Iam one of those.

'They call us Sabras, after the prickly fruit. They say we are tough and prickly on the outside and soft and sweet in the middle.' I remember how everyone looked at him with smiles and soft glances, and I could kind of see what he meant. It was obvious that he was held in high esteem by his peers.

"Avram continued.

'Everyone here has their own home.' A cheer went up from some of the people seated. 'And we all work. The children are cared for in the kindergarten. Parents take them in the morning and our nurses look after them. Our children are very precious to us and please be assured we take the best care of them. They are our future.' He was so sincere I knew I could believe him.

"He went on.

'We eat all our meals together and after dinner at six o'clock, parents take their children home. Some of us prefer to do the same job all the time but we do rotate the more boring ones, like food preparation and kitchen duties. Unless you would like a permanent position peeling potatoes or prickly pears,' he smiled arching his eyebrows.

"There was a ripple of laughter but I was devastated at the thought that I would have to hand you over to someone else each morning, even though I knew you would be well looked after. I felt there was no choice but I determined to see what I could do to keep you. We had never been parted since Frau Hoffman had handed you over, except for a few short hours each day on the ship. This would be different because it would be our new way of life.

'Tomorrow will be a day of rest for you and then we will all meet here again on Wednesday morning where you will be allocated your job,' Avram continued. 'Please go over to the table and tell Arya what your skills are and he will find the best place for you to work. And then take some time to explore our beautiful kibbutz.'

"I was lucky when they allocated the jobs because I told them about my two years of medical training. They asked gently if I'd done medical work in the camp and I nodded my head. 'You will be a great asset to us,' said Arya. 'We have so many people here who need to get well.'

"Of course, I wasn't a doctor but I was able to help, and with so many refugees who had poor health I was very useful. I wasn't strong enough to work all day so I was able to collect you early and we played all sorts of games together. You took your first proper steps at that kibbutz and learned more and more new words. Your first language became Hebrew.

"I have so many lovely photos of you playing in the sand pit and paddling in the swimming pool." Eva smiled as she reflected on the good times she'd had in what was then Palestine. She shook herself a little and continued,

"That day it seemed that so much had happened in such a short time. I was glad to walk back across the grass to our little house. When we got indoors, your eyes spotted the packet of biscuits.

'Sam, Sam,' you said, pointing at them and stretching out your hand. I watched your face light up as you bit into the crispy cookie. Memories like these are the jewels in my life.

"I was able to make friends, and my visit to the dentist, which I feared at first, was so rewarding. He looked in my mouth and said I would be able to have new teeth very soon. And, you know, he was right. At first the dentures hurt, but it wasn't long before I could wear them all day. I was no stranger to pain and I wanted to look more like a young woman and not a Bubba.

"Freedom is very subjective, Sam. I was away from the camp and the stink of Berlin but, in a way, I was in another kind of prison because after a while my life became so orderly and regimented. In the beginning, it was a comfort. I knew where I was and what I had to do, but after a few weeks the monotony set in.

"The only relief we had was the exercise we could take, walking around the grounds or playing tennis. I wasn't strong enough for that and so the highlight of my week was the regular Sunday night movie we could see in the big hall.

"There was always a scramble for seats but, whenever there was a news film or a documentary, I wanted to be in the front row. I had a perverse attitude to those films. They were full of the horror of the war and the post war days, yet I had a compulsion, a need to watch them.

"That Sunday night, a few weeks after I'd arrived in the kibbutz, I sat on one of the canvas chairs ready for the film. The lights dimmed and you squirmed a bit on my knee. All the children went with their parents to the movies. Now, of course, we wouldn't allow children to see such things but then we didn't have the knowledge it might harm them and we all wanted to see.

"Sam, I was so lucky to be watching that film. I looked up, just briefly, after trying to settle you and I saw a long line of prisoners coming out of Auschwitz. The picture had obviously been taken in January, when the camp was liberated. The men, still in their awful stripy prison clothes were walking with great difficulty through the gates, to where the American Army was waiting with trucks.

"Their faces were drawn with hunger and they looked like walking skeletons. The camera paused on one face for just a moment and the man looked straight at the photographer before lifting his foot onto the step. A soldier reached his arm out to help him and I could see it was Friedrich."

CHAPTER 18

"In that moment I thought I was going mad. I thought I was hallucinating. Friedrich was dead. I had been told this. He had been dragged off and the men in his barracks had witnessed it. He had left a trail of blood on the stony ground. There was no doubt he was meant for the ovens.

"I jumped out of my seat, screaming. Natasha came over to see what was wrong.

'It's Friedrich,' I cried. 'My husband. I've just seen him. He was dead but I've seen him.' You began to cry. You had never seen me so upset. Natasha took you from me and sat me down. Someone gave me a glass of water and the projectionist turned the film off. I held my hands out for you because I needed to feel your chubby arms about my neck.

'We can re run it,' someone said. 'And you must tell us when to stop it.'

"My hand was shaking as I lifted the glass of water to my lips. The movie ran for a few minutes and there was no picture of Friedrich. I began to think I had dreamed it. I was still missing him so maybe it was just wishful thinking. And then there he was again.

'Stop,' I shouted. 'Stop it now.'

"Everyone in the hall was holding their breath but I was oblivious. It really was Friedrich and I just remember handing you to Natasha before I slid to the floor. I came to in the infirmary, with Avram holding my hand."

'Sometimes this happens but rarely. Very occasionally, someone identifies a relative from one of the newsreels but never in quite such a dramatic way,' he said. 'Are you sure, really sure that the man in that film is your husband?'

'Yes,' I croaked. 'Yes, it really is Friedrich. If he's in that film he's alive'. I saw the look that Avram gave to Natasha then she said gently,

'We will do our best to trace him but so many died after they were liberated. They died from all sorts of things – malnutrition, being given too much food too soon, typhus, all sorts of things. Eva, darling, it wouldn't be good for you to get your hopes up too high. Avram will make some enquiries and we will hope for the best.' I had to be content with that.

"And then it was back to work. I was glad I had something to occupy my mind because there were so many things revolving around my brain. In the days that followed, you seemed to understand that you had to be quiet. Of course, you were always a good baby but, you know, normal…not silent. Now I could sense your eyes were following me everywhere I went. It was good to feel your warm body in my arms and, I admit, I let you sleep with me. I needed the comfort of you beside me.

"Every time I saw Avram, I questioned him if he had any news and eventually he told me to stop asking. He told me that if he heard anything, I would be the first to know. I had to be content with that but as the days and weeks went by, hope started to fade and I began to think I was mistaken.

"But you weren't, were you Ma?" Sam interrupted.

Eva's eyes lit up as she heard him say 'Ma'. Maybe she hadn't lost him.

"No, I wasn't mistaken. I was just impatient." She brushed a tear from her eye.

"The transport bringing new refugees to the kibbutz came at regular intervals. We had all got used to seeing people stepping down looking as dazed and bewildered as we had when we first arrived. I had just finished work and collected you from the kindergarten as another bus moved slowly along the road to the reception area.

"You liked seeing the buses and you waved and pointed to the people sitting aboard. They smiled, as most people did when they saw you, and then I saw the one face in the world I thought I'd lost forever. I thought I was hallucinating. I thought I'd gone mad. I rushed over to the reception hall, and I was standing there when the bus pulled up and people started to move down the steps.

"I heard a voice I thought I'd never hear again.

'Eva, Eva, is it really you?'

Eva's face was suffused with love; the telling of the story had taken her back to that precious moment when a miracle truly did happen.

"It was Friedrich. Thinner and with grey in his hair but definitely Friedrich. 'How?' I stammered. 'How did you get here? And why did no-one tell me? Avram promised…' my voice tailed off as Avram suddenly appeared by my side.

'We didn't tell you because we had no idea when Friedrich might arrive. We had to check everything first, to make sure it really was him. Then we had to organise travel from Jerusalem. I knew it would take time and I knew you would be impatient. We didn't want you to suddenly take off and disappear.'

'Avram was right, Friedrich,' I told him. 'If I'd known where you were, I would have moved mountains to get to you.' I just wanted to hug him and hold him and look after him.

"I could see he was tired but elated. I knew that feeling. I'd been there myself. And then, Sam, then I saw Friedrich's eyes turn to you. He asked in a voice which was trembling with emotion, 'Is he mine? Is this my son? I never thought… The conditions in that camp were so bad I thought you were dead and I thought there would be no child.'

"His shoulders shook and he staggered back against the bus, oblivious to the last few stragglers who pushed past him to get off. 'My child,' he said brokenly. 'My son,' and reaching out his arms for you, he wept.

"I was so glad you didn't cry when he took you. This meeting between father and son was so important, one Friedrich would remember for the rest of his life. You put a little hand up to his face and he kissed it through his tears.

'How old is he? What's his name? How did you get here? Are you ok? Is my son ok?'

'Too many questions,' I said, because to be truthful I had difficulty in speaking. I can't describe how I felt but I can only say I felt like Alice in Wonderland."

"Alice in Wonderland?" Sam looked bemused.

"Yes. Do you remember the story I used to read to you when you were a child? I felt as if I was in a downward spiral and my feet were off the ground as I fell, turning round and round and round."

Sam shifted on his seat. This story was taking a long time and, as he looked out of the window, he saw the faint tendrils of the rising dawn but he didn't want to stop Eva. He had a sense that if she stopped now, he might never hear the full story and, anxious though he was, he knew he wouldn't be able to settle until he knew all the facts.

"Go on," he urged. "What happened after that? Did you tell Friedrich whose son I really was? Did you both keep this secret from me?" he added bitterly.

"No, Sam. I couldn't tell Friedrich, even if in the heat of the moment I remembered whose son you were. Because you know that you are my son."

"No, I'm not," Sam interrupted. "I'm the son of a Nazi and his wife."

Eva struggled with this statement.

"Yes," she finally said. "Your birth parents were two Germans who undoubtedly wanted to see the elimination of all the Jews. But, Sam, you are the child of my heart. No-one could ever love a child more than your father and me."

Stricken at the hurt he'd caused Eva, Sam raised his eyes to look at her. She seemed to have aged ten years overnight. She looked small and defenceless against the tirade of his angry thoughts.

"I can understand you didn't want to give me back but why did you let the lie continue?" he finally asked.

"It's not as easy as that. First of all, I genuinely thought the Hoffmans and their children were dead. Frau Hoffman had made it quite clear that they would follow Hitler to the grave. I still don't understand why they decided to save you.

It makes me think that, underneath it all, they were not as convinced that Hitler was the great leader everyone else thought he was.

"Even so, they might have had relatives still alive and I knew that I could have made an effort to trace them. The truth, as you've rightly said, is that as time went on, I didn't want to hand you back.

"Don't think you replaced my child, Sam, because I was never able to care for him. I never fed him or soothed him when his teeth were coming through. I never had the opportunity to read him a bedtime story or play with him in the bath.

"With you I did all those things. In my mind then and in my mind now, you were and you are my son. And, don't forget, we were in a different country. How could I do anything to trace your family?" She looked piteously at Sam, who looked away not able to speak.

"So, how come we ended up in England?"

"Of course, of course. I will go on. Friedrich and I had spent such little time together since we were married. We only had one night at home after our wedding, and then there were years of separation, with only brief visits before we found each other in the camp. Even then, we weren't exactly together, separated most of the time by a wire fence.

"It felt strange to have him with me and I knew that we would have to learn to live together. Our house was small but still, it was our first home together. We pinned a curtain up to separate a part of the room for you to sleep in while we talked and talked about what had happened to each of us.

"Every now and then Friedrich would put his hand out to touch me – my face, my hands, my hair. He put his arms around me and held me close, and the healing tears came from both of us and mingled together until we couldn't tell whose tears they were.

"We talked about our families and all the friends we had lost. We talked about the people who had died before their time and who we would never see again. We knew how fortunate we were and we were determined to live good lives.

"We fell asleep, exhausted, late into the night and we were woken up by a banging on the door. Both of us still had memories of being dragged out of bed by guards, and we jumped up in such a hurry.

"The door burst open and the room became crowded with kibbutzniks who had had heard of Friedrich's arrival. Everyone was speaking at once, and Friedrich looked bewildered because he couldn't understand. I started to translate but he smiled over at me and said,

'I'm beginning to realise what all the noise is about. Everyone is pleased that I'm here.'

"The crowd parted a little to allow Avram to get in.

'It's been decided you can have a holiday, Eva,' he said to me. 'Take the day off and come and see me tomorrow with Friedrich.' I hadn't thought of work but I was so glad to have these precious hours with my husband.

'Out,' said Avram firmly to everyone in the room, and reluctantly, everyone moved out of the door. The silence was deafening after they'd left.

'Are these people always like this?' Friedrich asked. 'Shouting and noisy?'

I laughed. 'Yes, most of the time but kind and thoughtful too.' I realised how thoughtful when I saw a tray of food left outside so we didn't have to go to the dining room.

'Shall I take Sam to the kindergarten?' I wondered aloud.

'Do you have to?' Friedrich asked. 'Because I would like to get to know my son too. It's a bit of a shock – a nice shock, but I'm going to have to get used to having a wife and a child.' His smile was the smile I remembered. The dimple in his cheek was still there, although his face was thinner.

'Tell me about work,' he started. 'Do they have a doctor here because I would be happy to work in the hospital or start a surgery?'

"I told him there was only one doctor who was always overworked and under pressure because so many people had health problems after the war. I was sure another doctor would ease his burden and help everyone. And I was happy to think we might even be able to work together.

"The weather that day was wonderful. The flowers in the garden were in full bloom and in the distance we could see rows and rows of workers planting and weeding. There was a pleasant smell in the atmosphere and the sun shone benignly down on us. Everything seemed larger than life. We felt we had our future, and that our future together was assured.

"Friedrich started work in the hospital and was a great source of comfort to his patients, most of whom had come from concentration camps. He understood the problems they experienced, not just physically but mentally. He could dispense medication and assist patients with their physical recovery, but early on he realised that the mental scars would remain for far longer. With some people they might never fade but he did what he could.

"Our days followed a simple pattern. We all had breakfast together and then separated for the day. You went to the kindergarten where you blossomed in the care of the nurses and made friends with the other children. I know there have been reunions and you've kept in touch with many of them all your life." Sam nodded.

"Papa and I went to our separate jobs and then, in the evening, we all ate together in the big dining room. This was a bit of an eye opener for Friedrich at first, seeing such an abundance of food. Meat and fresh fruit were plentiful, and the kibbutz baker made all our bread.

"We especially enjoyed the Friday nights, where those who wanted to, came together for a service before our shared meal. One of the women would cover her hair and make the blessing over the two candles and then all the men would sing Eshet Chayil.

"The first time your Papa sang this to me I felt whole again. Previously I had listened, and thought that I would never, ever have anyone to do this for me. I would look around at the long tables covered in snowy white cloths piled high with food. And always I would feel the sadness of loss because Friedrich was not with me.

"Now I could see the smiling faces of all my new friends and would take my turn to make Kiddush and motzei. Big baskets took the pieces of bread to everyone so we could all share in the miracle of a free Shabbat.

"Afterwards, we would sing. There were several different nationalities – Polish, Hungarian and German, some Lithuanians and a few Russians, as well as the Americans and British. We sang our different melodies and then we sang our shared melodies, the traditional ones we all knew from our childhoods. All those differences and all the similarities too. I can't describe the peace that came over me each week.

"Friedrich and I would hold hands, with you sitting between us, in the circle of our love."

CHAPTER 19

"And then one Friday night, one awful Friday night, we heard the noise of gunshot. We had finished our meal and were settling in with the bottles of wine ready for the singing. There was a crash – I can't really describe it but it was a very loud noise, and then we saw flames. Somewhere on the kibbutz something was on fire.

"Avram took charge immediately. He rounded up all the children and sat them down in a corner with one of the teachers supervising. She started to sing quietly to them and they soon settled down.

"Some of the men went outside to put the fire out. They moved cautiously across open ground but no-one challenged them. The rest of us waited for Avram to speak.

'We have been waiting a while for something like this,' he said. 'We have been expecting it. We are not welcome here, and it looks as if we might have to defend our position.'

"We looked at each other. We had come from one war. Were we to find ourselves in the middle of another?

'I think that was a warning,' Avram continued. 'It sounds as if they are going. Maybe this was just to teach us a lesson but we need to learn from it. From now on we must be better prepared and better defended. Go to your own homes now and we will meet in the morning. Shabbat or no Shabbat we need to formulate a plan.'

"Friedrich and I were very quiet as we walked back to the room. Friedrich was holding you and you were looking around at the stars shining in the velvet sky, pointing at the brilliance.

'I'm afraid this is just the beginning,' he said. 'Maybe Palestine is not so safe for us.' He held his hand up as I started to speak. 'We should consider what we want to do. I didn't tell you before, but I have been offered a job in England. One of the big hospitals wants me to head the surgical department. It is such a wonderful opportunity, and there is a house with it and a garden. It would be wonderful for Sam. We would have safety and a better future.'

"It was all too much for me take in. 'When did you get this offer?' I asked. 'And why didn't you tell me?'

'I applied before I came here. I didn't know you and Sam were alive; there is no-one left from my family and I wanted a fresh start. And then I didn't stop the application. I suppose a bit of me wanted to know if I could get the job. After all the experiences I'd had in the camps, I wondered if I was employable.'

"I told him I couldn't move again. I was settled, and although there were some things I didn't like, I was realistic to know that everywhere has its down side.

"Friedrich listened to me and then said so gently,

'When the shots were fired tonight you were terrified. You put your hands over your ears and I thought you were going to suffocate poor little Sam. You held him so tightly.

Did it bring back memories, my darling?' he asked. I could only nod wordlessly.

'So are you telling me you really want to stay where this could be a nightly occurrence? Palestine is fighting for her independence, and there are many who do not want this to happen. We may have come from the frying pan into the fire. So, ask yourself if you would feel safe. Would you let Sam out of your sight?'

'I can't think,' I cried. 'Do I have to make a decision now?'

'I have only four days left before the hospital in England wants to know if I accept their offer. I have a number to call. Before tonight, I was going to refuse their offer but now…' his voice tailed away.

'Four days? How can I decide the rest of my life in just four days?'

"Friedrich looked kindly at me.

'From what you've told me,' he said, 'you've decided many things in even shorter times. Think about what you really want. I know the kibbutz is normally quiet and peaceful but you've said yourself it's regimented, and I know you don't like to have Sam away from you and in the kindergarten. In England we could have our own home. I think it might even be possible for you to finish your training and become a doctor.' His face was shining, alive and in that instant I knew I could trust him. Really trust him.

"I told him I didn't want to make a hasty decision, although I already knew in my heart what I would do.

"We should talk with Avram," I suggested. "Avram is the leader here and he will know what to do."

"Friedrich was very firm.

'It's not up to Avram, what we do with our lives. It's up to us, Eva, darling. If you really don't want to, or if you feel you can't, I will tell the hospital I won't take up their offer. I don't intend to lose you again so I will leave it up to you. I'm going out for a walk,' and he moved towards the door.

"This was a sobering thought. Friedrich would give up all his hopes and dreams for me. In that instant I knew I couldn't pour cold water on his ideas. I caught his arm.

'No, don't go. We can't be separated now. I will come to England with you and we will be a family. I ask only one thing. If it turns out to be a bad move, can we come back?'

"The relief in Friedrich's eyes was palpable. I hadn't realised how important this move was to him and I hadn't realised how much he was prepared to lose to keep us together.

'Thank you, my darling,' he said softly. 'We can tell Avram and the others tomorrow.'

"I put you to bed and then made tea and we sat outside in the twilight nursing our cups. We talked about this new change of direction. The offer from the hospital was a good one. They would pay travel expenses. Friedrich thought there would be no problem in them paying for me too.

"They hadn't known Friedrich had a wife. Eva suddenly laughed. Actually, Friedrich didn't know he had a wife. There would be a period of acclimatisation in London. Friedrich could speak English well but I definitely needed to improve my language skills. I would have to take classes but I would soon learn, and you were so young that learning another language wouldn't be a major problem.

"There would be a house with a garden for us, fully furnished. 'And, you know what, Eva,' Friedrich said happily, 'it's a good salary and if we save for a little while, I'm sure we will be able to buy our own house.' That was such an exciting idea. I hugged Friedrich and we looked at each other, each thinking the same thing. Another new start but a peaceful one.

"I don't think either of us slept much that night. Friedrich was content and happy but I had all sorts of things going round in my head. You were sleeping like a baby. Actually, you were a baby." They both laughed a little and Sam said,

"I have no memories of this at all. I can't believe that I don't remember…" his voice tailed off.

Again Eva smiled. "You were so little, Sam. So young. How could you remember?" She resumed her story. "I got up and made more tea, and Friedrich found me outside watching the day start. The skies were fairly dark and the sun was just peeping out. I could hear the birds chirruping in the bushes and further off I thought I could hear a frog honking. The kibbutz was beginning to wake up and, as the light grew brighter, the smell of warm bread drifted across and made me feel hungry.

"I knew that I would miss the kibbutz; the warmth of friendship as well as the warmth of the weather and the sense of belonging but, at the same time, going to London was the right thing I knew.

'Come on,' said Friedrich, handing me a wriggling little body. 'This one is hungry. Breakfast first then we see Avram.'

"No breakfast tasted sweeter than that meal we shared. We knew that we had made the right decision, but telling Avram was going to be difficult. We would be leaving the kibbutz short of a doctor and that was so hard for us to do.

The kibbutz had been our life line and we really didn't want to let them down, but when we looked at each other and at you we knew our future lay away from the conflict.

"You chewed happily on a crust – your teeth were coming through and you waved at everyone who passed our door. When we could no longer delay the moment, we dropped you off at kindergarten and went to the office.

"Avram was sitting at his desk, a pencil stuck behind his ear and a cigarette dangling from his lips. He was on the phone and waved to us to come in. He was punching the air with jubilation as he put the phone down.

'Yes,' he shouted. 'We have another group coming in tomorrow. They are mainly women from Ravensbrück but a few men also. Maybe you can help them settle in?'

"We looked at each other and it was Friedrich who spoke first.

'Avram,' he started.

'I know, you're leaving,' said Avram, interrupting.

'How did you know?'

'I've been through this many times with others. For many, the kibbutz is a haven and they wish to spend the rest of their lives here. For some, people like you, it's not enough. So, when do you go and how?'

"Friedrich explained that our expenses would be paid and that once we had organised our travel, we would travel by ship to England. I don't think there were any aeroplanes which went to Palestine in those days. Eva looked thoughtful. Actually," she added, "there must have been but we didn't consider flying. This journey would be a fresh start for us and would give us time to get our strength back.

"The whole kibbutz came out to wave us off. Avram drove us in the truck to Haifa and we boarded our ship. Had it only been a year since I arrived, frightened, worried and alone? Now I was setting off on yet another adventure but this time with my husband as well as my child."

"Did you never think about whether or not you were doing the right thing, taking me to England where it was unlikely any of my family could be traced?"

"No, Sam," Eva said firmly. "As far as you were concerned, Friedrich and I were your parents and there was no need to consider anyone else. I think I managed to somehow block any thoughts of the Hoffmans out of my mind."

CHAPTER 20

"There was a car waiting for us in Southampton and two tall men, very English, were waiting in the terminal. They shook our hands gravely and introduced themselves. They were the representatives from the hospital and became very good friends to Pa and me. They could speak German, which was a great surprise but it made it so much easier for me to relax.

"It was a long journey, or so it seemed, and you fell asleep on my knee in the back of the car. Your hands were hot and sticky and I wiped them with a handkerchief. I didn't want to leave marks on the beautiful car. Mr Lennard saw what I was doing and told me not to worry.

'I have two boys of my own,' he said. 'I know it's impossible to keep them clean. Don't worry. Just rest a little and we'll soon be there.' His kindness was wonderful and I leaned back against the leather seat and dozed a little.

"I came to when I felt the car slowing down. We were turning the corner into a narrow street with brick houses on either side of the road. There were neat little gardens with privet hedges in front and the occasional tree showering leaves onto the pavement.

"We pulled up outside a house with a green garden gate. The front door was opening and framed in the doorway was a pretty middle aged woman, brushing her blond hair out of her eyes with the back of her hand.

"Mr Lennard smiled and nodded.

'My wife,' he said. 'She came over to make sure the house was ready for you and to leave some food in the kitchen.' He got out of the driver's seat and walked round to the back.

'Out you come, young man,' he said and reached his hands out for you. You were still sleepy, but when you saw the puppy sitting on the garden path, you soon woke up properly.

'I don't know if you like dogs, Mrs Goldman, but if you do and would like to give this fella a home, he's yours.'

"You wriggled until Mr Lennard put you down and then you ran to the dog and put your arms around him while his warm tongue licked your face.

"I remember that dog," said Sam. "His name was Mischa and he followed me everywhere. I must have been about sixteen when he died, and I was heartbroken."

Eva paused and they both sat silent, thinking back over the past years.

"And then what?" prompted Sam. "What happened over the next forty years that I don't know about?"

"Nothing. Nothing. We just had an ordinary life. Papa went to work in the hospital. Rachel was born, you went to school…"

"Come on, Ma. Give me some credit for being able to work things out. I don't think for one moment that life was as simple as that."

"Simple?" said Eva thoughtfully. "Maybe not *so* simple. But a life, yes. And a good life.

"England wasn't quite what I had expected. In Berlin I had seen such huge devastation. Whole buildings razed to the ground. I never even considered that London had suffered also.

"When Pa went to work, I put you in the baby carriage and I went out to explore. We took buses rather than the underground so I could see about me. I saw huge bomb craters and houses with their sides open to the air. I could see the wallpaper on the walls of rooms which had once held happy families. I could see kitchen sinks balanced precariously and beds that had slid across the floor and were now hanging over the edge.

"In some places there were teams of men in overalls and hard hats working to clear the site. In other places the detritus of the houses had been left, forlornly, for all to see. I hurried past, not wanting to draw attention to myself. I suddenly realised that I had come from the country which had caused this damage and heartbreak." Eva paused for breath. "I know, I know, I didn't cause the damage and I know that I also had suffered, but to the outside world at least I felt I would forever be a German and possibly an enemy." She went on,

"You know, Sam, during the war, some German Jews were sent to camps in England because they were German. They had managed to escape to get here and still they were interned." Eva gave a staccato laugh. "How ironic was that?

"So, no, it wasn't simple and it took me a while to get used to England. I found the English humour strange; sometimes I still do." She gave a half smile. "I didn't always know why people were laughing, and in those early days, I did think they were sometimes laughing at me. When I went into shops, there was sometimes a bit of a silence before the ladies started to speak again and I did feel uncomfortable. Things improved when I was expecting Rachel."

"Ah, yes. Rachel," said Sam thoughtfully. "So she's not really my sister?"

"Not by blood, Sam, but in all other ways, yes."

"And you're sure Pa never knew about me? Never guessed?"

"What? That he hadn't fathered you? He *was* your father. I've already said, Sam. He never knew. You were his son and he was always so proud of you. And he told me that, for him, life was complete when Rachel was born.

"Two beautiful children, a boy and a girl. We were both worried that after our experiences in the camps there would be no more babies so Rachel truly was a miracle.

"No mother was more cared for than I was when I went into hospital to give birth. The nurses all knew Pa, of course, and they were all so kind. I was never left alone, not for a minute. In those days it wasn't allowed for fathers to be there when babies were born but somehow an exception was made for us.

"I think Pa 'just happened' to be walking past the room so he 'just happened' to be there at the right time. He held my hand and stroked my brow and when the nurse handed this tiny scrap of humanity to him, the tears overflowed and traced a pattern down his cheeks.

"He had missed this precious moment with you but he never said, never drew a comparison, and when we got home there was no difference in the way he loved you both.

I had worried that he might bond more with Rachel but he was the same with both of you.

"By now, my English was so much better although I don't think I've ever lost my accent." She grimaced. "It was easier for me to make friends and by the time Rachel was at kindergarten, I knew that I should try to finish my medical studies.

"Pa was all for it. He had always said I would be a good doctor and he encouraged me every inch of the way. The medical school allowed me to enter part way through the course and I graduated in 1953, the year of the Queen's coronation. Pa was so proud. I think that my graduation ceremony was more important than his own, certainly more important than getting a new queen. Although we didn't tell Her Majesty that." Eva smiled again and Sam hugged her.

"Afterwards we celebrated and Pa let you have your first taste of champagne. Rachel was too little and she had to be satisfied with fizzy lemonade."

"I remember that, Ma. She was not a happy girl when you told her she would have to wait till she was older before she could taste anything other than Kiddush wine." They both paused, lost in thought.

"It was a happy childhood, Ma," ventured Sam, "but how could you keep such a big secret all to yourself?"

"I made sure I had other things to do which kept me busy. We joined the local synagogue, Pa went onto the Board and I joined the Ladies Guild, and I had my work. We made friends, we played bridge, we had children's parties and dinner parties, and there was always a wedding to go to or a Barmitzvah."

"Ah, the Barmitzvah. How did you manage that, knowing that I wasn't entitled to it?"

"Of course you were entitled to it," Eva said indignantly.

"Well, not really, Ma," said Sam bitterly. "Don't forget. I'm not halachically Jewish now, and I wasn't halachically Jewish then. I really don't know how I'm going to explain all this to Rabbi Langer."

Eva looked shocked, trying to absorb what Sam had said.

"Is that how you feel?" she asked.

"How do I know what I feel? A few days ago I had no worries. I was looking forward to the interview." He made a face. "Well, maybe not the interview but certainly to the possibility of becoming the new Chief Rabbi.

"I felt secure and I certainly didn't have to question whether or not I was Jewish. I was looking forward to the future, and so was Helen. Now I find out I have no right to this. I'm not Jewish. How could I ever become the Chief Rabbi?

"Strictly speaking, I'm not even a rabbi, am I? And then there's my wife. She thought she was marrying a genuine yiddisher boy and what has she got? Certainly not that. At least Daniel and Esther are Jewish, through Helen. No-one can take that away from them." Once again, Sam put his head in his hands and wept. "How could you do this, Ma? How could you do this?"

Eva let Sam try to control his feelings. Neither spoke for a long time until he went on,

"There's always been a connection between me and Rabbi Langer. He did my Barmitzvah. How did that happen when you left him in Berlin?"

"He found me. I left a forwarding address at the kibbutz, and when he arrived at Haifa he made enquiries. The Jewish Agency told him where I was but by the time he got to the kibbutz we had already left. Avram passed on the details of our address and what we were doing in London, and Rabbi Langer wrote. He always kept in touch from wherever he was.

"He stayed in Palestine, living quietly until he was fully recovered from his experiences in Germany and the camps. Then he got a pulpit in France, where he stayed a few years, and then he moved on. Different communities, different times. I don't think he was able to stay in one place for very long, but we always knew where he was and occasionally he came to London and stayed with us.

"He felt so protective of you, I know. You were always his protégée and he came especially to England to conduct your Barmitzvah. After the service he told me that when you read from the Torah it was as if the angels were on your shoulder."

"I spent a lot of time with him when he was in England. I think he was the one person who took me seriously when I said I wanted to become a rabbi. If I remember correctly, Ma, you weren't too pleased. Now I understand why."

"You're right, Sam. I didn't want you to become a rabbi. A brain surgeon, yes, but not a rabbi." She looked at him through wet lashes. "I know, Sam, an old joke."

"And now I know why."

"How could I tell you the real reason? I tried to put you off but your mind was made up. I asked you to think about it, and then you got your A level results and you were offered a place at Oxford. I begged you to take it before you made any final decisions about the rabbinate. It was too good an opportunity to miss.

"You always were a thoughtful, sensible boy and I remember you saying to me, 'Mama, my mind is made up about becoming a rabbi but you're right about Oxford. I think I should go there but when I've finished my degree, I will go to Hebrew University.' I just hoped that university life would make you change your mind."

CHAPTER 21

"And then everything started to unravel. The local newspaper heard that you'd won a bursary for Oxford and were very interested in you. They came to the house to do an interview.

"I would rather not have let them in, but Papa was so proud of you. He couldn't understand why I didn't want to show you off too. I was so worried by now. I could see a look of Commandant Hoffman about you and I thought if a photograph went into the paper, someone in Germany might recognise you."

"In an English paper?"

"Never underestimate the power of the press, Sam. They came, they took pictures and wrote about this wonderful boy who had been born in a concentration camp, had won a scholarship to go to a prestigious university and who planned to become a rabbi. I became a nervous wreck. I think at that time Papa thought I was having a mental breakdown. He kept telling me that the war was long over and I was safe, but he didn't know the real reason for my anxiety.

"The story obviously *did* hit the German papers and Papa was even more pleased at that. I was terrified that someone would recognise me...or you. He said several times, 'The Nazis tried to eliminate the Jews, and look at what they couldn't extinguish. My boy, my son.'

"There were times when I was physically sick with worry and Pa didn't know what to do. He made appointments with doctors and psychiatrists but none of them could tell him what was wrong with me. But *I* knew. Guilt, Sam, guilt.

"I had kept an eye on what was happening in Berlin and when the Wall went up in August 1961, I heaved a sigh of relief. As far as I was concerned, it meant that if there were any of the Hoffmans left, they would have to stay in the East, even if I was sure they had all died in the war. They wouldn't be allowed to cross the guard post to get to the West. I could relax a bit. That wasn't what happened, though, Sam. Not at all.

"Just before you left to go to Oxford, I got a phone call. The voice sent a chill down my spine. It was Ernst Hoffman. I had never forgotten that voice – cold and menacing and full of hate.

'I saw the picture in the paper,' he said. 'Even here in the East we get the news. I saw the picture of my son. MY son, Eva,' he screamed at me. 'All these years I thought you were dead and then I read in the newspaper that my son is alive, going to Oxford University and planning to be a rabbi. A rabbi,' he spat out. 'Is this your revenge, Eva? Your way of getting back at me and the Reich? Your revenge for being in a camp?'

"I slumped against the hall table and you heard the noise. Do you remember, Sam? You came running because you thought I'd fallen. I told you I had just overbalanced and I was all right, and you looked at me strangely and then, in typical teenage fashion, said 'Okay, Ma.'

"Ernst Hoffman continued. 'Life has not been good to me. I am stuck in this tiny flat, with a job that pays peanuts; without money to enjoy life and without my son, the only son I have left. The son I entrusted to you. Why have you kept him? Why didn't you try to find me? No, don't tell me. Just tell me how you are going to make my life better.

'I need money. You have money. It seems only fair that you should share your money with me. If you don't, I will call again. Maybe I'll speak to your husband. Maybe Sam will answer the phone. Is that what you want, Eva? I can make it happen and it doesn't matter if you change your number or move house. I will always be able to find you.'

"I had to think quickly. Friedrich always said I had the ability to think on my feet. Now I had to choose what to do. I felt that my whole life was in ruins. You were at the start of your career – you had a brilliant future ahead of you. Friedrich was senior consultant at the hospital. If this got out, it would be a scandal and I didn't think we would recover from it. And then there was you. My darling son. I couldn't give you up. You and Rachel were my life. You are my life.

'What do you want me to do?' I know my voice shook as I asked him.

'I want money. I want to live like you, even though I'm stuck in this hell hole of a country. You can send me money every month and it will make my life better. I will be reasonable. Life is cheaper here than in the West so if you double my salary, I will get by,' he sneered.

'Double your salary,' I stammered. 'How can I do that without my husband finding out?'

'Come, Eva,' he responded. 'You can afford a few hundred dollars a month. You can set up a regular transfer with your bank and we will both be happy. You can keep my son and I can keep your money. A fair trade, don't you think?'

"I rummaged for paper and a pen in the hall table and wrote down the details.

'And don't try to stop this 'help',' he added. 'Don't forget, I know where you live.'

"I was in such a state of shock that I had to lie down. I lay on my bed, thinking and thinking and finally accepted that there was no alternative. I would have to do as the Commandant wanted or risk losing everything.

"I dragged myself off the bed and ran a comb through my hair and gathered up the things I would need for the bank. I wasn't due to go to my surgery till the afternoon, which gave me time to arrange a regular money transfer. Luckily, I had my own bank account and Friedrich would never have dreamed of checking it. I knew I could manage with Friedrich's salary, just, and I also had savings. And then I began to formulate a plan.

"There was no problem with the money transfer, although there was a little surprise when I gave the details. 'East Germany,' said the clerk. 'It will take a little longer to set this up, but we can do it.' I signed the forms and left, relieved that it was all over.

"I don't know how I got through surgery that afternoon. I was brusque, I know, with the patients and eventually my receptionist came in with some tea and asked me if I was ok.

"I told her I had a headache and she smiled sympathetically, dishing out some aspirin and said, 'Doctors make the worst patients. Go home.' She added, 'I'll clear up here. You've seen the last patient so take it easy and have a rest.'

"I took her advice and went home. We all sat round the dining table and I looked at each of you. Friedrich, tall and distinguished, absentmindedly feeding the dog scraps from his plate; Rachel, reading the latest pop magazine till I told her to put it away and you, eating hungrily as usual. I couldn't lose all this. Not after all the struggles I'd had to make this successful life.

"Every time the phone rang I jumped and I could see Friedrich looking at me with a worried expression on his face. He was always concerned that I might slip back into the dark pit of melancholy, but I reassured him that it was only a headache. It was a headache which lasted a week, until eventually I answered the phone again to Ernst Hoffman.

'It's arrived,' he said. 'It took its time but the money is in my account.' I heaved a sigh of relief. Now I could look ahead.

"Oxford was an eye opener for you, I know, but it was also an eye opener for me. Pa and I took you just before term started. You bounded up the stairs to your room, heaving suitcases and a cricket bat and your guitar, smiling at the other boys and throwing yourself on the bed in delight.

"We left you to it. This was the first steps for you to take in adulthood."

174

"What about my Barmitzvah?" Sam intervened. "That was my transition from being a child to becoming an adult."

"Only in Jewish law. In the secular world I think leaving home is the big transition.

"Life settled into a semblance of normality. You wrote, occasionally," Eva smiled, "and you telephoned, usually when funds were running low."

Sam grimaced at that. He knew she was right. He had often needed a top up for the bursary.

"And then you graduated and, once again, it made news. The reporters asked what you were going to do. Stay on and do a Masters? Teach, what? And you said you were going to Hebrew University to become a rabbi.

"This really was newsworthy and there were wonderful headlines again and more photographs. Papa was delighted, and took us all out to celebrate. We drank champagne, and this time Rachel had some. We toasted you. 'L'Chaim', we said. 'Long Life'.

"And then the inevitable happened. There was another phone call and that same insidious voice told me that he needed more money.

'What would happen if I called the Hebrew University principal and told him all I know? How would that affect Sam's future?'

"Once again, my life came crashing down. I increased the payments without arguing but I knew, deep down, that this was going to happen over and over again. It was time to put my plan into action.

Sam paled at that. "Ma, you didn't…"

"No, of course not, Sam. I didn't arrange for him to be killed. Who do you think I am? James Bond?"

Sam rubbed his hands through his hair, settling back in his seat.

"Well, you have to agree, this sounds a bit like a spy story."

"No," Eva said firmly. "Not a spy story. Just my life.

"All the time I had been paying Hoffman, I had spent time finding out about him. You know, after the war a lot of war criminals had been found and put in prison. There were the Nuremberg trials when high profile Nazis were tried and sentenced but there were also many, many other cases where the not so well known were taken to court.

"I spent a lot of time in the library researching, trying to find out what happened to the Hoffmans. I was so sure that they had all died, and the shock of knowing the Commandant was alive had prompted the thought that maybe other members of his family were still living.

"I spent hours – hours and hours, going through old records, old newspapers, and reports from survivors. And then one day, I came across a report of the liberation of the camp I had been in. It was only a small camp, a camp for workers, although the ovens were there as well as the hangman's noose." Eva shuddered and Sam stroked the back of her hand until she had calmed down.

"I learned that Frau Hoffman and the children had been at home when the Russian army arrived. The officer demanded to see the Camp Commandant and he was taken to their house. There was no reply when the soldiers banged on the door and they forced their way in.

"Obviously, the house was in silence so the soldiers systematically searched each room. In the master bedroom they found Frau Hoffman and the children asleep on the bed.

Of course, when they tried to rouse them they found they were not asleep but dead.

"The empty cocoa cups were on the side table and there were traces of chocolate around the mouths of the children. Frau Hoffman had her arms around them all and lying on her chest was a large photograph of Hitler. She was loyal to the end.

"It seems that the soldiers looked at each in dismay. I can imagine what was going through their minds. How could a mother take the lives of her children? There was a little whimper and they saw the baby move.

"There was a collective sigh from the rough soldiers and one rushed forward to scoop the baby up. The little boy had been sick, and this had saved his life. The paper didn't say what had happened to the baby, just that he was very ill and not expected to survive. He had survived his mother putting cyanide in his drink but he wasn't likely to live. He was taken to a local hospital and expected to die. There was no trace of the Commandant.

"Testimony from survivors later detailed the way in which the camp inmates had been treated. Some tortured, others put to death for what Hoffman referred to as 'crimes' and many sent to the gas chambers when they were no longer able to work.

"It brought back all the memories of the time I had spent in the camp. Of friends made and lost, of kindness shown and ill treatment given. Nowadays some people talk about something called survivor guilt and, as I sat in that library, day after day, breathing in the smells of manuscript and old books, I felt as if my heart was breaking. I am sure all this contributed to my mental health problems.

"It was clear that Hoffman had left his wife and children to die alone. I had thought he would do anything for Frau Hoffman but, in that moment, I realised the true nature of this man. He didn't have the courage of his convictions to either die with his family, or live with the consequences of his actions.

"He had escaped and disappeared, who knew where. Now, many years after the end of the war, I had that information and I knew what to do.

"I felt that now was the time to act. I had made copious notes and I collated them into a proper file. There were many agencies still searching for Nazi war criminals and it was easy to find a contact telephone number.

"I made that call, knowing that I could help the organisation locate this evil man."

"But weren't you worried that they might find out I was his child? That he might work out that you were the person who had informed on him?"

"Of course I'd thought about it; of course I was anxious, but the whole of this story is so preposterous that I felt no-one would believe it."

"You say that, Ma, but you had paid blackmail money for years. What changed your mind?"

"I don't really know, Sam. I think in the beginning I just panicked. I wasn't thinking straight. I felt I had so much to lose, not just you but your father, also. I had to consider Rachel too. This time, I felt I was stronger, more able to deal with any repercussions, but I'm not saying it was easy to pick up that phone and make that call. It wasn't but it was the right thing to do."

"Did you tell Pa?"

Eva looked horrified. "Why would I do that? All that time, keeping such a secret. I would have been meshugah to let it out now. No, of course I didn't tell Friedrich. I made the call and then I pushed everything to the back of my mind."

"Hoffman's capture made the national press so I knew he would be put away. There was a big trial and many people came to testify against him. There was a phone call from the prosecuting lawyer and I was asked if I would take the stand, but I told them 'No'. They had found me through the list of prisoners kept by the camp. Fortunately, Pa was at the hospital when the call came and I never told him about it.

"They didn't know it was me who had told the authorities where he was so I wasn't concerned about that. I had called anonymously, naturally. I didn't want Friedrich or you and Rachel to hear my testimony and I didn't want to have to explain how I escaped.

"Strangely, Pa had never asked me properly. He just knew that you and I managed to survive till the end of the war and got out with the remaining prisoners. Hoffman was sentenced to life in prison and I felt I had been given my freedom all over again. Pa never as much as showed me any of the newspaper articles. He knew any mention of Nazi war criminals and concentration camps had a really bad effect on me.

"You became a rabbi and I was so pleased when you got engaged to Helen. I knew her parents from shul and we were actually quite friendly. I think both families hoped you would make a shidduch, so when you and Helen came home after going to the theatre with that look on your faces, we knew. Pa and I looked at each other and Pa said,

179

'Time to get the champagne out, Mother.'

Sam reminisced.

"Rabbi Langer married us and it was just perfect. When I saw Helen coming to me under the chuppah with you and Helen's Mum leading her, I thought I would burst with happiness. You walked her seven times around me and I was the one who felt dizzy.

"After the ceremony, when we shared our first meal alone together, we planned our lives. Children, a good pulpit, some teaching. It was all going to be so perfect. And now what?"

"It is perfect. Your life is perfect."

"Have you any idea what you're saying?" said Sam incredulously. "How can my life be perfect when the whole of my world is a sham? And you did this. You did it." He banged his hand on the arm of his chair.

Sam looked around. Eva had been talking for hours and the early morning sun was coming in through the net curtains. He looked at his watch. It was 5.30am. They had been up all night and he could feel his eyelids drooping. He needed sleep and time to process what he had heard.

Making his mind up, he got up from his chair and bent over to kiss Eva.

"I need to go home, Ma. I need to talk to Helen now that you've told me the story."

"You haven't heard it all, Sam," she replied. "There's more."

"More? There can't be."

"But you're right, Sam. You need to speak with Helen. Come back this afternoon and I'll tell you the rest."

CHAPTER 22

There were cars parked on both sides of the streets as he let himself out of the front door, and that same feeling of uneasiness came over him. He looked up and down but the vehicles seemed empty and there was no-one standing around. Still, he couldn't rid himself of the feeling that he was being watched.

He unlocked his car and got in. For a moment he sat still, his head resting on the steering wheel until eventually he turned the key and started the engine. Nothing moved in the street. It was silent and calm and he drove smoothly away.

Within twenty minutes he was unlocking his own front door. He tiptoed up the stairs and went into the bathroom to remove his clothes. There was a faint aura of Helen's flowery scent, lingering after her bath, and when he went into the bedroom he could see she was sound asleep.

Moving the blankets aside gently, he carefully slid in beside her. She stirred slightly and threw an arm over him, then settled into sleep again.

The alarm went off but Sam slept on, so Helen left him and went quietly downstairs, carefully avoiding the squeaky step. He slept until the smell of toast woke him up and, dragging on his dressing gown and pulling his hand through his hair, he joined his wife at the kitchen table.

She was sitting nursing a cup of coffee and smiled up at him as he sat down beside her.

"Tough night?" she asked.

"You won't believe it and I just don't know where to start."

They looked at each other and Helen laughed and said,

"Start at the beginning, like your Ma always says."

"Okay, Helen, but it's going to be hard for you to digest. In fact, I can't get my head round it myself. Ma still hasn't finished telling me everything and I said I'd go back this afternoon. I'd like you to come with me but in the meantime I'll try and tell you the bare bones."

There were times during the telling when Helen breathed deeply and there were times when her tears fell unchecked. Sam's voice broke when he told her that he was the son of a Nazi war criminal and her hands went to her mouth in horror. He stopped for breath and then said,

"But the children are Jewish, whatever happens to me, that can't be taken away."

Helen looked wildly round the tidy kitchen. A moment of normality in a world which had got out of control.

"What do you mean, whatever happens to you?" she asked tremulously.

"I mean just that, darling," he said. "Whichever way you look at it, I'm not Jewish. I wasn't Jewish when I was Barmitzvah, when I took semicha and when we got married. My whole life has been a sham." His voice was choked.

"You can't be Jewish by association," he went on. "How many times have I counselled parents who want to adopt a non Jewish child?

"I've always told them that adoption is no problem but the child has to convert. No matter how young the child or baby is, they still have to have an official certificate to say they are Jewish. The child cannot be Jewish just because he or she has Jewish parents and lives in a Jewish home."

"But this is different, Sam."

"How is it different? Actually, it's worse. If Eva had talked to Rabbi Langer right at the beginning in Berlin, he could have sorted something out, I'm sure."

Helen was struggling with what Sam had told her.

"I'm not sure you're right there. If a child is to be adopted, the birth parents, or at least the birth mother, has to agree and sign some sort of papers. That didn't happen with you, I think."

Sam thought rapidly.

"Not exactly, but I've seen the letter Eva was given. It is quite clear that Frau Hoffman gave Ma the right to look after me."

Helen poured more coffee, her hand shaking. Sam got up and walked about the room. He looked out of the window to disguise how upset he was. He took a deep breath.

"And I have to ask you this, Helen. How does this affect how you feel about me?"

"Nothing could change how I feel about you even if you had horns and a tail, and you don't…do you?"

"Not as far as I know," Sam said with a faint smile, "but it might be easier if that was the problem. This is something more serious. Even now, there's more for Eva to tell us. I had to leave because it was all getting too much. I said I'd go back this afternoon with you. Is that okay?"

"Of course, but how do you feel about a walk in the fresh air to clear our heads first? Go and have your shower and get dressed and I'll make a sandwich to take with us. I think we still have a lot to talk about."

For a brief moment Helen sat at the table, thinking through what Sam had told her. She knew they would have to tell Daniel and Esther and also her parents and Rachel too. As far as she was concerned, Sam was the love of her life and would always be so, but she wondered if her parents would still feel the same about Sam. They had such bad memories from the war. Like many Holocaust survivors, they had a dislike of all things German. Would that now extend to Sam, she wondered.

The phone rang, disturbing her thoughts and she crossed to the dresser to answer it. It was Eva.

"Has Sam explained?" asked the older woman.

"Yes, he has and we plan to come over after lunch. Sam thinks you have more to tell him."

"I do, I do, and I'm worried about how he will take it. I'm glad you are coming with him. Oh, Helen," she wept. "What do you think of me after doing such a terrible thing?"

"Let's not talk about this now. It can wait till we get over to you," and Helen replaced the receiver thoughtfully.

Honeywell Park was only a short walk from the house and Helen and Sam didn't need a car to get there. Once again, Sam had the feeling that someone was watching him but the streets seemed as quiet as ever. People were at work and children were at school and there was only the occasional passer by, who smiled at the couple holding hands.

Sam felt a frisson of anxiety running through him as he walked under the iron gates of the park. The lettering made him think of the words over the gates of the concentration camps. He'd never thought of that before but his senses seemed heightened after the events of the last few days. Things which he'd never considered before as alarming kept popping into his head.

The flower beds were well tended and the nodding heads of the flowers waved cheerily in the slight breeze. In the distance there was a white painted bandstand and they headed towards it. It would offer a little shelter from the wind and they could continue talking.

Helen unwrapped the greaseproof parcels of sandwiches and passed Sam one. He bit into it appreciatively, enjoying the tang of the pickled cucumber on the salt beef. He took a long swallow of coffee from the flask and then turned on his seat to look at Helen.

"What do I do?" he asked.

"No, Sam, what do we do?" she answered softly. "We're in this together. It affects both of us and all the family so we need to work out just what we can do."

"Talk to the rabbis?" Sam said, with a question in his voice.

"At some point, yes, we do have to," Helen suggested. "But maybe the kids first. Or my parents."

"Or actually, we need to find out what else there is to know."

He crumpled up the sandwich wrapping and tossed it in the nearby bin. Helen stood up and brushed crumbs off her navy skirt. She wrapped her patterned scarf around her neck and hauled Sam to his feet.

"Time to go. We need to get back to our house and then we can take the car. It's too far to walk to your mother's."

They were even more thoughtful on the way back. Helen tried to reassure him. "It'll be ok. Whatever happens we have each other. We've weathered other storms…"

"But nothing as serious as this. This isn't a storm, it's a hurricane."

Sam bent over to unlock the car.

"I'll just nip inside and get my jacket. It's getting a bit chilly," said Helen and, as Sam looked up, he thought he saw the shadow of someone moving in front of the curtains in the front bedroom. He had locked all the doors and windows when they left but he could see that the window at the side of the front door was slightly ajar.

He didn't want to alarm Helen by telling her he thought there might be an intruder in the house.

"I'll get it for you. I need the keys for Ma's house anyway," he said rapidly. "I left them on the hall table. You get in the car and I'll be back in a minute."

The house was still, dust motes dancing in the sunlight which came through the stained glass window over the top of the front door. Helen's jacket was where she'd left it on the newel post at the bottom of the stairs. A discarded slipper seemed to have lost its partner, until Sam saw it hiding under the hall table.

Everything inside looked just the same as when they'd gone out but he knew, he just knew, that someone had been in the house. He pulled the little window at the front door closed. He was sure he'd closed it. He had closed it, hadn't he? Or maybe he had so much on his mind and he'd left it open.

He ran lightly up the stairs, trying to be as quiet as possible. The door to the master bedroom was wide open and the room looked completely empty. There was no-one there. No-one had been in. His imagination was running riot and had been ever since he'd seen the man in Berlin. He suspected that was the next bit in Eva's story. It was time to unravel the rest.

He paused at the hall table to pick up the keys. The china bowl where they were kept was empty. He looked around and then felt in his pockets. Nothing. There were so many little things which were different. Was he so confused that he'd forgotten to lock a window; had he left the keys at Ma's? He shook his head. This situation was really getting to him.

Helen was waiting patiently for him in the car.

"All ok?" she asked.

"Well, I'm obviously a bit disorganised after Ma's revelations," he said. "I can't find the keys for her house and I could swear I shut that window before we left."

"Oh, Sam," she chided. "You've had a lot on your mind. Don't start magnifying the problem. It's understandable that you're a bit out of kilter. Come on. The sooner we get to Eva's, the sooner we'll find out the rest."

Glancing around, Sam put the car into gear and moved slowly off. There was no-one in the street. No-one there at all.

CHAPTER 23

Sam pulled the car onto Eva's driveway. The house looked as it always had. Solid, red brick with neat flower beds at the front. It was tidier than when he was a child. Then there were usually bikes and toys scattered on the front lawn and the door was always open.

His parents' home had always been busy and welcoming. On Friday nights there was usually a crowd around the big dining table. No matter how hard Eva and Friedrich worked through the week, Friday was sacrosanct. The house was immaculate and the table set beautifully for the Shabbat meal.

He sighed as he rang the bell. He heard the distant chimes and waited for Eva to answer. He rang again, glancing over at Helen with concern in his eyes.

"I can't imagine why Eva's not answering the door. She knew we were coming."

"Maybe she's changed her mind and she doesn't want to talk to us," suggested Helen.

"Maybe. I'll go round the back and see if the kitchen door's open."

Suddenly, Sam's shouting broke the silence of the sleepy street.

"Helen, Helen. Come quickly."

She ran down the side of the house and through the big wooden garden gate. Sam was kneeling on the kitchen floor, cradling Eva's head. "Call the ambulance," he shouted. "I think it might be her heart."

Helen went into the hall to find the phone. The doors were all ajar and she could see that someone had ransacked the drawers and cupboards. She made the call, giving clear and concise directions and explaining that her mother-in-law was collapsed on the kitchen floor.

She answered the paramedic's questions; yes, Eva was breathing. Yes, her airway was clear. No, they hadn't been in the house when it happened. They had called round and found her. She replaced the receiver thoughtfully and went to break the news to Sam that there had been an intruder.

"What? Someone's been in this house and done this to Eva?"

"We don't know that she was attacked, Sam, but someone has definitely been in. Every drawer in the sitting room has been opened and the contents are on the floor. I didn't go into the room as I expect the police will want to take fingerprints. Should I check upstairs first, do you think?"

"I can't take all this in. Now the ambulance is on its way, we need to call the police. Will you do that, Helen? I don't want to leave Ma."

The police officer on the phone was calm and reassuring.

"Don't touch anything," he instructed. "I'll send someone around as soon as possible."

Helen told him they were waiting for an ambulance and she wanted to go with her mother-in-law to the hospital.

"Right," said the officer. "In that case, leave everything as it is and call us when you get back. And I hope your mother-in-law is all right," he added sympathetically.

Eva began to stir and Sam soothed her.

"Just lie still, Ma." Helen came in with a cushion, which she put under Eva's head. "The ambulance will be here soon. Do you remember what happened? Did you slip on something, a wet floor, maybe?"

Slowly, Eva began to speak. "No, I was in the sitting room and I heard a noise. I came into the kitchen and there was a man standing by the cooker. He had a hood on his head and he shouted at me to sit down. What could I do? I sat.

"Then he went into the hall, and I could hear him moving around. He went into all the downstairs rooms, then I heard him going up the stairs. I could hear crashing and banging but I was too scared to move."

Helen sat down on the floor and put her arms round her mother-in-law. "He's gone, now. There's no-one here. You're safe. We'll come with you to the hospital and wait till you've been checked out, and then we'll talk to the police."

"The police? No, please don't call the police." Eva was agitated, running her hands through her thick white hair.

"We need the police, Ma. They'll find who did this and, besides, I've already called them."

"Cancel it," said Eva desperately. "Please, for all our sakes, cancel that call."

190

"We can't do that, Ma. It's been logged and, anyway, I want to get whoever did this."

"No, please," Eva said again. "I know who it was. It was your brother."

"My brother?"

"Yes, your twin. Hans. It was him."

Sam tried to digest this. "What did he want?"

"He wanted the letter Frau Hoffman gave me, putting you in my care. He wants to publish it. He wants to let the whole world know you are the son of Ernst Hoffman, war criminal and not Sam Goldman, Rabbi."

And with that, Eva began to sob uncontrollably while Helen and Sam looked on helplessly. They were interrupted by a cheery voice calling out,

"Any one at home? Paramedics here. Can we come in?"

The world stopped. For a moment, they all stayed still as if in a tableau, then Sam pulled himself together. "Yes, we're in the kitchen."

Two burly men came in, carrying medical bags. They saw Eva still lying on the floor and bent down to talk to her.

"Can you tell us what happened, dear?" asked one, undoing his bag as he spoke.

"I was in the kitchen," Eva began hesitantly. "No, I wasn't. I was in the sitting room and I heard a noise and *then* I was in the kitchen. There was a man in here and he told me to sit still. I could hear him ransacking my home and then he came back and shouted at me." She started to sob again. The ambulance man patted her hand.

"It's okay. Take your time. Did he assault you?"

"No," said Eva. "I got up from the chair and he came over to me. I thought he was going to attack me and I moved

191

back and I just tripped on my bag. It was on the floor beside the table."

"Did you lose consciousness?"

"Yes, I think so. Just for a few minutes." She looked worried. "Actually, I don't know for how long."

"Let's get you into the ambulance, then, in case…"

"In case I have concussion. I know the routine. I'm a doctor, or at least I was a doctor, although I'm retired now. I'll just get up."

She swayed a little as the two men helped her up. "Into the chair, dear."

"I don't think so," retorted Eva. "I'll walk."

"No, you won't, Doctor," the ambulance men said in chorus. "Rules, Doctor. You're the patient and you have to get into the chair."

Eva swayed again, then gave in reluctantly. She was wrapped in a red blanket, strapped in and the two men wheeled her down the path and into the ambulance.

"I'll go with her, if that's ok," said Helen. "You take the car, Sam, and I'll meet you at the hospital."

The emergency department was, as usual, busy but the receptionist looked up when she saw the procession arriving.

"Hello, Dr Goldman. Long time no see," she said, as she saw Eva, "Been in the wars? Let's get you checked in and I'll get someone to see you."

"This is a lot of fuss about nothing," protested Eva but nevertheless she was happy to sit by the bed in a cubicle.

"Do I have to go through it all again?" she asked, somewhat petulantly.

"No," replied the young doctor, taking a light out of his pocket. "Your son has told me what's happened." He finished looking into her eyes and ran his fingers over her scalp. "I don't think there's anything to worry about but, at your age, we need to be extra careful. I suggest you get your family to take you home and have a rest. Don't do anything strenuous and if you are worried about anything, give us a call. Do you need any painkillers for the bump on your head?"

"No, I do not," said Eva forcefully, "but I will be glad to get home."

She was silent on the way back in the car, waiting for Sam to ask questions, but he concentrated on his driving.

They both helped her out of the car and into the house, and Helen suggested she should have a rest on the bed. Eva was too exhausted to argue and allowed herself to be led upstairs. She kicked her shoes off and lay on top of the eiderdown. Helen covered her with a blanket.

"I'll bring you up a cup of tea," she said, "in an hour or so, unless…" she turned to look at Eva and saw she was already asleep. She tiptoed out of the room and joined Sam in the kitchen.

"I can't leave her like this. I don't suppose she'll come back with us, but we could always ask."

"You're right, Sam. She can't be on her own. Leave it to me and I'll persuade her. You know she'll do anything for you so if I tell her you're very worried about her safety, I'm sure she'll listen. In the meantime, what do you think happened and do you think the man who broke in really is your brother?"

"I have no doubt," Sam said wearily. "This latest development has opened a whole new can of worms. We need to talk to Daniel and Esther, and your parents, and I should speak with Rabbi Langer and withdraw from the interview panel."

"Don't be hasty about that. I'll call the kids and get them to come home. It's nearly the end of term anyway so they can miss a couple of days. As for my parents, they don't need to know just yet. My mother would only worry and my father would get angry. No, not with you. With this stranger brother. Leave it to me. I'll make the calls."

"Leave Rabbi Langer to me, though," said Sam. "I'll tell him about Ma and ask if we can have a postponement even though I know I should just withdraw. I need time to sort things out properly. I'm sure he will understand."

While Helen was on the phone, Sam went upstairs to check on Eva. He found her awake but still lying on the bed.

"I'm fine," she said, somewhat crossly, as Sam tried to persuade her to stay there. "I'm going to have a hot bath and then I'll come down for something to eat. Go on, go back downstairs."

Sam dialled Rabbi Langer's number and waited for the old man to pick up the phone. He outlined what had happened to Eva and asked if the interview could be postponed for two weeks at least. It wasn't easy for Sam, lying by omission, but he only spoke about what had happened to Eva. The old rabbi could sense how important this was but he felt he should point out to Sam that the interviews were also important to the other candidates.

He listened to the worry in Sam's voice and, making his mind up, he said he would give Sam ten days only. If, after that time, Sam felt unable to return to Berlin, there would be no choice for the panel but to reconvene, interview the other two men and make their decision based on that.

Sam agreed immediately, knowing that he wasn't in the running anymore. He just wanted time so that he could get the whole story from Eva before he put a stop to his career as a rabbi.

Helen told him about her conversations with Daniel and Esther.

"They were very surprised when I asked them to come home. I could sense the worry in Esther's voice, in particular. She said she knew we wouldn't ask her to leave Uni before the end of term unless it was important and why wouldn't I tell her what the matter was. She asked if it was Granny, and I said she was okay. I didn't tell her about the burglar – no need to worry her but she does sense that, whatever it is, it's serious.

"Daniel, on the other hand, said he would leave after his lecture tomorrow. Apparently, it's the last one this term and he was planning to leave early anyway."

They were sitting in the living room, knees together, while they talked. The sound of the bath water draining away intruded into their conversation and Helen decided she should see what she could rustle up to eat. She knew Eva was hungry so she went into the kitchen and opened the fridge and various cupboards.

Sam joined her, putting plates on the table and setting out cutlery. By the time Eva came into the room, sandwiches had been made, potato salad and tomatoes put into bowls, a fruit cake found and the kettle was boiling noisily.

"Do you feel strong enough to carry on?" Sam asked. "Helen knows everything so no need to start at the beginning this time."

"Do I feel strong enough? Not really. Do I want to carry on? No, I do not but there's no alternative. You deserve to know the whole story."

She put her knife and fork tidily together on her plate and replaced her cup very carefully onto the saucer before she started to speak.

CHAPTER 24

"Hoffman was sentenced to life in prison and the judge informed the jury that it really would be a life sentence. Pa might have thought he was keeping the papers from me but when I was at the surgery I devoured all the news. When the judge gave that verdict, I heaved a sigh of relief.

"I felt that I could put all the anxiety behind me and carry on with my life. I felt safe and I thought that the feelings I had about the awful secret – the secret I had kept inside me for so many years –could subside. I would be able to put it to the back of my mind again.

"I knew that Hoffman would die in prison and with him my secret. And I *did* push it to the back of my mind. All those years," she said quietly. "All those years.

"I had no reason to believe that anything else would come out of the woodwork. Until about a month ago when I had a phone call from Hans, your twin. And, my God…excuse me, Sam, but that's how I feel, what a shock that was.

"How could I know that he'd survived? I knew Frau Hoffman's intention was that they would all die together. In the aftermath of war, who would have taken care of him? To be truthful, I never even considered that he might have survived. I had put everything to the back of my mind so that call was totally out of the blue.

"It was awful. He demanded to come and see me. He knew my address from his father's papers, where he had found a record of all the money I'd paid until Ernst Hoffman was arrested. He screamed down the phone that it could only have been me who had informed the authorities where his father was. There was so much venom in his voice and I was so scared, but I knew I would have to arrange a meeting.

"You had him in this house?" Sam asked incredulously.

"Of course not," Eva responded. "Do you think I'm totally meshuggah? I arranged to meet him in the Fortnum and Mason's tea room."

"What?" said Helen. "Why Fortnum and Mason?"

"I reasoned that if we were in a public place there was less chance of him hurting me or making a scene."

Sam and Helen exchanged glances. Only Eva would arrange to meet a potential killer in Fortnum and Mason.

"And he agreed?"

"Well, not at first. At first he shouted and blustered and threatened me, but I stood my ground. If he wanted to meet me, and I told him I didn't know *why* he would want to meet me, it would have to be on my terms and in a very public place.

"I admit I was frightened of what might happen. If he came to the house and hurt me, and I really thought that was a possibility, he would never get the answer to his questions. On the other hand, he was so enraged I felt it was better to keep him away from where I lived.

"You told me what a shock it was when you met him, Sam, and you didn't know who he was. Can you imagine what it was like for me when I saw him?

"I was in the Tea Room first. I wanted to get a look at him before he saw me. I waited for him come in. He was wearing such an odd collection of clothes but the face, the face was yours. No beard, of course, but otherwise…" Her voice tailed away before she continued. "I stood up and he saw me and came over. I poured tea.

"How banal that sounds when I was shaking like a leaf. He saw my hand tremble and smiled, but the smile didn't reach his eyes and made him seem even more menacing.

"He looked at me and I realised that the face I was looking at wasn't yours. I just saw Ernst Hoffman."

Sam took Eva's hands in his.

"Apart from vengeance, what do you think he wanted?"

"I know what he wanted. He wanted the letter that Frau Hoffman wrote to me. It was proof that I had not returned you after the war. That I hadn't made any effort to trace the family."

"Do you have a phone number or address for him? I don't think we should ask you to tell us any more. I can see it's upsetting you. I think it would be better if I talked to him direct. What do you think, Helen?"

Helen looked worried. She picked at a thread on her skirt.

"I don't know, Sam," she replied. "You don't know anything about this man and he certainly seems to have a violent side. You only have to look at the mess he's made of the house. What do you think the police will say when you tell them you know who it is?"

"I'm not sure I will tell them," Sam said slowly. "We don't really know it was him. What evidence is there?"

"Really, Sam? I think we do know, but let's wait till they get here and we can decide."

The bell rang and they all looked at each other. "Are you both okay with me not saying I have an idea who the intruder was?" Sam said hurriedly.

"I don't know. I can't think but, yes, let's keep it to ourselves for the moment." Eva was obviously upset and it showed in her voice.

Helen opened the door and ushered the two policemen in. They asked Eva to tell them what happened and she went through the story again.

"Have you any idea who might have done this?" asked the Sergeant.

Eva replied carefully.

"How could I have any idea? Why would anyone want to break into my house? I just feel lucky I wasn't injured more seriously." She looked anxiously at the constable, who was in the process of shutting his note book. "Do you think you will catch him?"

"Well, Dr Goldman. We've had several calls recently about opportunistic burglars and we haven't managed to apprehend anyone yet. And, from what you've said, he hasn't taken anything. You obviously disturbed him so you were very, very lucky not to get hurt.

"We'll keep looking and we'll keep the case on file. If anything happens, we'll contact you. In the meantime, try and put it out of your mind."

Sam took them to the front door and watched as they got into the squad car. The driver adjusted the mirror and the policemen drove off. He went back inside and sat down again.

"So, do you have a number for him?"

Without speaking, Eva got up and went to her handbag. She unzipped it and took out her purse. There was a piece of paper in with a telephone number and she handed it to Sam.

"Is he staying in a hotel?" Sam asked.

"I don't know but he's been in England for about a month so maybe he's renting a flat. A hotel, even a bed and breakfast, would be expensive."

"Right. Well I'm not going to do anything now. Helen and I are going to stay here, unless you want to come home with us." He lifted an enquiring eyebrow, as Eva shook her head. "I worry about you being on your own. You know after Pa died we asked you to live with us. Perhaps now is the time to consider it."

"No, this is my home and I won't be chased out."

"I thought so but we'll talk about this later. Is the spare room made up?"

"Of course it's made up," Eva said with a flash of her old spirit. "I'll just make sure there are clean towels."

Sam and Helen exchanged glances. "Before you do, tell me a bit about when Pa was ill. Did you never feel you should tell him the truth?"

"Never, Sam. It would have broken his heart. I don't think he would ever have thought I was capable of doing something which goes against everything he thought was right and proper.

"He went to his grave thinking you were his son, and you *were* his son. No-one could take that away from him." She went on, "We were married a long time and went through a lot together. We had shared memories and shared struggles.

"When Friedrich died I thought the end of the world had come but, I know from experience, that human beings can somehow summon up enough strength to continue. I had hoped that we would have many years of retirement together so when the hospital rang to say Friedrich had been taken ill, I wasn't too worried.

"We had been through so much and I felt he was strong. I was wrong. His heart, his wonderful caring heart, just stopped and there wasn't anything to do about it. Another year and he would have retired and I was so angry with God that I had been cheated of that special time. But there's no point in being angry with God, is there. He has his own plans for us. You, above all people, should know that."

She left the room and the sound of drawers opening and closing drifted down the stairs.

"She'll be putting things back in order." They looked around at the mess. "We should also do the same. Better tonight than coming down in the morning."

Eva called down the stairs. "I've put clean towels in the room and I'm going to bed. Suddenly, I feel very tired. Goodnight both of you."

She closed the door to the sitting room and Sam and Helen could hear her heavy steps going upstairs.

"More tea," asked Helen, "before we start?"

"No, I think some of Ma's precious sherry. I don't suppose there's any whisky in the cupboard? Thought not. At the moment a stiff drink is what I need while I think about how to handle all this. I shall call this man tomorrow and arrange to meet."

"In Fortnum's?" Helen enquired mischievously.

"No, not in Fortnums," Sam said, with a twinkle in his eye. "Maybe a library somewhere. At least there wouldn't be raised voices."

"Very clever, Sam. What about the one on the High Street?"

"Too near home. I wouldn't want anyone to see us together. What about the Meeting House in Marylebone? I've been to several conferences there and there's a coffee shop. It's quiet and I don't think I would bump into anyone from the community. We really need to talk without being interrupted."

"That's an inspired idea. Call him in the morning and arrange a time but remember, I intend to come with you."

"I'd rather you stayed here with Ma."

"No need. Esther will be back by lunchtime and she can stay with her, so if you arrange a time in the afternoon we can both go. I have no intention of letting you see this man on your own," Helen added firmly. "And now, bed. Just make sure all the doors and windows are locked. I don't fancy another visit from our unknown burglar."

CHAPTER 25

The following morning seemed normal. The birds were up early, chirruping in the back garden and rustling the leaves of the trees. The post dropped through the letter box, a couple of circulars and a letter addressed in a very strong handwriting. Rabbi Langer's, Sam noted but addressed to Eva. Helen, in the kitchen, boiling water and slicing bread looked up as Eva came into the room.

Wordlessly, Sam handed Rabbi Langer's letter to his mother and waited while she took a knife from the drawer so she could slice the envelope open. She scanned it quickly and then looked up at Sam.

"It's not a problem for you," she finally said. "He just wants to know if everything is in order and can he help with anything. He's not stupid, he knows something has changed, otherwise you would have been at that interview. Maybe we should call him. He's still in Berlin and will be there for a while. I think he's waiting to see what you are going to do."

"I will call him, if you want, Ma, but I'm not going to tell him anything till I've spoken to this man. My twin," he said, testing the words on his tongue. "My brother, my twin. Time, I think, to make that call to him."

Slowly he dialled the unfamiliar number, apprehensive yet excited that maybe the mystery of what Hans wanted would be resolved. A deep voice answered and asked who was calling.

"It's Sam Goldman. May I speak with Hans, please? Hans Hoffman?" The unfamiliar names lingered on his tongue.

He heard the noise of the phone being laid down and the voice shouting,

"Hans. Hans. A call for you."

There was the sound of footsteps coming nearer and then the phone was picked up.

"Yes, who is it?"

"It's Sam Goldman. We met in Berlin. I would like to talk with you. Can we meet?"

"Meet?" asked the rough voice. "Yes, you know I would like to meet. We have much to talk about. Where do you suggest?"

Sam gave him the directions to the Meeting House and asked,

"Would three o'clock be okay for you? I don't want to leave my mother so I need to wait for my daughter to come back from university so she can stay with her."

"Your mother is a strong woman. She would be okay on her own but, yes, that will be fine. I will see you at three pm. You will recognise me, I think," he added with a sinister laugh.

They had just finished breakfast when the doorbell rang and Esther flew in, dropping bags and books and a flute case on the hall floor. A mass of dark curls framed her heart shaped face and her dark eyes sparkled as she looked around.

"So what have you been up to Granny?" she asked with a smile in her voice. "Still in your dressing gown and it's almost lunchtime." She looked at her father.

"Dad?" she said. "What's going on?"

"Esther, you need to be patient. I want you to stay here with Granny till we get back. Have something to eat and then, when we get home, we'll explain everything." He held up his hand to stop her protesting.

"No, Esther. Now's not the time. I promise to tell you later. It would be even better if Daniel was here so I don't have to keep on explaining, but I'm not sure what time he might arrive."

There was an unfamiliar firmness in his voice so Esther stopped protesting and moved over to give Eva a hug.

"It's good to be here. We can catch up on what I've been doing at Uni. There's so much to tell you."

Helen shrugged into her jacket and picked up her handbag.

"Right. I'm ready. I've called a taxi so you don't need to worry about parking and, besides, I don't think you should be driving."

The driver dropped them at Euston Station.

"I can't get any nearer, guv," he said, "but it's only across the road and down a bit." Sam took his wallet out and paid him.

"Let's get a coffee first, Helen. I need something to fortify myself and we have time."

Helen looked at her watch.

"There's a little place over there, and you can have a bite to eat. You didn't manage any breakfast, did you?"

"Heaven preserve me from Jewish mothers," Sam said but he was smiling and agreeing. They waited until their salads arrived before Helen spoke.

"Have you decided what you're going to say to him?"

"No, not really. I just want him to tell me what's going on. After meeting him in Berlin, I've had this strange feeling I've been followed ever since. I even thought someone had been through my stuff in the hotel and then I thought I was imagining it. Now I don't think so, not after what happened yesterday."

They finished their food and paid the bill. The traffic was busy as they dodged between the cars to cross the street. Helen reprimanded Sam, telling him he should go to the pedestrian crossing but he just grabbed her hand. When there was a gap they darted over to the other side. As usual, there was someone on duty at the Meeting House and they gave their names and signed in.

"If you go into the coffee lounge, there is someone waiting to see you, Rabbi," said the doorman. "I'll bring some drinks. Tea alright?" Sam took a deep breath and walked across to where Hans was sitting.

"So, you came. I wondered if you would. I wondered if you would have an official guard with you but I don't see any signs of a nice British policeman," he added sneeringly.

"No, we came alone. I suppose I could have told the police about you but I prefer to find out what is going on first. Why have you been following me and why did you break into my mother's house? I need to know what happened. Did you hurt her?"

"Slow down," Hans said. "Too many questions for your brother."

Sam recoiled.

"I can't think of you as my brother."

"That's your problem," the other retorted, "because you are so! I will tell you but I hope you have time to spare. And it will take some time. Will she be all right?" he asked pointing to Helen. "She may not enjoy this story."

"Enjoy it or not, we want to hear it. But first, what did you do to my Mother? She says she tripped but I'm not sure."

"I didn't do anything to your mother. I got into the house with your keys. I took them from the bowl in your hall when I had a look around. Nice house! Elegant. Not like mine."

Sam took a sharp intake of breath. So someone had been in his house. He hadn't imagined it.

"What were you looking for?"

"All in good time. All in good time," said Hans.

"When did you find out about me?" Sam began. "Or have you always known?"

"Wait," interrupted Hans. "You will wait. This is my story and I will tell it my way. You don't get to ask any questions, at least not yet."

Sam and Helen looked at each other. They could sense the anger in the other man's voice. They settled back and waited for him to begin.

"You were the lucky one, Otto."

"Otto?" Sam asked faintly.

"Otto," replied Hans clenching his fist. "Otto is your name. Not Sam," he added sneeringly. "Not Rabbi Sam. But I told you before. Just sit and listen."

They shuffled awkwardly in their seats and waited. Hans started again.

"Yes, 'Otto', although it was a long time before I knew about you. Like you, I was born in the concentration camp." He laughed grimly. "Of course like you. We are twins, are we not? Your mother was our nanny, of sorts."

Sam snorted derisively. "Nanny? I don't think so. Skivvy, more like. Prisoner definitely."

Hans looked over at him.

"Whatever. She worked for my parents and she lived in our house. According to my father, she was a good worker and my mother – the mother I never knew, liked her."

When Sam heard Hans mention his father, he started to speak and Hans raised a hand.

"I warned you. If you interrupt, I shall leave. It is in your best interests to sit and listen. I won't tell you again...brother!" He went on,

"Nobody knew that twins had been born. They had prepared well for one of us to survive and it was a lottery as to which one. It was easy to keep that secret. We are identical, and they made sure that no-one ever saw two babies. Not even Eva.

"My father told me that mother begged and pleaded to save one of us. She could see which way the war was going and, although she and father were staunch followers of Hitler, mother loved all of us children. I assume you know about the others. Our brother and sister."

Sam nodded and Hans went on.

"Mother knew that Eva was sneaking out each day to see her own child and she found out when that child died. She made her mind up quickly. Eva and one of the babies would have to leave. And quickly. Father told me all about how he took Eva to Berlin and how she reacted when she realised that the child she was left with was you. He had seen her face in his rear view mirror when he drove off.

"I knew there was a letter explaining everything." His face was contorted with anger. "I want that letter. It proves that Eva kept you. I want to take that to the authorities and have her denounced as a child stealer."

He paused, his face red, and banged his fist on the table. The cups rattled and a couple in the far corner of the room looked round in alarm.

"I know what's in that letter. I know that Eva was supposed to return you after the war. She kept you and you had the life I should have had."

"So you're angry because your mother gave me to Eva and not you," said Sam slowly. "I thought you were angry because I wasn't returned."

"Yes, I am angry that you weren't returned…and I'm angry because you had a better life than me. We're twins. We shouldn't have been separated. Did you never feel that there was a part of you missing, even if you didn't know what it was?"

He put his head in his hands then continued.

"I'm confused. I don't know how I feel. I was so angry with Eva. I think I could have killed her, and I was so angry with you but now, when I'm fairly certain you didn't know anything about it…I can't think any more. Ever since I found out, I've wanted to smash up your life. Now, I want you to feel what I feel."

Sam glanced over at Helen. For the first time he felt some sympathy for the man sitting across the table from him. He wanted to calm him down and diffuse the situation.

"Would it help if you started at the beginning and told me about yourself and about your life? For example, your English is so very good. Did you learn it at school? You seem to know a lot about me and I know nothing about you."

CHAPTER 26

"Oh, yes. I know all about you," Hans sneered. "You had a mother who loved you and took care of you. You had a father who was so proud of you. You left the chaos that was Berlin and went to Palestine, with plenty of food and people who cared for you. And when that wasn't good enough for your parents, you moved easily to England and lived a charmed life.

"University, marriage and children. You were the blue eyed boy. The concentration camp kid made good." Hans coughed. He looked very pale and Sam urged him to drink some tea.

"Ah, tea," he said sarcastically. "The British answer to everything. If you have a problem, drink tea. If you lose your job, drink tea. Well, okay. I will drink your tea and then I will tell you what my life has been like.

"I was a few months old when my mother tried to poison me. How does that make me feel?"

Sam shifted uncomfortably in his seat but didn't reply.

"Well, how do you think I felt when I found that out? She was prepared to sacrifice her children because of her love for Adolf Hitler. I was told so many times that I was lucky to survive. I can tell you that when I was a child I didn't feel lucky.

"The soldiers who found me knew I was the son of the Camp Commandant. No-one could find him. He had disappeared off the face of the earth. You know, I was nearly murdered by my mother and I was abandoned by my father. I don't know which is worse.

"I was taken to an orphanage for babies and small children. Somehow, the welfare people found my grandparents – my father's parents. They were living in the suburbs of Berlin. Who knows, Sam, it might even have been near where you were. It could have been the same street."

Both men sat thoughtfully, thinking this over and then Hans continued.

"Berlin in 1945 wasn't the same as Britain in 1945. It wasn't even the same as Palestine where you were. It was a city reduced to rubble. The war between countries might have been over, but the war to survive was just beginning.

"My grandparents had been told that their son, their daughter-in-law and the children were dead. They were struggling to keep alive foraging for food and trying to keep clean.

"Suddenly, they were given a child to care for. How do you think that made them feel? Grandmother told me later they were shocked. Their flat had been bombed and they were existing in an air raid shelter which somehow had managed to survive the allied onslaught.

"You, of course, were comfortable in a warm house on a kibbutz, whereas I was delivered to them like a parcel by a social worker who told them what had happened to the rest of my family."

"But how could anyone leave a child just like that?" Helen interrupted.

"How? There were many others who were in even worse situations. Berlin was in ruins and there was nowhere for people to go, unless they had relatives in the country. There was no way the welfare people could find anywhere better for me to live. It's a miracle they found my grandparents and if the military hadn't known about my father, I don't think that would have happened.

"You, Sam. You went to Palestine and lived in comfort, while we were living in poverty. There was no way we could stay in this air raid shelter so my grandparents took me to live with a cousin on the outskirts of the city. We all shared a room but at least there was a kitchen and a toilet. I don't remember all this but my grandmother told me often enough about how hard it was to just exist.

"My grandfather had fought in the first world war and he had wanted to fight again in the second but his health wasn't good. He'd suffered from a gas attack in 1917 and never really recovered."

Sam risked an interruption. "My grandfather also fought in World War I, also in Germany. He won an Iron Cross for that."

"*Your* grandfather. *Your* grandfather. Don't you mean Eva's father, the Jew, who is very definitely not your grandfather?"

There was a stunned silence as the venom in Hans's words percolated through and then Hans continued.

"It took years for Berlin to recover from the damage. Large parts of the city were destroyed completely. Do you know what that means?" Without giving Sam time to reply, he rushed on.

"A city in ruins means no water supply, no gas or electricity. No phones, only a few shops and a great shortage of food. German citizens were given a food ration of only about 1,200 calories a day. Do you know how many calories a day you need to thrive?" Hans voice thickened with anger.

"You need around 2,500 calories just to maintain your weight so this was a government 'diet'. It was a starvation diet." He snorted disdainfully. "It wasn't our choice. Of course, the concentration camp survivors got more food." There was so much bitterness in Hans's words, and he repeated them before continuing. "There were camps for German prisoners of war, where men were held in the most atrocious conditions."

Sam interjected swiftly. "Maybe so but at least they weren't extermination camps."

Hans raised his hand again. "Enough! I won't go on if you argue with everything I say. Can you not sit still and keep your mouth shut?"

Sam shook his head in despair and motioned to Hans to continue.

"Even those men that were in forced work parties didn't get any extra food. The Americans were told not to supplement the German diet by sharing their food with them. They were told to destroy any left over food. Unbelievable but true. Can you imagine? They were told to destroy perfectly good food, while we were starving.

"Germany was suffering from incredible shortages and there were some countries who offered to trade goods like coal and steel for food. The Allies refused. Can you understand now why I am so bitter? Children were starving and there was a way out but it was refused. Most of this happened when I was too young to know but I heard all about it from my grandparents. They never forgot and they made sure I wouldn't either."

Sam tried again to intervene.

"That may be so but you can't blame Eva for that. Or me," he added.

"But I do blame her," Hans responded. "She took you and you didn't have to struggle like me."

"Not fair," said Sam. "Eva didn't 'take me' as you put it. She didn't have a choice. I was given to her."

"And she could have given you back. Let me go on...

"I do recall a speech made by Ernst Reuter. My grandparents took me to the ruins of the Reichstag building. Hundreds and thousands of people were there and the atmosphere was electric. It was autumn, September I think, and the air was crisp.

"I was shivering in my thin coat and when I looked down at my legs, sticking out of my short trousers, my knees were blue with cold. Grandma had made those shorts out of an old pair of grandfather's trousers and they were rough and scratchy on my bare skin."

He paused and absent mindedly rubbed his knees, reliving that day. He continued, "Reuter stood in front of the silent crowd and appealed to the 'people of the world' not to abandon 'this city and its people'. We were at rock bottom. We had nothing.

"We walked slowly home, holding hands in the throng of people and I saw Grandma wipe a tear from her eye.

'I never thought my beautiful Berlin would end up like this,' she said sadly, and grandfather put his arm round her to comfort her. They were Berliners, born and bred.

"When I was about eleven I changed schools. I think I was quite clever enough – I was in the top class for English language but there was no opportunity for serious learning. All of us children were undernourished and I couldn't concentrate on my studies a lot of the time because I was always hungry. There was still rationing in Germany until 1955. Did you know that?" He looked at Sam.

"In England, we too had rationing. It was around 1953 or 1954 when it ended so I know what you were going through." Sam spoke very quietly but it only enraged the other man.

"Don't tell me you know what we were going through," he hissed. "You had rationing? You were short of food? I don't think so. I really don't think so. In 1953 we saw the coronation of Queen Elizabeth. Don't look so surprised, Otto, we too had the opportunity to see television in the East even if not many of us had a set of our own.

"I watched all the pomp and ceremony. I saw people sleeping in the streets to watch the processions. They were doing it out of choice. In Berlin, people were still sleeping in the streets because they had no homes. How can you compare your smooth, easy life with the one I had?"

Hans's elbow jogged the table and the cups rattled in their saucers. The ladies sitting in the far corner averted their eyes and tried to ignore the noise. Sam realised that this café was not a good choice. It was too quiet, too discreet and they were drawing attention to themselves.

Sam was beginning to feel like a nomad, moving from place to place. Glancing around, he realised that they would have to find somewhere else to continue. His eyes caught Helen's and she gave an almost imperceptible nod. He smiled inwardly. They were always on the same wavelength.

"Hans," he started impulsively. "Would you like to continue this at our home? We could have something to eat and it would be more comfortable." Helen nodded in agreement.

Hans looked surprised.

"At your home? Oh, I get it. You're frightened that people will see the big Rabbi having an argument in a public place."

Sam reddened – Hans had hit the nail on the head. "It's true I wouldn't want anyone from my congregation interrupting us," he murmured, "but, even so, it would be more comfortable, you know."

Hans looked at his watch.

"Actually, yes. I would like to visit my brother and his family in their own home. What about tomorrow? I could come to you around eleven am?"

"Yes, that works for me. Helen and I need to get back to see Ma is ok, and we need to speak to our kids. We have a lot more to talk about but it can wait till the morning. I think we've all had a pretty tough time lately, including Ma."

They all stood up and Sam replaced his hat carefully on his head. "See you tomorrow, then," he said. Hans didn't reply. Helen and Sam watched as Hans hurried off through the double doors.

CHAPTER 27

The shadows were beginning to fall as they walked down the steps to the street. A taxi drew up at the kerbside and Sam helped Helen in and gave the driver the address. Within twenty minutes they were at home and, as they walked up the path, the front door flew open. Inside in the hall, Esther was waiting and they could see Daniel behind her coming out of the sitting room.

"We have Granny here," whispered Esther. "She was reluctant at first but I told her that you were very worried about her and if she didn't come here, you would have to stay with her and leave both of us. She knew I was manipulating her but she accepted there was no choice. She gave in gracefully. She's having a lie down in the spare room. So now, Dad, please tell us what's going on."

This was going to be so hard for everyone. Esther and Daniel would see a side of their grandmother they might find difficult to understand.

Sam took his hat and coat off and placed them carefully on the coat rack. He went into the sitting room and poured everyone a glass of brandy.

"I suspect we're all going to need this," he said passing them round.

"I don't know how or where to start," he said helplessly. "What I am about to say will sound so incredible that you might even think it was a plot of a book but it's all true. I haven't heard everything but I will tell you what I know."

Esther and Daniel looked at each other. They had a feeling their tranquil life was about to be shattered.

"First of all," started Sam, "I don't want you to think ill of your grandmother." They looked at each other again. Whatever Sam was going to tell them, they hadn't considered it would have anything to do with Eva.

Briefly and succinctly, Sam outlined Eva's story. Everyone was silent, trying to process what was being said. Even Helen, who had heard it before, found herself in tears at some points and she moved to sit in between her two children. She put her arms around them and held them tight. Esther was shaking and Daniel look bemused.

"Dad," he started. "I can't take this all in. Are you really telling me you were stolen from the Hoffman family and that Hoffman himself was a war criminal? Not to mention the fact that you have a twin brother. And you never knew any of it?"

"Not until Granny told me. We met Hans Hoffman today, and we've asked him to come tomorrow to tell us the rest of the story. There's still so much we don't know."

"Is it wise to have him in the house?" Daniel said loudly. "What do you know about him? He might be a criminal like his father."

"He might be," Sam said mildly, "but we cannot judge him. We need to talk to him again and see if we can find a way out of this awful mess."

"Awful mess?" responded Esther. "Dad, it's more than that. It's chaos. It's unbelievable." She rushed from the room and Helen made to go after her. Sam caught her arm.

"Leave her be," he said. "It's a shock for her and she needs time to digest it."

"Dad, where does this leave us? Esther and me."

"It leaves you where you always were. You're Jewish, Mum's Jewish, I'm your father and no-one can take that away. I'm the one with the problem. I'm the one who's a rabbi, when I'm not even a Jew."

"Of course you're Jewish, Dad. How could you not be Jewish?" Daniel said. Esther came back into the room, wiping her eyes and went to sit by her brother.

"It's not as simple as that, Son," said Sam wearily. "Technically, I don't have a Jewish mother, so I'm not Jewish. It doesn't really matter that I was brought up as a Jew, with a Jewish family. The important thing is that my birth mother was not Jewish." Daniel and Esther tried to digest this. They had never had to think about a problem such as this before.

"And what about Auntie Rachel? Does she know?"

"Not yet," replied Sam, "but she'll have to be told. That can wait a while, though. She and Uncle Ivor are on holiday. They won't be back until next week. Frankly, at the moment, I can't face telling anyone else and until I've spoken with Hans tomorrow, it would be better if I didn't. I'm going up to see Ma now. I assume she's in bed?"

"Yes," said Esther. "She went up to her room not long after we brought her back here and she says she's tired and doesn't want to come down again. I took her up something on a tray so if I were you I would leave her now, Dad. She'll call if she wants you."

"No, Esther. I need to talk to her. I need to tell her that Hans is coming tomorrow. It would be too much of a shock for her if I waited until the morning."

Esther raised her shoulders in a gesture very like her grandmother's.

"It's up to you, Dad. Just be aware she might want to be left alone. I don't think she's in a good place just now."

Sam knocked tentatively at his mother's, relieved when she told him to come in.

"I have to tell you something, Ma, and I want you to listen before you interrupt me." Sam looked at the figure of his mother, lying under the bedclothes. "Just stay there and I'll tell you."

He crossed to the chair by the bed and sat down.

"I met Hans this afternoon and he started to tell me about his life. We were in the café at the Meeting House – the one on Marylebone Road. It started out reasonably well, then I realised it would be better to be somewhere even more private so I…I mean Helen and I, invited him here. He's coming at eleven tomorrow morning."

Eva sat bolt upright.

"In that case, Sam, I'm going home. Help me out of bed, please. I'll get dressed and you can call me a taxi."

"Don't be silly, Ma," Sam said gently. "You don't have to be in the same room but I don't want you going back to your house."

223

"What could happen to me? The man that broke into *my* house will be here in *your* house so I'll be quite safe."

Sam nodded thoughtfully.

"That's one way of looking at it, but you might want to ask him questions yourself, Ma."

Eva shook her head vehemently. "I don't think so but I'll stay till the morning and then I am definitely going home."

Daniel was pouring himself another brandy when Sam went into the living room.

"Want one, Dad? I think you might need it." He handed a tumbler to Sam with a generous measure in it. "Soda?"

"You're right. I do need a drink. I'll take it as it is."

He looked around at his family.

"You've heard what's happened. I don't think I need to go over it again. What I do need to consider, though, is where I go from here." He turned to Helen. "I am so proud of you, my darling," he said. "You've discovered that the man you are married to is actually someone completely different and isn't even Jewish." He raised his hand to prevent anyone interrupting.

"Isn't even Jewish," he repeated. "And not once have you suggested that our marriage is over. I would understand if you wanted a divorce in the circumstances."

Helen looked aghast.

"I've never heard anything so ridiculous in my life," she said hotly. "We will stay married, even if we have to get married all over again!"

Daniel and Esther groaned. "Not another wedding," Daniel said, but they were smiling. Each of them had independently wondered what would happen to their

224

parents' marriage and each of them was relieved there was a future for them.

"I suggest we all get some sleep," Helen said. "I think tomorrow is going to be a very difficult day."

Later, in the stillness of their bedroom, Sam asked Helen if she had meant what she said or was it just to keep the kids happy.

"How could you ask that, Sam?" she said tearfully. "We've been married for over twenty years. How can you doubt my feelings for you? I love you, whatever and whoever you are.

"There's just one question I have. When you first saw Hans in Berlin, did you believe straight away there was a problem?"

"Yes, I knew right from the start there was something I needed to investigate. Even though I didn't know what the problem was, I knew there was something I had to find out."

She moved across to take him in her arms.

"We'll get through this together, whatever it takes. Let's get some sleep now, ready for what tomorrow will bring."

The house settled into its night time quietness but Eva, in her room lay sleepless, reviewing her past and all the decisions she'd made concerning Sam. She thought about how she'd kept the dreadful secret all his life. She'd made that choice when she had allowed Rabbi Langer to perform Sam's circumcision.

After that there had been no going back. Her punishment for doing this had been that she'd been unable to confide in anyone, a burden which had always weighed heavily on her.

Sam and Helen lay entwined, arms around each other, recognising that their relationship would have to change and

225

move into a new phase. Helen smoothed Sam's hair away from his brow. "It'll work out alright. Have faith, Sam. God will help us," she added sleepily.

Esther sat at her desk, listening to the creaks and groans of the house settling, going over and over in her mind the events of the day. Eventually, she shut her books and switched off the light before getting into bed. She fully expected to stay awake but soon she was sleeping soundly.

Daniel waited until everything was quiet, then cautiously opened his bedroom door. Avoiding the creaky step, he tiptoed down the stairs, went into the kitchen and opened the fridge door. Treasure trove. A plate of pickles, some sliced meat, a piece of melon and a large carton of orange juice, which he drank without transferring it to a glass. Wiping his mouth, he went back up the stairs, crawled into bed and was asleep in seconds.

CHAPTER 28

The dog barking woke Sam. Poor Tess hadn't been taken out for a walk as usual yesterday evening. No doubt she was desperate to be let out into the garden. Sam pulled on his dressing gown and went to see to her. He opened the back door for her and she bounded out, tail flying. He decided he would make breakfast for everyone. He was busy setting the table when first Helen and then Eva came into the kitchen.

Eva spoke first.

"I've changed my mind, Sam. I won't be going home just yet. I want to hear what this man has to say. He needs to apologise to me for breaking into my house and scaring me like that."

"He'll be here around eleven so we need to get a move on. We should decide whether or not Esther and Daniel join us."

"Don't you think if we were all in the room that Hans would feel overwhelmed? Better that you and I talk first with him and then Eva can join us." Helen turned to Eva. "How does that feel to you?" she asked.

Eva nodded her head. In reality, she wasn't sure that she would be able to meet Hans face to face so this was an easy way to take that step. Sam could always tell her later what was said if she decided she couldn't manage it.

By eleven o'clock Eva was looking anxiously out of the window.

"I don't think he'll come," she said eventually. "Too much for him. Anyway, what is there to say? From his point of view that is."

Several cars were moving up the street and a light rain was slanting at the window. The sky was overcast and grey, very much like the moods of the waiting people. And then Sam saw Hans turn the corner and walk slowly down the pavement, looking at the house numbers. He paused as he came near, as if he was assessing the kind of property Sam and Helen owned. And then he was ringing the bell and standing back under the porch.

Hans waited until he could hear footsteps coming down the hall, wondering why he'd agreed to this meeting. He had no intention of making a friend of Sam. The anger and bitterness he felt at learning of his twin's existence was never far from the surface of his personality.

The door opened and he stepped over the threshold. Helen and Eva were standing in the doorway of the dining room, two young people were sitting on the stairs and Sam was waiting for him to come in properly.

"A reception committee," Hans said angrily. "I have no intention of talking to a crowd," and he turned to leave.

"It will just be Helen and me talking with you," Sam said soothingly, "although my mother does want an apology from you for what happened the other day." Hans had the grace to look a little shamefaced. "I didn't mean to scare you," he said apologetically, "but you have something I want. I am hoping you are feeling better now."

Eva nodded grimly and said abruptly,

"I'm going upstairs. I don't wish to listen to any of this." She called to the two youngsters. "Leave your parents to deal with this. It is their problem, not yours." They obeyed, moving into the kitchen.

"Can we make a new beginning?" said Sam carefully. "You must realise by now that Eva did not kidnap me or steal me from your parents. It was they who gave me to her."

"And you have the letter which explains why. I need to see that letter. What have you done with it?"

"All in good time. I will show it to you but you must accept that it is Eva's letter – not mine and not yours."

"I don't care who the letter belongs to; I want to see for myself what my parents intended."

"Later, I think. Let's go back to what you were telling us yesterday," urged Sam.

"You know, Otto, I envy you."

Sam flinched when Hans used the name 'Otto'. Hans continued,

"I hate you but I envy you. You have had unconditional love all your life. I have only ever had conditional love. My grandparents were old. They had been damaged by the war. They had lost their son and grandchildren and then they were given a baby to look after in a city which wasn't healthy for adults, never mind children. I grew up knowing I had to look after them.

"They would send me out to collect firewood when I was only five or six years old. I would scramble around the ruins of collapsed houses and I knew I wouldn't be welcome back at home unless I had a bundle of wood for them. If I didn't take enough, Grandfather would slap me or Grandmother would shout at me.

"I desperately wanted a good education but I had to leave school when I was fifteen. I had to find a job so I could give money to my grandparents, who had very little. At a time when you were working hard for university entrance, I was trying to be a man and put food on the table. I bet you never had to worry about that." He rubbed his fist across his eyes.

"People think that when the war was over, Germans were helped by the British or the Americans, and it's true that a lot of construction work went on, but the ordinary people – people like me, had to fight for everything we wanted.

"I couldn't have new clothes, or eat decent food. I had to make do with what we could buy second hand or what was left in the shops at the end of the day." He looked across at Sam.

"There were no Christmas presents, although I don't suppose that would have been a problem for you," he sneered. "I was ten years old when the zoo opened in Berlin but I didn't get the chance to go and see the animals. Too much work scavenging, and no money. I would love to have seen the animals.

"At one time I thought I would like to be a veterinarian but that would have meant a lot of study and a lot of money to pay the fees. I wasn't privileged like you, brother. I went to work on a building site to put food on our table." He held out his hands and Sam could see they were thickened with hard work, scarred and scratched, with calluses on the fingers.

"While you were gently pushing a pen around and getting drunk at university, making friends and going out with girls, I was doing real work. Man's work.

"And then things changed. Grandfather was getting sicker and we were still sharing an apartment. Grandfather's cousin was getting tired of us. I knew that. We had been there a long time and she wasn't getting any younger. She started to make life difficult and we knew we had to move.

"And then a letter came from the authorities. My grandparents had been allocated one of the new flats built with public funding. You would call it a 'council house'. We called it home. For the first time we had a place of our own.

"Large housing estates had been built and we felt we were so lucky to get a new property. It was like all our birthdays and Christmases in one. Needless to say, we had no money for furniture, not even beds but we managed with cast offs and hand outs.

Hans paused for breath. He had been hurtling through his story and he nodded his thanks at Helen for the glass of tea. He stirred the sugar in slowly and looked across the table.

"This is not easy for me, you know. I was just as shocked to find out about you as you obviously were to find out about me. But there it is. We are brothers.

"What were you doing in 1961, Otto?" he asked. "I'll tell you what I was doing. I woke up on August 13th to find I was living in East Germany. The day before, I had been living in Germany. Now my country was divided and we were prevented from leaving. Berlin was totally divided into East and West. Can you even think what that meant?

"We were not allowed to go over to the West. People tried to leave, of course, and if they were caught they were shot. I don't suppose you had a problem if you wanted to travel to Scotland," he added wryly. "Never mind another country. For us it was impossible."

There was silence in the room as Helen and Sam tried to imagine what that must have been like. To be prevented from travelling to another part of their own country was unthinkable yet it had happened to Hans.

"Some things did improve but, for us, life didn't get better. We were living under a communist rule and salaries were low. There were always rumours about how good life was in the West and how salaries were large but there was no way for us to get there and see for ourselves.

"There were times when people from West Berlin were allowed to visit those in the East. They came to see relatives or friends. We didn't have any relatives or friends in the West so we couldn't find out what it was really like to live in a free society, but we could always identify them. They looked smarter and better dressed than those of us in the East." He stopped to think. "You might find this strange but I envied the men their jeans."

"Their jeans?" asked Sam. "Why would you envy someone their jeans?"

"Because we in the East didn't have any. I think the government thought they were a subversive element. When we could see television, we saw the film stars and the pop stars wearing them and we wanted them too."

Sam and Helen looked shocked. They couldn't envisage a society where young people couldn't buy jeans, or were considered subversive if they did.

"And so I continued to go to work and live with my grandparents."

"Did you never marry?" asked Helen.

"Yes, I got married."

"Children?"

"Children? No. I wasn't able to father children. The doctors said it was because I was severely malnourished during the war. Very different from your experiences, I think," he added bitterly. "I would have liked children of my own, a family, and a normal life. Instead I've always had to struggle."

Helen asked gently, "Where is your wife now?"

"My wife was killed."

There was silence before Helen probed a little. "Killed?"

"She was on her way home from her work in the café, when she was attacked. They must have thought she had the takings in her bag because they took it. Before they ran off, one of them hit her and pushed her and she fell and banged her head.

"She didn't come home at her usual time so I went out to look for her. I found her lying there in the alley, bleeding. She was almost unconscious but she knew it was me. She just whispered, 'I knew you'd find me,' and then," Hans paused, his voice thickened with tears. "Then she died in my arms. There was nothing I could do."

Helen's hand went to her throat, as she tried to take in what Hans was saying.

"Did the police ever catch her attackers?" enquired Sam.

"No, they just said it was a random assault. They did look for a while but nobody had seen anything. It was dark, what else could they do?"

They were all silent, thinking over what Hans had said. How tragic that he had lost his wife in such awful circumstances. Sam cleared his throat.

"How old was she?"

"How old was she?" snapped Hans. "What's that got to do with anything? She was killed, I tell you. She died in a rubbish strewn alley. What does her age matter?"

"You're right," soothed Helen. "Age doesn't matter at all when you lose someone you love."

Slightly calmer, Hans muttered, "She was twenty-seven. Too young to die."

"And you've been on your own ever since?" prompted Sam.

"Yes, I never wanted anyone else after Trudi died. She was not just my wife, she was my best friend. I went back to live with my grandparents. They were becoming even more frail and I didn't want to be on my own any more. They were happy to have me back because the money I earned helped them too."

Once again there was silence. Sam was so aware that, in comparison to Hans, he had led a charmed life. He had enjoyed the opportunity to study, to become a rabbi, to marry and have children. Even now, after this horrific discovery, he knew that he had the love of his family. What did Hans have?

"So when did you find out about your father?" he asked Hans tentatively.

It was after my grandmother died. We had already lost my grandfather, and I was supporting my grandmother. We still lived in the little flat and I continued to work on the construction sites. The Iron Curtain stopped us from going into the West, of course, but life was getting better.

"There was more food in the shops; there were concerts and the cinema." He laughed. "I even went to the zoo, somewhere I had always wanted to go. I took Grandmother with me and she couldn't believe it when she saw all the animals, penned up in their cages. Of course, I felt as if I, too, was in a cage. A cage of family loyalty and a cage made by the Wall.

"When my grandmother died I stayed on in the flat. I didn't have anywhere else to go, and I suppose it was easier to just stay there. There were two bedrooms and I thought I might get someone to share with me. I was so lonely, even though living with my grandparents had never been easy.

"The first thing I had to do was clear out their room. Have you ever had to do that?" Hans asked. "It's not a good thing to do. Getting rid of clothes and stuff like that is not a problem but sorting through old papers and photographs for me was heart rending.

"I had never seen pictures of my mother and father. I had asked, of course, when I was a child but my grandparents had always said they didn't have any. When I found a shoe box full of old photographs, I was so angry with them."

His fists clenched and his jaw stiffened. For a brief moment, he looked very like the picture of the soldier he was pushing over the table towards Sam.

"This is our father," he said. "*Our* father," he repeated. "Yours and mine."

Sam was reluctant to look but curiosity got the better of him. He picked up the worn black and white photo of a man in military uniform. He was standing very erectly against a large wooden door. His uniform was immaculate and his boots, even in an old photo, looked highly polished. His leather belt held a pistol and he was holding a cigarette in his left hand.

Hans spilled more pictures onto the table. More of the Commandant alone, several with a tall woman standing or sometimes sitting beside him.

"Our mother," Hans said briefly.

Sam looked closely at a family portrait. His birth parents and his brother and sister. They were all sitting on a tartan picnic rug, on a lawn. The children looked very serious but the woman was smiling. Her husband's hand lay carelessly over her shoulders and her face was turned slightly towards him. The camera had captured the look of adoration in his eyes, as he gazed at her.

"There are no pictures of you or me," Hans went on. "By the time we were born, the war was at a difficult point for Germany so I don't suppose many photographs were taken."

Sam spread all the pictures out and Helen moved closer to see them. There was no doubt of the relationship between Sam and the Hoffmans. The facial likeness was quite marked.

"Go on," he urged Hans. "Did you find a lodger?"

"Hold on," Hans replied. "Let me tell you about my discovery."

CHAPTER 29

"Sorting out the paperwork took a long time and then I came across a bundle of letters. If I hadn't read them," he said ruefully, "we wouldn't be sitting here today. But I did and it was like opening a can of worms.

"The letters were from my father. At first I imagined they had all been written before or during the war. The earliest ones were on top of the pile and I read them eagerly. They told about Father joining the army in 1933, when he was twenty-one. He had been captivated, it was clear, by Adolf Hitler. His letters home were full of this charismatic leader who was going to make Germany the most powerful nation in the world.

"Hitler was going to eliminate all the weak citizens and the ones who didn't fit in to his plans. This included the Jews, whom he described as 'vermin'.

"I had been brought up by grandparents who thought the same so this was nothing new to me. In fact, I agreed with it all. I wished that all the Jews had been wiped off the face of the earth."

Helen and Sam looked at each other, glad that Eva wasn't in the room to hear this. Hans was so vehement, it was obvious that he followed the doctrines of his parents and grandparents. They felt uncomfortable but Sam still urged Hans to speak.

"Father wrote regularly to his parents. The pile of letters was huge so I knew it would take a long time to get through them. I settled down with a beer to read more.

"There were regular accounts of his training and then his deployment to a crack regiment. He rose swiftly up the ranks it seemed, mainly because of his determination to follow Hitler's ideas.

"When the war began, he was one of Hitler's favoured advisers. He was with him at all the important moments; the Wannsee Conference, the meetings with Eichman to agree the Final Solution and so on.

"He described how there were many attempts on Hitler's life and how he managed to move swiftly in front of his idol when an officer raised his pistol to shoot the Führer. He was so proud that the bullet meant for Hitler lodged itself in him. As a result, he suffered a damaged lung and that put paid to any ideas he had about continuing active service. He was rewarded by Hitler for his loyalty and given the Iron Cross like his father before him.

"When he described this in his letters, his anguish was tangible. Not about losing his previously good health but about the fact he wouldn't be able to fight on the front line. He so desperately wanted to be at the Front, to make sure that Germany would become the supreme power.

"Hitler appointed him Camp Commandant, with the authority to run the camp as Hitler himself would have done. Hitler had said he had every confidence that Ernst Hoffman could reduce the number of Jews in Germany and therefore the world. Father wrote proudly to my grandfather about this, detailing all the measures he would implement which would make sure the prisoners suffered.

"When I read this, I agreed with the idea but, as time went on, the letters became more sadistic. He seemed to delight in inventing new ways of eliminating Jews.

"There were also letters which described happy things but not many. His main focus was getting rid of 'vermin'. He did write about the births of Dietrich and Giselle but not of us. I suppose that by the time we were born the postal services were fractured. I had hoped that by reading these letters that I would get some insight into what kind of man my father was.

"They were in chronological order and tied with string. The last one in the pile was dated August 1944, before we were born. I was bereft. Realisation hit me that the reasons the letters had stopped was that he had been killed, and I cried for the father I had never known. I cried for the mother I had missed all my life and for the brother and sister I couldn't even remember.

"And this was despite knowing that my parents had decided to kill us, rather than leave us alive to face the uncertain future of Germany. I mourned their loss, all the while acknowledging that however evil their plans were for us children, blood was thicker than water.

"And then I came across another box of letters. I recognised the writing straight away. More letters from my father.

"Once again, they were in a neat pile, held by an elastic band. The postmark on the top one was 1975. I got another beer to steady my nerves. One minute I had thought my father was dead, the next I could read letters from the fairly recent past. Why had there been a thirty year gap in communication? And why did it start again?

"I can tell you that my hands trembled as I slid the closely written sheets out of the envelope. The postmark on the outside was of a prison in Leipzig and inside it was obvious that some words had been censored. There was enough, though, to read and understand that Ernst Hoffman was in prison and had been for a long time. This obviously explained the long gap since the last letter.

"My grandparents had moved a couple of times so I was curious as to how father knew where they lived. All was made clear.

"Even though the war had been over for years, there were always agents trying to trace, find and take to trial those Nazis who were considered to be war criminals. Ernst Hoffman had been on the run for a long time before he had been caught.

"Grandfather had written to him because news of his trial was in the papers. There were many people who were happy to testify against him. Some were camp survivors, others were guards who themselves were on trial. Probably they hoped for a lighter sentence if they testified against other Nazis who had committed crimes which were even more serious.

"The first letter I picked up was a response to the one grandfather had written. Father was not trying to excuse his actions. He was proud of them, proud of the way he had treated the prisoners in his care.

"He described how he kept the prisoners working till they dropped and how every little misdemeanour was punished.

240

He had developed a scale of punishments, ranging from starving the inmates to executing them. Of course there was censorship in the prison but it was easy to work out what the blacked out words were and this gave me a picture of my father which I wasn't happy to see.

"My world was crumbling about me and the more I read the sicker I became. Even though my father was now an old man and incarcerated in prison, he was still convinced that his ideals were the right ones.

"I agreed with many of his principles. I still do. I could see no reason why Jews should be allowed to live but I was in favour of a planned controlled extermination plan. The Commandant wished to inflict as much pain as possible before all life was extinguished."

As Sam listened to Hans's words, a shudder ran through him. He was in the same room as someone who still wished for the annihilation of all Jews, even though the war had been lost by the Germans over forty years ago.

He looked at Helen and could see the disgust and horror in her face. He knew her so well, that he could work out what she was thinking. She looked at Sam in despair at what she was hearing but he shook his head and motioned to Hans to continue.

"We have heard so much, darling," he said. "We have to hear the rest. We need to know the complete story," and so Helen sank back in her chair, trembling hands raising a glass of water to her lips.

Hans went on.

"After a while I stopped reading. I couldn't absorb any more but the one thing I knew I had to do was meet him. He had given me life and I wanted to see what kind of man had fathered me, even though I had read some of his letters.

"There is a phone box across the road from the flat and I was lucky that night."

"Lucky?" interrupted Sam.

"Yes, lucky. Sometimes the phone was unusable because it had been vandalised. I crossed the street, which was very quiet and managed to find some coins in my pocket.

"The street lamp near the phone box was broken and so the light was dim but I managed to slip the phone book out of its shelf. I flicked through the pages until I found the number of the prison. It was in Leipzig and I was able to find a telephone number to call. The number rang and rang.

"It was some time since my grandfather had died and I wondered if my father, also, was dead. I worked out that he must have been nearly seventy years old, and would have been in prison a long time.

"I was about to hang up when I heard a woman's voice saying firmly,

'You are through to Leipzig Prison. Which department would you like?'

"I couldn't stop shaking, as I asked to speak to the governor. She asked me what it was about and I just told her that it was a personal matter and that I could only discuss it with the governor himself.

"Reluctantly, she asked me to hold on and then a few minutes later I heard the click of the receiver as the phone was picked up.

"I asked if a man by the name of Ernst Hoffman was held in the prison. There was a silence and then the governor answered.

'I'm not allowed to give out information like that,' he said. 'Please tell me who is calling.'

"I have reason to believe that Ernst Hoffman is my father," I told him.

'Really,' he answered. 'How do I know you are telling the truth?'

"I thought quickly. 'I know he has had a visitor once a month for a number of years,' I told him. 'That was my grandfather, Hans Hoffman. I am named after him.'

Once again I waited until eventually the governor replied.

'I do recall someone visiting this man so, yes, I can confirm Ernst Hoffman is held here. Is there any further way in which I can help you, Herr Hoffman?'

"Boldly, I asked if it was possible for me to visit my father.

'There is a protocol here,' said the governor. 'I will need to ask him if he will see you. As far as I know, Prisoner Hoffman had only one relative – as you say, the father who visited him. However, those visits stopped very abruptly. If you give me your phone number, I will call you and let you know his decision.'

"I told him I would have to call him back as I didn't have a phone in my flat and asked when would be a good time.

'Call me tomorrow,' he said. 'After two o'clock and I will have an answer for you.'

Hans looked at Sam.

"Do you ever feel as if your life is spiralling out of control?" he asked. "As if you're falling into a deep pit…down and down and down?"

Sam recalled what Eva had said about feeling like Alice in Wonderland. He looked directly at Hans. "Until this week

– no," he said. "But now, I know exactly what you mean. Just as I seem to process one thing and come to terms with it, something else happens."

"Well, that's how I felt then. As far as I knew, my parents and brother and sister had died in the war. Grandfather had always spoken of my father as a war hero. He was immensely proud of him and I'd always thought he'd been killed in action. Which, of course, is what my grandfather wanted me to believe.

"I don't think anyone would acknowledge that their son was a Nazi war criminal, no matter how much they might have loved them. And I'm sure that in the early aftermath of the war, my grandfather did believe that the Commandant was a war hero. It was only when he read the newspapers that he learned that Ernst was to go on trial for his life for the atrocities he'd committed.

"And then I began to understand why he had never talked much about Ernst. As a child I had often asked about my father. There were many boys at school who had fathers who were heroes but all I knew was that my father had died in battle. I think my grandparents couldn't speak because their grief was too much to bear.

"And until he found out about Ernst, that was the way it was. I suppose I was about eighteen when the truth was published in the German papers, and I really don't know how I was unaware of it. After that, I expect he was so revolted that he couldn't speak about Ernst.

"When I think back, I do remember a time when any newspaper was put quickly on the fire if I came into the room but I wasn't particularly interested in reading about war criminals and, if I had seen the news, I don't think I

244

would have made the connection. Hoffman is a fairly common name," he added.

"However, it's pretty obvious that Grandfather did not want me to meet my father. In a way, he was protecting my opinion of the war hero."

Hans stopped and looked away and then added quietly,

"And he didn't tell Ernst about me. He knew it would make Father's life so much happier if he knew that one of his children had survived and yet he decided to withhold any information about me. That was his way of punishing the 'war hero' for the war crimes.

"And then, the most momentous meeting of my life. I was faced with seeing my father face to face. Of course, I thought he would know about me. Now it was my turn to find out about him."

CHAPTER 30

"I was put through to the governor's office the next afternoon. He was waiting for my call and said only mildly.

'Prisoner Hoffman has agreed to see you but I have to warn you, he was very confused. He seemed to think you were English or at least that you lived in England. We have told him you are German, that you speak German and so on but I'm not sure that he believed us.

'However, he seemed to recognise your name so we have made allowances for his mental state. We will make an exception and you may come to see him on Saturday. It is not good for a man to be in prison without any visitors. Where are you coming from?' he enquired.

"He briefly explained that I should take the train from Berlin to Leipzig and then probably it would be better to take a taxi to the prison.

'It's about eleven or twelve kilometres, too far to walk and public transport is not wonderful,' he added. I would be allowed to see the prisoner for one hour only, between two and three pm. There was a whole list of rules; no food, no drugs, no alcohol, no weapons. No physical contact with the prisoner. So many rules until my head was spinning. It was almost too much for me to take on board.

"I don't know how I managed to go to work that week. I was doing heavy stuff on a building site, laying foundations for new houses. I didn't feel I could talk to anyone so I kept all the worry inside. Friends asked me if I was ok. How could I answer? How could I tell the truth?

"I just nodded and smiled and let them think what they wanted. I have a reputation on the building sites for being a hard man. Now wasn't the time to let that slip. Even so, I was like a boiling kettle, waiting for the lid to fly off.

"On the Saturday I woke early. No, that's not strictly true because I don't think I slept much. I shaved, looking at my face in the mirror, trying to see if I could find a resemblance to the pictures of Ernst I had seen...was it only a short time ago?

"As I scraped the razor over my chin, I peered at the spotted glass but I couldn't see anything that looked like the man in the photograph. He was erect, firm of jaw and with piercing eyes. My eyes were bloodshot with lack of sleep, heavy and tired.

"I decided I would get an early train, to avoid any travel problems. I knew there would be somewhere to eat once I was in Leipzig and then I would take a taxi to the prison. I had little money and it was a struggle to pay the train fare but I considered that this was probably the most important meeting of my life so it was an expense I would just have to afford.

"Have you ever been to Berlin?" he asked Sam. "Before this last week, I mean."

"No, never, except those few months when I was a baby," responded Sam. "It's not somewhere my family ever wanted to go. In fact, it would have been better if the meeting I was due to attend could have been arranged in another place."

"Ah, yes," Hans nodded. "This all important meeting. You see, Sam, we do have something in common, apart from the circumstance of our birth. We attend important meetings. Or maybe not, in your case. We'll see." His eyes glittered as he said this and again Sam felt there was a malevolent atmosphere in the room.

"Well, let me tell you what it was like. Berlin Hauptbahnhof on a Saturday morning is busy, very busy. Lots of people are going home for the weekend to see their families. I had only rarely travelled by train so I didn't know how to negotiate my way round the station. Everyone seemed to have a purpose, rushing here and there. They were carrying flowers and parcels and suitcases.

"I, on the other hand, had to ask where the platform for my train was and when I finally found a seat, the carriage was crowded and I felt overwhelmed." He laughed wryly. "Can you imagine, the hard man was overwhelmed because he was travelling on a train." He laughed bitterly.

"It's not a long journey to Leipzig. Maybe an hour and a half. Not really long enough to get comfortable and relax. As the train went through small villages, stopping at country railway stations, people got off to be greeted by friends or relatives with warm hugs.

"More people would get on and I was relieved when I could stand up and make my way down the carriage to the door. There were so many people on the train that, for a moment, I thought I might not manage to get off before it moved away but I managed.

"I stood on the platform, with no-one to greet me, and I felt so alone. It was mid morning, a clear day with no rain and the sun giving a little warmth, but I felt cold. Cold inside and yes, frightened about what the day would hold.

"In a short time I had gone from someone who revered his father, the dead war hero, to a nervous anxious man about to meet his war criminal father for the first time since he was a baby. I wondered if I would be able to cope with this meeting.

"The station buffet was warm, offering hot coffee and sandwiches. I decided that I would have a drink and something to eat then take a walk around the town. I hoped it would clear my head and let me get my thoughts in order. I knew I would have a lot of questions, and maybe walking around would help.

"As I left the station, I saw a double-decker commuter train pull in. I had travelled there on a regular train so I found it very interesting to see that there were stairs inside and seats on top for passengers. I decided I would try and catch one of these trains for my journey home, so I could have the experience of being upstairs. I think I was trying to distract myself from what lay ahead by focussing on such a trivial thing.

"I was surprised to see how poor the roads in Leipzig were. It was a long time since the war – plenty of time for work on the infrastructure to have been put in place. There was graffiti daubed on many walls – I think there had been some sort of demonstration there, and this was left over from it.

"People in general didn't seem to be well dressed. This was a contrast to Berlin, where the locals looked more affluent and the shops had displays of more up to date clothing.

"Many of the houses were in a dilapidated state and the new buildings I saw were all high rise flats, built as cheap accommodation for the workers. It wasn't all depressing though. I passed several street entertainers, playing musical instruments and the shops were brightly lit. I could see church spires in the distance and a tram passed by me, full of shoppers and children.

"By this time it was approaching one o clock so I hailed a taxi to get to the prison. It was originally a hospital, I think, and then it was a women's prison but since the war it's been used as a general prison. I don't think they have many war criminals there though.

"Have you ever been to a prison, Sam?" Hans asked.

"As a matter of fact, I have. I go regularly to visit Jewish prisoners."

"Yes, and I suppose you sit in a comfortable chair in a nice clean office. Probably you have a nice cup of English tea." His face showed disdain.

"Well, not exactly…"

"Not exactly," sneered Hans. "Not exactly!" I can tell you that the prison where my father, *our* father, was being held was nothing like a clean antiseptic British prison."

There was a knock at the door and Daniel poked his head round.

"I can see you're still talking so we've decided to take Granny out for lunch. She says she's hungry so we thought we'd take her to The Copper Kettle. Can we bring you anything back?"

"No, it's all right. We have enough in the fridge so we'll fix something ourselves." The door closed behind him and there was silence again until Hans shouted,

"Why do you have this obsession with food? All you do is eat, or think about eating or planning your next meal. What is it with you?"

"I suppose it's the traditional Jewish way of life," Sam answered mildly.

"But you're not Jewish," screamed Hans. "You're a German, like me. So answer me properly. What is this fixation with food? I've spent most of my life feeling hungry but still I don't obsess."

Neither Sam nor Helen replied. They sat quietly, waiting for Hans to calm down. There was no doubt he was under a great deal of stress. Helen passed him another glass of water and waited while he drank it.

"Why are you both so reasonable?" he shouted again. "Here I am, in your home, yelling at you and you are kind to me. You offer me food and drink. What's the matter with you? Don't you feel any hatred towards me for the way I've been behaving?

"The way I came into your hotel room, your house and your mother's house. The way I went through your drawers and cupboards. Are you not angry?"

"No," said Sam. "I can see you are under a great strain and we are just waiting to hear the rest of the story. We know you will tell us in your own time."

251

Hans slammed the glass down on the table. "Don't patronise me, brother," he said. "But, yes, I will continue. You might as well hear it all."

CHAPTER 31

"I can tell you now that I was terrified to meet my father. All my life I had thought he was dead and now I was to meet him in the flesh. Of course, at the prison I had to go through all the formalities. He was classed as a high risk prisoner so the guards were very thorough.

"They searched me. They even made me put all the contents of my pockets out onto the table. I had to leave my keys and money in a box so that I couldn't hand over anything dangerous or anything that he could trade with other prisoners.

"I was escorted into a large room where there were several tables and chairs.

'You can sit,' said the guard. 'Please keep your hands on the table at all times and do not touch the prisoner.'

"It seemed ages before Ernst came in. I was shocked. I suppose I was expecting someone who looked like the man in the pictures grandfather had kept.

"In reality, an old man came in, shuffling along because his ankles were in chains. He was wearing a navy prison uniform and his hands were in handcuffs. He was clean shaven and the moustache he'd had in the photographs that was a copy of Adolf Hitler's, was gone. His neck was wrinkled and flabby and he was an unhealthy colour.

"He sat opposite me, looking carefully at me before he spoke. 'They said you were my son,' he said eventually, 'but my sons are dead. I have no children alive. No-one to mourn me when I die, unless…' he paused. 'Unless you are Otto.'

'I am Hans,' I told him. 'Didn't Grandfather explain about me? I don't know why he wouldn't tell you about me.'

"I had never understood why my grandfather hadn't told me my father was alive. Now I learned that he had never told my father that *I* was alive.

"Ernst stood up, almost knocking the table over and the guard looked sharply at him. He sat down again quickly.

'I had a son called Hans once,' he said, 'but he died. You cannot be Hans. But Otto we gave away. I know he is alive. Maybe you are Otto.'

"I was so confused. I knew, of course, that what he said about me was true. I should have died, but who was this Otto he'd given away?

'I see,' he said again. There were tears in his cloudy eyes. 'You are Otto and you are alive. My son is here.'

"He put his head on the scarred wooden table and wept and the sound of his sobbing was heartbreaking. There were other prisoners in the room, all with their visitors and they looked at him, and then looked away.

"I said again, 'I am Hans, Father. I did not die. It was a miracle but I did not die.'

"He shook his head. 'So where is Otto?'

"The guard came over then and told me visiting time was over. I felt as if it had hardly started but he told me I had to leave.

'You will be able to come again,' he said. 'You should fill in a form at the office and list yourself as next of kin. Then, if anything happens to Prisoner Hoffman we will inform you. You will be able to visit once a month on a Saturday but now you must leave.'

"Father shuffled off without a word. He seemed unable to accept that I was Hans. He was obviously confused. Hell, I had seen turmoil in those eyes. I hoped that the next visit would be more productive so that I could learn more about this mysterious Otto.

"I watched him leave the room but he didn't turn back, didn't show any emotion, and the iron gates clanged shut behind him. I was escorted to the office where I filled in the necessary forms and made an arrangement to come again.

"I decided to walk back to the station. It was a long walk but I couldn't face the thought of seeing people or sitting in a crowded bus to get back to the station. I hoped the trains would be quieter by the time I got a connection back to Berlin. I kept going over and over in my mind the conversation I'd had with Ernst but none of it made any sense.

"I looked at the station notice board to check the time of the next train back to Berlin and I was surprised to find that there was a train to Colditz in a few minutes. It was so strange, after the day I'd had, to see a train to Colditz where British prisoners of war had been kept when I had just visited my own father in prison."

Hans looked across the table at Sam and Helen. "Sometimes life is like that. There are connections we make ourselves and then there are connections which happen naturally. Colditz prison, Lepzig prison –so similar yet so different."

All three looked at each other, lost in their own thoughts. Hans coughed and cleared his throat.

"You have to understand this had been for me an exhausting day, emotionally as well as physically. The long walk had tired me out and I dozed a little on the journey back. In fact, I was asleep when the train pulled in to the station at Berlin.

"I felt drugged with tiredness and disorientated, and I struggled to open my eyes. I stepped heavily down from the train and the lights on the ceiling in the station spun round. I felt sick and dizzy. There was a woman passing by and she stopped to ask me if I was alright. I told her that I was feeling a little unwell but I would be better when I got home.

"Back in the flat I stood under the shower for a long time before I fell into bed and slept. My mind was no clearer in the morning. I couldn't work out why Father thought I was someone called Otto. I knew I would have to go back again to visit him in prison.

"It's strange how sometimes it seems that time is passing quickly and at other times it passes slowly. The month dragged by until, once again, I was standing outside the prison, joining others who were waiting to see family or friends.

"This time I knew what to expect; the waiting, the search and then the awful room where prisoners sat at tables opposite their visitors. When Ernst sat down, I asked him the all important question.

'Who is Otto?'

He stared at me before replying. 'I don't understand what is going on. I think I am confused,' he said. 'You are Otto because you can't be Hans.'

'What do you mean, I can't be Hans?' I retorted. 'I am Hans. Who else could I be?'

Ernst stared at me for a long time.

'I will tell you why you are Otto,' he said. 'You are Otto because I gave you to Eva to look after. Hans was killed in the war, when his mother put cyanide in his cocoa.'

"I knew the story. I knew that all the Hoffman children should have died and that it was a miracle that I had lived. It was obvious that Ernst hadn't been told that I'd survived. I felt so confused and I couldn't make sense out of what Ernst was saying. Who was Eva? And who was this other child that Ernst said he'd given away?

"I couldn't even begin to understand why my grandfather hadn't told him I was not only alive, but living with him and my grandmother in Berlin so near to Leipzig.

"Slowly, things were becoming clearer. I had worked out that Otto was not only my brother but my twin, but I wanted to hear that from Father's lips. I wanted confirmation of what I was thinking.

"I asked Father how many children he had. He looked surprised but answered readily. 'Dietrich and Giselle and Hans and Otto, the twins.' Mystery solved. I got up to leave and he asked me piteously if I was going to come back.

'No,' I shouted. 'Never again,' and I left the broken hulk of a man that was my…our father. I was in a state of shock.

I couldn't believe that my parents had planned my death and Otto's survival.

"But of course, after that I couldn't keep away. Something drew me to the prison every month because I wanted to find out the whole truth. I needed to find out all about you. It had been a shock to find out that I had a brother and even more of a shock to learn he was still alive. And I needed to know how Father knew about you.

"Hatred of the Jews never left Father. In many ways it was irrational, but I knew that in other ways he was right and I could agree with him. I could see that in his mind, there were real reasons why Hitler should have decided to implement the Final Solution and every time I visited I learned more about his life and his army service.

"I asked him why Otto had been the one whose life he wanted to save and he explained.

'No-one knew that twins had been born, apart from the midwife and we soon sorted that out,' he said grimly. 'By then, we knew that Germany was going to lose the war and we had already decided what we would do. We would all die together.

'But your mother talked and talked to me, trying to persuade me to let one of the babies live. She said that if we let one boy live, he could grow up to carry on where we had left off. She said she knew that this war was lost but Germany would rise again and, in the end, I could see that she was right.

'We planned it very swiftly. Your mother knew that Eva had given birth but she had never told me. She knew what I would do; I would get rid of Eva and the baby. Your mother

258

had obviously been planning something when she realised that Eva's baby was too weak to live.

'Your mother told me we could trick Eva into thinking we were helping her and her child escape. She might think it was strange but we knew she would clutch at straws. She would do anything to save her baby.

'Of course, Eva wouldn't find out until it was too late that the child she had was Otto. We had to hope that Eva would not harm him but that was a chance we would have to take.

'As your mother described what we could do, I listened, reluctantly at first. Then I realised that if we saved one child there could be a future for Hitler's Germany. This child, our son, would grow up to be a follower of Hitler and could carry on his work.'

"It was at that point that I realised that Ernst was truly mad. Whatever the prison said about him having dementia, or confusion, I could see that he was still in the days of the Reich and was completely insane. I listened, though, as he went on with his story."

CHAPTER 32

'I took Eva to the suburbs of Berlin,' he said, 'and left her with money and papers in front of a dilapidated block of flats near the Reichstag. I felt sure that I would be able to find it again if things calmed down. I hoped for a miracle which meant we would all survive. We were prepared to take a chance that Otto would live because he was the stronger boy. That is why we gave him to Eva and not you.

'I could see that Eva was terrified as we drove from the camp. She desperately wanted to see and hold her son but there was no way I could allow her to see the child. If she knew her own baby was dead, I didn't know how she would react.

'I had seen many women, crazed out of their minds, throw themselves on the wire fences to commit suicide when their children had died. Eva might try to kill herself if she found out the truth but, worse than that, she might kill Otto. I couldn't have cared less if she killed herself but not my own precious boy.

'Your mother took charge. She was so organised.' As he spoke about his wife, Ernst's eyes lit up and seemed to become clearer. He smiled at something in the distance and I followed his gaze as he waved. There was no-one there, of course, only the other prisoners and their visitors, and they avoided looking at him. I prompted him to continue and he went on.

'We had cyanide capsules given to us by the Führer so she gave Dietrich and Giselle and you hot chocolate mixed with the poison. I intended to be with her – I needed to be with her but the camp was overrun with Russians and there were bullets flying everywhere.

'I had driven back to the camp, avoiding burning houses, overturned jeeps, and bodies in the road. I didn't stop to see if anyone was alive – I wanted to get back to my family.

'I drove in through the gates which were hanging open. Everywhere was in chaos. There had been a heavy barrage of gunfire and I couldn't cross the parade ground to get to the house. I sat in the car, just watching. Then I saw the Russian soldiers coming down the front stairs, carrying the bodies of my children.

'I knew they were all dead and there was nothing I could do. If the Russians caught me, I knew I would be hanged. My pistol was in my pocket and I took it out and looked at it. For a moment I thought of using it. I considered taking it out of the holster and shooting myself so I could be with my beloved wife and children.

'But I am a soldier and taking my own life in that way would have been the opposite of everything my military training stood for. Reluctantly, I put it back. I say reluctantly, because at that moment, all I wanted was to die.

'There were prisoners everywhere, running and screaming and panicking. I managed to get hold of one and I hit him sharply. He was weak and fell to the ground in front

261

of me. I dragged him behind one of the barracks and I changed clothes with him.

'The smell of his uniform made me retch but I knew I had to overcome that and so I put it on. Then I just sat on the ground until a couple of Russian soldiers came over. I pretended to be weak, and I staggered as I tried to get up.

'We've got a live one here,' they said and picked me up. They helped me onto one of the trucks which was standing at the entrance of the camp. No-one noticed that I wasn't as skeletal as the rest of the men.

'I watched how the other prisoners behaved. They were like zombies so when I was asked my name, like the others, I just shook my head. The soldiers moved among us, giving drinks and bread. I snatched at the crust as if I was starving, like all the other men on the transport.

'They took us to a hospital – I don't know where it was, but it was full of camp survivors. I tell you, there were beds everywhere full of men just lying there and staring blankly into space. Some were even on stretchers on the floor.

'We were given showers and clean clothes. I had to pretend to be afraid of the showers like the others but I copied the behaviour of the inmates. No-one realised that I was different, and I watched and learned. Eventually, I was shown into a ward with clean beds and allowed to sleep.

'The next morning a trolley came round with breakfast. Several of the men didn't get out of bed and an orderly went over to wake them. No need, they had died in the night. Some people died because they ate too much food too soon but there was no fear of that happening to me.

'I called myself Jakob Stein. I had disciplined one of the prisoners a few months before and the man's name was

Jakob Stein. It seemed a good idea to use the name of a man I knew was dead.

'There was no-one to challenge me or argue with me. After all, who would do as I had done; change clothes with a Jew so that they could live.

'Everyone was being interviewed by the Americans. When it was my turn to tell my story, I said that all my family had died and I was alone in the world. Who could disagree with me? Someone found clothes for me, someone else gave me the papers I needed and suddenly, I was free.

'I managed to hitch a lift on a lorry that was going to Berlin. Everyone wanted to help the poor Jews so it wasn't difficult. The city was almost unrecognisable but I knew where I had left Eva and Otto. The roads were covered with debris and it wasn't possible to drive safely, so the lorry driver dropped me some distance away, pushing money into my hands. He was an American relief driver and shocked at what he saw, I guess.

'I walked the last few hundred metres. There were no pavements, no street names but it didn't matter. I knew roughly where to go.

'The block of flats was still standing, just, but there was no sign of Eva and Otto. I went up the stairs and knocked on a few doors until at last one was opened. The old man inside told me that there had been a young woman living in the basement but she had left a while ago.

'He didn't know about any baby, though. He'd never heard a child crying. He suggested I go and enquire at the town hall but I knew I couldn't do that. They might question me more closely than anyone else and I couldn't risk being found out. It seemed possible that Eva had managed to survive but I had to accept that Otto had not.'

"Ernst looked at me, and for a brief moment there was a spark of recognition before his eyes glazed over again. He rubbed his head and his wiry grey hair stood up.

'Hans, I must tell you, after that I went into a deep depression. I had lost everything. My wife, my children and my Führer. There was no way I could move from Germany to another country like the others who had been in charge of camps. I knew there was an escape route for people like me to get to Argentina but I couldn't do it. Here, I had the chance of survival. The damaged city of Berlin would be my refuge, at least for a while.

'There were always jobs for men prepared to do the hard manual work required on reconstruction sites. I spent the next few years moving from city to city, job to job, always worried in case someone would identify me as Ernst Hoffman when the name on my papers was Jakob Stein. I knew that when people got too friendly with me that it was time to move on.'

Hans looked directly at Sam and Helen.

"As I listened to him, I got a mental picture of a lonely man, frightened to make relationships, frightened to make contact with people, frightened of his own shadow. Quite different from the militaristic soldier in the Führer's army. And the coincidences in our lives were astonishing. We could have by-passed each other on any one of the building sites; we could even have worked together.

"I had thought my life was hard but what my father was describing was infinitely worse. He had gone from being a respected soldier of the Reich to a down and out vagrant. He was a man wanted for war crimes and he knew it. He knew that the years ahead would mean he would have to hide in order to stay alive.

'Why didn't you try and find your parents?' I asked him.

'How could I?' he replied. 'I knew my name would be on a wanted list. Even though I knew that the way I had organised the camp was the correct way, I knew that others might not agree.

'I knew about the Nurenberg trials, of course. Soon after the end of the war, many of our leaders were convicted of war crimes. They were either hanged or imprisoned for life. Some of the men on trial were my friends, and I watched in the shadows as they were all convicted and given life imprisonment or even the death penalty.

'I felt anything was better than that. A soldier should not die by the rope but they were denied a firing squad. I could not contemplate that for myself and yet here, now, I find myself in prison.

'So, no, I didn't make contact with my parents. So many missed opportunities,' he finished sadly. 'I could have found Otto if I had gone to Berlin sooner. I could have found you, also, my son, if I had tried to find my parents.' Tears leaked from his eyes but he ignored them. 'It never occurred to me that you might have survived. Don't forget, I had seen the bodies of my children carried out of the house.'

'But you obviously knew about Otto at some point,' I told him. 'How did you find out?' And then the bell rang for the end of visiting time and I knew I would have to wait another month to find out why.

"Those visits became the focus of my life. It was like living in some kind of serial… Do you know what I mean by a serial?" Sam and Helen nodded. Hans went on,

"You know, something which happens regularly but the end of each episode leaves you in limbo. Every time I saw father, he told me something else but still he didn't tell me how he knew about you and how he ended up in prison.

"He told me about his early life, about how he grew up with his parents. He was born before the first world war and so, for a long time, he didn't see his father. When his father came home, decorated with the Iron Cross, our father was old enough to admire him.

"He wanted to be a soldier too. Listening to all these stories was frustrating for me but I knew this was the only way I would learn the real truth about what happened to us." He looked over at Sam. "Yes, us," he repeated. "I needed to know everything about *us*." He stood up and Helen looked alarmed, but Hans was only stretching his legs. He sat down again and carried on speaking.

"I knew that my father was the only person who could tell me the whole story. There were times when I tried to push him into telling me more but he wouldn't answer my questions. He would go off at a tangent talking about all sorts of other things but not the things I wanted to hear.

"Listening to him talking about his life in the army, I began to understand what had motivated him to join the military. He wanted to be better than his own father. I think he always had that competitive spirit and his background was so regimented that it was all he knew. When Hitler came on the scene he transferred his allegiance from Grandfather to him.

"He went to all the rallies, he signed up for everything which might help him get closer to his idol. And it happened. Hitler became aware of him and wanted him near.

"From that day on, he followed his master. Whatever Hitler said or planned to do, Hoffman agreed. He came up with ideas that Hitler approved of and adopted as his own. It became obvious to me that if Hitler told father to cut his arms off, he would do it.

"He liked to talk and he liked to boast about how he had got rid of the Jewish vermin. He made it seem so rational but I was beginning to see it was the ravings of a madman."

"How long did you visit him for?" asked Sam.

"Oh, a while, until the prison wrote to me to tell me he'd died."

CHAPTER 33

Hesitantly, Helen interrupted. "And Eva said he knew about Sam," she asked tremulously. "What did Hoffman tell you about that?"

"Let me tell you, then," said Hans and the anger was apparent in his voice. "When I was a teenager, I was already working on the building sites. You have seen my hands," he said stretching them out. "You can see that I have had to work hard. So, what was Sam, the Golden Boy doing?

"He was passing exams and getting his picture in the papers. This was a big story in Germany and there were pictures of this concentration camp survivor in all the papers. A miracle baby, they called you. There was a picture of you with Eva, and my father recognised her. Of course, she must have looked older but he knew it was her.

"He told me it was as if the light had gone on. He could see that if he blackmailed Eva he would have an income for life. At that time, I think he was struggling to find work. He wasn't getting any younger and he told me that he wanted to enjoy the sort of life that Eva was obviously having.

"It wasn't possible for him to go to England, otherwise he would have confronted her in person. The Berlin Wall had been put up in the sixties and there was no way he could get a visa to travel. I think he tried a few times but he was rejected.

"He decided the only thing he could do was to telephone. It was easy to find out the information he needed although more difficult to actually place the call. The operator was very curious as to why he wanted to speak to someone in England but he managed to distract her.

"He told me he got a great sense of satisfaction when he spoke to Eva. She knew immediately who he was and, in the background, he could hear voices. He thought one of them was Otto.

"At first, Eva was unable to speak. She told him she couldn't send any money, but when he threatened to go to the press with the story, she soon changed her mind."

Hans looked at Helen and Sam. "Your mother," he said contemptuously, "didn't want her perfect life exposed as a sham. For a while everything worked well. There was a regular money transfer each month and my father's circumstances improved dramatically.

"He moved to a better flat and began to enjoy himself. He went to concerts and made a few friends and I think for the first time for a long time he relaxed. And then there was another newspaper article about you. Funny, isn't it how a few words in a paper can alter the course of your life.

"He was getting greedy now. He wanted more money to keep quiet – the arrangement had worked well so far, so he contacted Eva again. And Eva agreed to pay more. She argued with him but he was adamant.

'If you don't help me, you know what I can do,' he reminded her.

269

"And then, a few months later there was a knock at the door. When he opened it, he saw two well built men standing outside in the corridor.

'Are you Ernst Hoffman?' the taller one enquired. 'No,' he stammered. 'My name is Jakob Stein.'

'May we come in?' they asked. Apparently they were very polite so reluctantly, he opened the door wider and they went through.

'Nice place you've got here,' they said. And the minute they said that he knew it was all over. It was obvious that the salary of a working man could not have given him all the little luxuries he had in his flat. They even accused him of having hidden Nazi gold. That would account for the comfort in which he was living but he couldn't explain it.

"He'd had a good run for his money but his time was up. He tried to bluster his way out of it. Time and time again he said his name was Jakob Stein. He was unmarried, he'd been in a concentration camp during the war and his papers had been lost.

"They didn't believe him.

'Pack a bag,' they told him. 'We'll continue this at the police station.' They gave him time to put a change of clothes into a small suitcase and then told him to get his passport and papers. He told them he didn't have a passport. He was a humble bricklayer. What use would he have for a passport? Anyway, there was nowhere to go.

'We won't worry about a passport, then. Just bring your identity card and any other papers you have which can prove who you are.'

"The cell at the police station had only a bed and a bucket. There was no privacy but it gave him time to think when they locked him in.

"He had been living as Jakob for a long time, enough for his false identity to become almost real to him. He sat on the edge of the bed trying to find a way of convincing them he was who he said he was.

"Eventually, they took him to the interview room. They asked him if he would like a hot drink and when he said 'yes', an officer brought in a thick mug of strong tea. He told me he was expecting to be tortured, interrogated, shouted at but this didn't happen. The two men just looked at him and stayed silent.

"Eventually he shouted at them,

'Why have you brought me here?'

'You know why,' he was told. 'We know you are Ernst Hoffman and you are wanted for crimes against humanity, murder and torture, and false imprisonment.'

"He tried hard to talk his way out of it, saying over and over again that he was Jakob Stein, a concentration camp survivor. He was exhausted when they took him back to the cell but secretly jubilant that he hadn't cracked and told them anything.

"I think he thought they were very weak because there had been no attempt at physical persuasion. He was contemptuous of their interrogation technique, I know. He told me that he would have made a prisoner tell everything. He said that inflicting pain always brought results and when he looked at me I could see the light of madness in his eyes.

"He spent the night lying on the hard bed, waiting for morning when he was sure he would be released. The only person who knew he was alive was Eva, and he knew that she wouldn't tell anyone if she wanted to keep her secret safe. He also knew he couldn't say how he was able to afford his flat and all the things in it. Any attempt to involve Eva would mean a definite confirmation that he was indeed Ernst Hoffman.

"He knew that Eva wouldn't want anyone to know of the link between her and the sadistic commandant everyone thought he was. And, of course, she lived in the West. There was no way she could travel to Berlin and identify him so he felt relatively safe.

"In the morning he was shocked to learn that he was to take part in an identification parade. He told me, at that point he *did* expect to be confronted by Eva and probably an Eva who wanted vengeance. He felt she was the only one who would recognise him so perhaps the authorities had arranged a visa for her to come to Berlin to identify him.

"He was lined up with half a dozen men, all of whom looked like him. He was still tall and the hard work had developed his muscles but he had tried to change his appearance a little. He'd shaved off his moustache and the lean face he presented to the world now was different to the smart soldier he had been. And, too, he was older.

"When the policeman brought in a woman, he could see she was trembling but she had no hesitation in saying in a loud voice,

'That's him. That's the Commandant.' But it was not Eva staring at him.

"And then the policeman brought in another woman who identified him and again, it was not Eva. There was a steady stream of people, who all spoke against him. He told me he

272

was amazed that so many people had survived the camp. And all of them looked him in the eye.

"Finally, an old man came up to him while he was standing in line, looked at him directly and spat in his face.

'I don't know where you've been hiding all these years,' he said, 'but you can hide no more. There are plenty of people who can identify you and hundreds who will testify what a brutal sadistic camp commandant you were.'

"At that moment," Hans said thoughtfully, "I think Father realised that all was lost. The officers in charge exchanged a smile and led him back to the cell."

'There is no doubt in my mind that you are Ernst Hoffman, Camp Commandant,' said the interrogating officer, 'but the jury will make their own decision,' he was told. 'You will be transferred to a proper prison now and brought back here to appear in court tomorrow.' At that point, Father felt he was facing the death penalty. He had been identified by too many people.

"He told me that, as well as his fears about this, there was also his worry that any of his fellow soldiers still living would condemn him for cowardice. He had escaped by assuming the identify of another – a Jew, to boot, and he would be vilified for this.

"There was plenty of time for him to think over a defence. First of all, the case against him would depend on the credibility of the witnesses. Would the judge believe them, or would he dismiss their preposterous allegations out of hand?

"Ernst knew he would have to admit to being the Camp Commandant. There would be no doubt about that. There would obviously be plenty of witnesses. His defence would

273

have to rest on whether he could prove that he was a fair and just officer.

"He thought back to his time overseeing the prisoners. How could anyone prove he had been harsh, when he had only been following orders from higher up, orders which in his opinion were the right way to treat the 'vermin'?

"Nothing, he decided, could change that. It had been the opinion of Adolf Hitler, and Hitler had been the leader of Germany. The only way to reduce the influence of Jews in Germany and the world was to eliminate them, and by following Hitler's ideology, he had only been doing his job.

"Satisfied that his defence was not only adequate but superb, he was able to enjoy the meal brought to him by a guard and settled down to sleep. He felt he had got things straight in his own mind. He was ready to face his accusers."

CHAPTER 34

"An official car, a black limousine, took him to the courthouse the next morning, where he was charged and then remanded in custody. He said this was a shock for him because he had expected to be released and he jumped from his chair shouting,

'Why are you sending me back to prison? I am innocent of the charges against me. I was fulfilling the wishes of my Führer and helping to rid the world of undesirables.'

"He told me that there was a silence in the courtroom before the judge banged his gavel on the desk.

'Take him down, now,' the judge said. 'Take him out of my sight.'

'Of course, he was a Jew,' my father told me. 'What could I expect?'

"They transferred him straight away to the prison in Leipzig, no doubt because they knew he would be found guilty and would be incarcerated there for the rest of his life. This was always supposing he wasn't given the death penalty. I have no doubt this was on the cards for him.

"The trial date was set for early July, three months away, giving the prosecution and the defence time to prepare their case. Once the story of his arrest had been in the papers, people from all over Germany came out of the woodwork ready to testify.

"Every time a new name was listed, the defence attorney asked Ernst if he knew who it was. He always said 'No'. This was true, of course, because he never knew the names of any of the prisoners, apart from Eva that is. Once in the camp, names were taken away and numbers given and there was no way he could match numbers to faces.

"His solicitor went over and over the depositions made by witnesses. There seemed to be a common denominator in them all – the unnecessary cruelty of the sadistic Commander.

"They described how prisoners were placed in solitary confinement, how they were starved and beaten, how families were separated and so on. All of these accusations would be explored during the trial but in the meantime, the defence lawyer asked Hoffman if any of them were true.

'True?' he asked. 'How could they be true? They were prisoners being punished.'

"The defence lawyer asked about the children. 'Why were they punished? Why did they have to die?' he wanted to know. It was obvious he wasn't sympathetic to Ernst.

"Father told him that children don't always behave themselves and, in that case, they should also be punished. He looked at me when he said this and it made me think back to my own childhood and how Grandfather had been quick to beat me if I did anything which displeased him.

"The defence lawyer had been appointed by the court because no-one wished to take on such a case voluntarily. He was fairly young and inexperienced, which was not in

276

Hoffman's favour but he had the advantage of working in a large chambers, where there were several more experienced solicitors. None of them wished to defend Hoffman but they were there for advice should the case get too difficult.

"Hoffman was summoned to the governor's office on the day of the trial.

'Your lawyer has sent you a suit so that you don't have to appear in court in prison clothes. He seems to think it might help your defence.' He passed over a brown paper parcel and when Hoffman opened it he found trousers and a jacket, a white shirt and a dark tie.

'Take him to the men's bathroom to change,' the governor said to Father's guard, 'but make sure you keep the handcuffs on him.'

'That's going to be a major problem,' grumbled the guard. 'Don't know how you'll get a suit on if I can't uncuff you.'

"Father described the procedure in great detail. In fact, it took up almost the whole of a visiting time. He thought it was amusing. I was impatient for him to complete his story; it had crossed my mind that he might not live to finish it but nothing I said made him deviate from his own words. He said he hadn't made it easy for the guards and he laughed out loud at that.

"In the toilets, Father pulled off his trousers and replaced them with the new ones. The guard cuffed him to a radiator, while he slid an arm out of one sleeve. When he'd finished, the handcuff was attached to the other side of the radiator and he did the same thing with the other sleeve. That way he was able to put on the shirt and jacket. The guard himself had to knot Father's tie, which he did with a great show of reluctance.

"Father told me that he complained to the guard, telling him that he was innocent until proved guilty.

'But we all know you're guilty, mate,' the officer replied. 'So that doesn't apply to you. You're guilty until you're proved guilty,' and he roared with laughter at his own joke. 'Changing your clothes and putting on a smart suit won't make you a gentleman. You'll always be a thug.'

"I suspect by this time that Father was having serious mental problems. He could not understand why others were unable to see what he was doing was right."

"And you," Sam interrupted. "What do you think?"

"Oh, of course I agreed with him that Jews needed to be eliminated but I am thinking now that maybe, just maybe there were other better ways of doing it. Now, I am so confused." He rubbed his head.

"I see," said Sam thoughtfully. "And do many people in Germany still share your views?"

"Yes, of course," said Hans proudly. "Just because the war is over doesn't mean the problem has gone away. I expect there are some good Jews," he added grudgingly, "but not many. And we need to rid the world of the rest."

Helen stood up carefully and brushed her skirt with her hands. She was trembling and white as a sheet.

"I need to go into the kitchen," she said. "I'll be back in a moment."

Hans looked at her as she left the room.

"What is the matter with her?" he asked Sam, who looked at him searchingly for a few moments, and then said,

"How can you ask such a question? Surely you must know that the systematic destruction of six million Jews and six million others who were incarcerated in concentration camps is wrong. Helen's parents are Holocaust survivors, as were my parents. What you have said has resonance with her. However, she will be back. I know she wants to hear everything. We will wait a few moments for her."

There was a murmur of voices from the hall.

"Ah," said Sam. "Daniel and Esther are back, with my mother."

He called to them.

"Come in for a moment. We are not yet finished but soon, I think."

Daniel pushed a paper bag over to him.

"Esther thought you might want a sandwich. Granny has already gone upstairs. We'll leave you to it, as long as you will tell us everything later."

"I will, I promise," said Sam. "We're just waiting for your mother to come back in before Hans carries on with the story."

"More tea," Helen said brightly as she put the tray down. She was smiling bravely but Sam could see she had been crying and he took her hand. Together they waited for Hans to speak again.

"My father said the court case was a sham. Even his lawyer told him to be prepared for a guilty verdict because it was a foregone conclusion that he would be convicted. Father he did not believe it.

"He told me he went along with what he called 'The Farce' but he fully expected to be declared innocent. He had eventually admitted that he was Ernst Hoffman, the

279

commandant of a camp where he was carrying out the orders of the Führer. He could see no reason why he should have been declared guilty. Time and time again, he said he was a soldier doing his duty in a time of war.

"His answers to the questions posed by the prosecution were always the same. His name, his title and his fervent statement that his methods were not sadistic; they were the only way that this epidemic of vermin could be treated.

"He said that sometimes after he said this, there would be gasps from the spectators and the judge would admonish them. He was very pleased, he said, when that happened because he felt those people were on his side.

"I don't expect you to agree with that, Sam. I think you will say that the people were horrified and disgusted, but how can we know because we were not there," Hans suggested.

"There had been many appearances from camp inmates, none of whom father recognised, all of whom recognised him. Each recounted some atrocity or other which they said father had committed or, if not him, a soldier under his command. Each of them said the name of the man in the dock was Ernst Hoffman.

"The judge spoke directly to the jury before they retired to consider their verdict. 'Under no circumstances are you to be ruled by emotion,' he said. 'This trial has had a great deal of publicity and you have heard some horrific stories. It is not your place to condemn or judge the prisoner. Your job is to decide whether or not the case against him is proven. If you feel, without a shadow of doubt, that in the first instance the man in front of you is Jakob Stein, labourer, and not Ernst Hoffman, Camp Commandant, it would mean that he has not committed any crimes at all. He would be allowed to leave this court room as a free man. I think that it is unlikely you will be able to do this as the prisoner has already admitted that he is not Jakob Stein but I need you to agree this and to tell the court.

'On the other hand, if the evidence you have heard means you are convinced that the man in the dock *is* Ernst Hoffman, you then have to consider each indictment on its merit. You must ask yourselves if the evidence which you have heard proves that treatment handed out to the prisoners was contrary to any human rights to which they were entitled. You must also ask yourselves if the imprisonment of any of the prisoners in the concentration camp was lawful. Finally, there are several indictments from individual witnesses, reflecting their own ill treatment. You must consider each of these separately and then make your decision known to the court.'

"He asked if they had appointed a foreman, and a woman in her thirties nodded.

'In which case, court is adjourned.'

"You may feel, Sam, that this was a very quick hearing but in fact it went on for some days. Father was not in the least worried by this time. He was in his own fantasy world where his actions were justified. He was quite sure that the jury would find him 'not guilty'.

"His lawyer told him before he was taken back to the cell that if the jury came back quickly, it would more than likely mean a guilty verdict. If they were in any doubt about it, they would be arguing and that would take longer.

"Father said he just smiled and said,

'Oh no. I don't agree with you. They will come back very quickly because they know I am *not* guilty. They won't have to argue; they will already have made their decision.'

"He was very confident, he said, that justice would prevail. He looked at me and smiled. His eyes glittered in a strange way and I felt very uncomfortable. The man in front of me was my father and I had been prepared to believe him and agree with him. I had been prepared to honour him and look up to him but things had changed.

"There was a shift in my feelings and I felt it was very difficult to come to terms with this.

"And, to be sure, there were some things I did agree with. However, I now found myself in a dilemma. I was learning that not everything Ernst had done was acceptable – not just by the survivors of the camp…but by me."

CHAPTER 35

"Of course, the defence lawyer was right. The jury did return very quickly and sat in the jury box looking very solemn.

"The judge asked them if they were all agreed and the foreman stood and said,

'Yes,' in a very firm voice.

'How do you find the prisoner?'

'Guilty on all charges,' replied the woman, 'with a recommendation for the death penalty.'

"The judge looked at her over the top of his rimless glasses.

'It is not for you to decide what punishment the prisoner should receive,' he said, 'but I will keep in mind what the jury feels would be a just sentence. Court will adjourn and reconvene for sentencing in one week.'

"Apparently, the court room exploded with cheers and shouts of jubilation. I have seen the drawings done by the court artist and they show Father looking absolutely stunned. A few black lines captured his features perfectly.

"There was a look of incredulity on his face, as if he could not believe what had happened. He told me that he was expecting to be acquitted and he could not understand why the jury had found him guilty. Even now, after all these years he does not understand. As far as he was concerned he was doing his duty. More than that, he was convinced he was right.

"The press was waiting outside and managed to get some pictures of him. They published them in the early editions, along with a biography of him and the verdict. They gave him a nickname and it was emblazoned on the front pages.

"They called him 'Hoffman the Hunter' because of the way he had hunted down the people in the camp. It was ironic, really, because he had been caught by some of the best Nazi hunters in the world.

"He had to wait a week in prison but I don't think he was worried about what might happen to him. Even though he always said over and over again that he was innocent of the charges, underneath it all I think he was prepared for a guilty verdict. When he was telling me this, he still looked confused.

'I don't know why they found me guilty,' he said over and over again. 'I was just following orders. I was behaving as a good soldier would in times of war.' He told me he was prepared for the death sentence, although he would ask for a firing squad, rather than the hangman's noose.

"When he was called in front of the judge for sentencing, he said he was surprised that the court room was empty. The publicity surrounding the case had made the judge decide to sentence Hoffman in camera.

"Father said that he was brought up the steps from the cell below and into the bright lights of the court room. He was blinking like an owl because the light downstairs was so much dimmer than the ones above.

"He waited for the judge to speak and it seemed to take an age as first, papers were shuffled, then glasses adjusted and then the judge took a long drink of water.

"Finally he looked directly at Father, and he began to speak.

'The verdict given by the jury last week found you guilty on all charges. It is my duty now to give you a fair sentence, in accordance with the laws of Germany. I have read all the papers pertaining to your case, including reports from the psychiatrist and medical officer.

'This is a difficult decision to make, Herr Hoffman, because it is obvious now that your faculties are somewhat diminished. However, when you were committing these acts of atrocity, it seems clear that you were in full possession of your mind. You had made a conscious decision to follow the commands of a leader who was determined to eliminate a group of people who had never broken the law. You did not have to do this. You could have refused.

'In this court we are, sadly, unable to refer to the Geneva Convention when trying and sentencing defendants. However, we are bound by another set of rules which covers those crimes committed during times of war; crimes which are unacceptable to us all. As such, we have been able to sentence you as a war criminal.

'We have taken into account your mental instability and as such, feel that the death penalty is inappropriate. Your physical health appears to be as good as any other man of your age, and it is the feeling of this court that your expectation of life has not been affected. You are, therefore, sentenced to life imprisonment, which in this case means you will stay in prison for the full length of your natural life.'

"He banged his gavel on the desk, and instructed the gaoler to take Father away.

"Father's memories of this are a little hazy. He seems to think that he was pushed roughly down the stairs and out the back door of the courthouse into a waiting van.

"The press had published the sentencing date so there was a large crowd of people outside. The police had cordoned off the steps, which seemed to indicate he would be brought out the front but that was all part of an elaborate plan to keep him away from the media, as well as those prisoners he had harmed in the camp. They were cheated out of a final opportunity to hurl abuse at him. He left through the back door, without any chance of anyone seeing him.

"He was taken back to Leipzig prison straight away but this time his entry was completely different. This time he was a convicted prisoner, not someone on remand. The same guards were there who had processed him when he had been first arrested. They treated him with contempt, searching him roughly, pushing him into the shower and throwing his prison uniform at him.

"He was still bewildered. He couldn't believe that he was back in the prison and he started to continually ask when he could go home.

"Initially, he was placed into the hospital wing so that the prison doctor could observe him. They were not sure if he was acting out a mental illness or if he had sunk abruptly into a state of dementia. The head doctor eventually came to the conclusion that he was, indeed, in a state of melancholia and was possibly in the early stages of a dementia which would get progressively worse.

"After a week he was moved to a cell in the main prison. Despite the usual overcrowding in prisons, the governor decided that he would be better off on his own. There had, in the past, been attacks on war criminals by other prisoners and he wished to avoid any further publicity.

"Every few months he was moved to another cell, in accordance with the policy of the prison. It wanted to avoid prisoners making relationships with other prisoners. He recalled quite clearly that he wasn't given any notice of a move.

"A guard would come in, tip his mattress on to the floor, pull his few belongings off the shelves and tell him he would be punished for not keeping his cell tidy.

Sam interrupted mildly.

"I can sense that you feel sorry for your father but he was sentenced as a war criminal for serious crimes against humanity."

Hans replied angrily, "He was obeying orders."

"You may think that," Helen added, "but he had a choice. What he was doing was wrong, so wrong, and he could have refused his orders. He could have run the camp on fair and kind lines. It seemed he did nothing of the sort. He made it a policy to treat Jews as badly as possible.

"Did he not understand that the people in his camp were not animals to be brutalised and killed when their usefulness was over?" She paused for breath. "My parents were also in a camp. They went through unspeakable torments and, like Eva, they have never spoken of it.

"I don't know the details, any more than Sam did. In a way, you have done us a favour because your visit has meant that Eva has told us about her experiences."

She turned to see Eva standing in the doorway. "Your father was an animal," she said quietly to Hans. "He took delight in inflicting pain on the inmates. He took delight in watching *us* turn into animals." She glanced at Sam and Helen.

"Oh yes, it happened," she said. "People fought for a crust of bread. Some even killed. And when that happened and they were found out, of course, Hoffman took delight in hanging them in front of everyone as a reminder that he had infinite control over the whole camp."

Hans reddened but stayed silent. Faced with Eva's controlled anger, he could say nothing. She came further into the room, and Sam put his arm around her and helped her to sit.

"I can see you feel confused about your father's actions," she said to Hans. "Do you not have any compassion for those he murdered?" Again, Hans flushed.

"He didn't murder anyone," he asserted. "How can you say that an officer doing his duty was a murderer?"

"There is a difference between punishing a crime and the indiscriminate murder of innocent people. People who, through no fault of their own, were rounded up and systematically destroyed."

Hans dropped his head, trying to assimilate what Eva had said. A plethora of emotions crossed his face.

"Even so," Eva said in a whisper, "there's no point in continuing this conversation. I think we've heard all we need."

"Not quite, Ma," Sam said. He risked a look at his mother. "Did you hear Hans say that Ernst died while still in prison in Leipzig?" he asked.

Eva's voice shook as she said, "No, I didn't hear that. In that case, let us listen to the rest. I will stay because I think I am part of this. And I want an end to it. I want to draw a line under all this, all this…this…anger and bitterness."

She waved her hand at Hans and said imperiously,

"Carry on with your story. I am interested to hear how your grandfather got in touch with the Commandant."

Hans coughed and cleared his throat.

"The power of the press," he responded. "When Father was first arrested, the press had a field day. Here was another so called war criminal and they wanted to get the message out that, even after all these years, war criminals would still be arrested and held responsible for their actions.

"Father had been in prison for a few months before the governor called him into the office and told him that he was eligible to have a visitor. He had received a letter from someone who said he was Ernst Hoffman's father and who wished to see him.

"In the beginning, Father refused. He didn't want to see his father. He didn't want to relive again what had happened to his children but, eventually, he agreed.

"He described that first meeting as the worst in his life. Grandfather just looked at him. He couldn't understand how the man in front of him, the son who, when young, had such a promising career as a professional soldier, was now in prison, labelled forever as a sadistic killer. Like me, he believed that some of Ernst's actions could be justified but, like me also, he could see that most were not.

289

"And yet, every month until just before he died, Grandfather travelled from Berlin to visit Ernst in prison. He tried to find out what had made Ernst take the path he had but he couldn't get anywhere with those conversations. In return I think he was selective about what he told Ernst.

"For example, he never told him that I was alive. I think it would have meant the world to my father and I suspect that is why Grandfather never spoke about me. It was his way of punishing his son. The son who was such a disappointment to him.

"Ernst was, a lot of the time, still re-living the war years. His dementia had got worse. Loud noises bothered him to such an extent that he would cower if he heard a door bang, or hear shouting along the corridor. He thought the noises were gun shots or bombs falling.

"Sometimes he would speak maniacally, other times he would be withdrawn and silent. I saw this for myself when I visited him and I have no doubt that he had been like that ever since he went to prison.

"I don't know if Grandfather ever knew about you. I don't know whether Father ever told him. There were no more letters between them. That had all stopped when Father first went into prison so there was no way I could find out any more.

"And the death of both of my grandparents meant I only had the word of a deluded man to believe, but there seemed to be some truth in what he said.

"The Berlin Wall was the thing that prevented me discovering anything else. There was no way I could leave East Germany, I knew. In my mind, I wanted to go to the West and travel to London to see if I could find you. The only way that might happen would be if the Wall came down.

"I needed more information so I decided that the best way forward was to get Father's confidence. I would continue to visit regularly and find out what I could about my twin."

CHAPTER 36

"Sometimes after Ernst got started, his words were like a waterfall racing down the hillside. He told me all about your education, how you'd been to university and how you had married someone equally as talented. He knew Helen was a teacher. He even knew about your children.

"On the one hand, I could sense the perverse pride he felt about you, even though you had been brought up as a Jew and had qualified as a rabbi. On the other hand, I could sense his hatred of all things Jewish. When he spoke with pride about you I felt less than a man.

"You were the twin who had been educated, I was the twin who worked as a labourer. Did I feel jealous? I suppose I did. You had the opportunities which had not been available to me, just because of a split second all those years ago, when you were left with Eva and I was left to die.

"Sometimes, he would rant and rave about you. How you had denied your birth and how he wanted to kill you and all your Jewish relatives, especially your two Jewish children. He would describe what he would do to you, and my blood ran cold as I listened. The light of madness was in his eyes and there were times, many times, when I was so glad he was handcuffed to the table. I never interrupted; never told him that you didn't know you were his son. What was the point? I couldn't compete with his insanity.

"All the time this was going on, Berlin was getting nearer to reducing the Wall to rubble. I saw it as a race. If I could get all the information I needed, I would be able to go to England.

"When I asked Father what your name was, he became very suspicious of my reasons for asking. I told him I was just curious and wondering if it was a Jewish name.

"That set him off again, until eventually he spat out, 'Goldman. That's his name. Sam Goldman but to me he will always be Otto, the traitor.'

"I was jubilant because now I was on the first steps to locating you. I felt as if I'd struck gold. I was confident that I would get the rest of the information I needed if I was patient. I listened to the clack of the wheels, saying 'You've got it now, you've got it now', as the train took me back to Berlin. I was so pleased I could see the light at the end of the tunnel.

"Two weeks later I came home from work cold and tired. I checked the mailbox in the entrance hall as usual, and took a handful of letters to the flat. There were a few brown envelopes; a bank statement showing how little money I had in my account, a reminder from the Gas Board that my payment was overdue and a white envelope addressed in black ink.

"The words on the page jumped out at me. The prison was sorry to inform me that my father, Prisoner Hoffman, had died. It was thought he had suffered a heart attack and there would have to be a post mortem.

"I was welcome to attend the funeral, which would happen later that week. He would be buried in the small cemetery in the prison grounds. Afterwards, the governor would like to see me in his office."

Sam put his hand out to touch Hans's shoulder but it was shrugged off. "I don't think you can feel sorry that father died," Hans said. "How could you?" he added harshly. "You never knew him."

"You're right. I didn't know him but I can feel compassion for your loss."

"You're assuming now that I was sorry my father had died? Was I upset? No, I was angry, so angry. He had cheated me out of finding out any more about my twin. Death had taken that opportunity from me.

"I decided I wouldn't go to the funeral. There was no point. Ernst Hoffman was my birth father but there was no real connection between us. It would be a mockery for me to become the grieving son.

"And yet, as the day of the funeral drew near, I realised that I needed to go. It was time to let go of the past and move into the future. I needed to see him buried so there would be a proper ending.

"It was the first time I had ever been to the prison on a weekday. The funeral was early in the morning and the trains were crowded. I felt out of place in my dark suit; I felt as if people were looking at me, trying by smiles to show sympathy to a mourner. It felt wrong and I wanted to shout out loud, to tell the passengers that I was only going to my father's funeral so I could leave all thoughts of him behind.

"I stood, swaying as the train went over the points and willing it to get to Leipzig as quickly as possible.

"There was a line of taxis outside the station and so I didn't have to wait. Outside the prison there was a guard on duty and I had to give my name and reason for being there.

"There was no sympathy from the man who opened a side gate and let me through, and the only difference from my previous visits was that I didn't have to go into the main block. I was directed round the back of the building to a small green area. It was bleak, only basic crosses with names on at each grave and no flowers at all.

"There was a small group waiting; the governor, a priest, the doctor and one guard. The service was brief – no hymns, no singing, just a straightforward committal, not even a few words said about Ernst Hoffman. It was as if he had never lived, never had a life.

"For a moment the proceedings left me moved. It crossed my mind I should say something but the moment was lost as the grave diggers started to do their work. I will always remember the smell of the damp earth and the sound of the sods hitting the coffin as shovelsful dropped onto the plain wood.

"The governor came over to speak to me.

'I have your father's personal effects in the office. There's not much; the clothes he was wearing when he was sentenced, some personal papers, his wristwatch and so on. I would be grateful if you would come with me now and I can hand them over. It's up to you to do as you want with them.'

"By now the sun was high in the sky. There was the promise of heat in the air and I could hear birdsong in the distance. We walked silently back to the main building and through the corridors to the governor's office.

"He opened a cupboard door and took out a couple of glasses and a bottle of schnapps.

'I always find these affairs melancholy,' he said. 'Will you join me in a drink?'

"I nodded, glad of the offer. The spirit coursed its way down into my stomach and warmed me. I waited until the governor unlocked a drawer in his desk and took out a large brown envelope.

'These are Hoffman's effects and the parcel over there,' he pointed to a chair in front of the window, 'contains his clothing. The envelope has been sealed since he came here,' and he showed me where the sealing wax covered the flap of the envelope.

'Your father's signature across the wax shows that the envelope has not been opened and that nothing has been removed.' He gave me another envelope. 'This contains the death certificate, which you might need.' He slid a book across the desk and asked me to sign to say I had received everything. And then it was over. No more Saturday trains, no more prison visits, no more father.

"Back in the flat, I opened a bottle of beer and sat down to look at the contents of the envelope. As the governor had said, there was a watch, my only inheritance from a father who had tried to deny me life.

"And then the tears started. Grief for what might have been, for all the lost years and for the knowledge that nothing could bring them back."

Helen tried and failed to suppress a tear, which rolled down her cheek, and Hans glanced across at her.

"What would you know?" he said roughly. "Your parents are both alive and, presumably, took care of you and loved you all your life. Not so, me. Anyway, I've nearly told you everything. Not much more, now."

"I'm crying because your life was so sad," Helen said, wiping her eyes. Hans looked away, ignoring her, before he started again.

"I tipped everything else out of the envelope onto the table. There was a bank book and a couple of newspaper clippings, a wallet with some Deutsch marks in, and a photograph of a woman dressed in a pretty frock; my mother. Not a lot to show for a life, I thought. I opened another bottle of beer.

"I don't drink a great deal normally but I decided that this was one of the nights I was going to get drunk. Strangely, the more beer I swallowed, the less drunk I became.

"I was stone cold sober when I opened the bank book. I wasn't expecting to see that there was very much money deposited so when I saw the amount I was astonished. I looked closely at the entries.

"There had been a regular amount deposited every month for years. It had stopped some time after Father was sentenced to life imprisonment but the interest had accumulated. It was a tidy sum. I would have to go to the bank and find out more.

"The newspaper clippings were pictures of you, Otto. Your graduation and your wedding. You looked fine. Happy and relaxed and I was so jealous. I wanted what you had enjoyed all those years and I determined that somehow I would find you and spoil what you had now.

"I had that power. I still do." He looked sideways at Sam and Helen, gauging their reactions. Their faces didn't show any emotion, as he continued with the story.

297

"I opened the parcel and shook out the clothes. The suit Father had worn in court, and the shirt and tie. I went through the pockets but they were all empty, until I came to the last one, the small concealed pocket on the inside of the trouser waistband.

"I found his ring, the one all SS officers wore. The Totenkopf. That and the watch were my only inheritance and if I had just given the clothes away I would have missed it. I gathered all the papers together and put them back in the envelope, ready for my visit to the bank in the morning.

"The bank manager was kind and courteous. He listened to what I had to say, and then put his fingers together as he considered his reply.

"I have the death certificate," I told him, pushing it across the desk, and he picked it up and read it.

'These are strange circumstances and, normally, I would have to take this to a higher official but, because the person who held the account was in prison at the time of death and because you are so obviously his son, I will do whatever I can to help.'

"I breathed a sigh of relief.

'All I need is the name of the bank in England which was paying money into my father's account each month, and the name of the person whose account it was coming from.'

"I held my breath as he crossed to a large filing cabinet in the corner of the room."

CHAPTER 37

'That's easily done,' he said as he pulled open a drawer. He rifled through the files, until he found what he was looking for.

'Here it is,' he said, passing a sheet of paper to me, after first crossing a line of type through in thick black ink. He glanced up, 'I am unable to give you the address of the payee. That would be contrary to client confidentiality but you will be able to trace the person through their bank.'

"The letter heading was the name of a bank, and the name of the payee was listed as Eva Goldman.

'If you fill this form in,' he added passing over a pen, 'I'll make sure that the funds remaining are transferred to your account.' I couldn't believe it had been so easy to get the information I wanted. I couldn't believe I was the beneficiary of the money in my father's account. And then I was out in the street, elated that I would be able to contact Eva.

"I knew I would have to be clear about what I wanted. I wrote down the steps I should take in getting the truth from Eva. I would have to contact her bank first, then I would need that all important conversation with Eva and finally, when it was possible, a visit to England.

"I was so sick of having to use phone boxes that I determined as soon as Father's money came through, I would invest in a phone for my flat. This traipsing over to the phone box was a nuisance and waiting for letters was even worse.

"Eva's bank was not very helpful at first but I told them I was a relative who wanted to give her information about a windfall; some money that was due to her.

"Strange, isn't it that when money is involved, doors are opened. I asked if I could write a letter to her that could be forwarded on and they agreed. The bank manager stressed that he couldn't give Mrs Goldman any advice about whether or not to reply but he would be able to give her advice about investing the money.

"I smiled to myself at that. The conversation we would have wouldn't be about a windfall. It was going to be a bombshell.

"It wasn't long before she wrote to me. I had made my letter to her vaguely threatening so that she would feel insecure and I'm sure that's why she agreed to let me call her.

"We arranged a day and time. There was no reason to think that you would be in the house with her and I'm sure she agreed a time when she knew she would be alone.

"Before I spoke to her, I asked myself what outcome I wanted from the conversation. Did I want her to start 'supporting' me the way she had supported Father or did I want revenge, where she would be denounced as a baby snatcher and the whole world would know that you are a

German, not a Jew? How damaging this would be for the Jewish community in England." For a moment there was a cold, calculating look in Hans's steely blue eyes.

"Money would have been good but revenge was going to be better. I knew that the key to this was the letter my mother had written. I had to have that letter. I needed to see if it was clear that Eva should have returned my twin to his own family after the war.

"I had to go to England and talk to Eva face to face. Thanks to father's money, I would be able to do it." He looked again at Sam. "Of course, I suppose that half of that money belongs to you," he added sarcastically, "but we can talk about that later." Sam shook his head vehemently. He didn't want anything to do with money from Ernst Hoffman.

"People didn't really believe that the Berlin Wall would come down. Most of us in East Berlin were waiting to see what would happen. There were constant meetings between politicians but, to my mind, when it actually happened it was an anti climax. It was November – the ninth of November to be precise."

"Ninth November," exclaimed Sam. "Ninth November is the anniversary of Kristallnacht."

"Ah, Kristallnacht," repeated Hans. "What good Germans hoped would be the beginning of the end of all Jews. However, that was over fifty years ago and nothing to do with what is happening now.

"So! The night the Wall came down men and women were out in the streets and there was singing and dancing. People were hitting the wall with hammers, trying to get a bit of stone to keep as a souvenir.

"At midnight, an announcement was made, telling everyone that the crossing was open to all. There was a general outpouring of East Germans crossing into the West. Some could remember when Germany was all one country but the majority were young people who had lived under the shadow of the Wall all their lives.

"I would like to say I was celebrating with all the rest of the revellers but the truth is that I was asleep in bed. I had been to work and had a hard day.

"No-one knew exactly when the Wall would come down. There was no timetable of when it was to be demolished, otherwise I would have stayed awake. In fact, the Wall came down because of a mistake. Instead of giving a date in the future, the minister at the press conference said the Wall could come down immediately. I think there was total mayhem but it didn't affect me.

"As it was, I woke up to a new world. I started to go to work but several people stopped me on the way. They were going into the West to see what it was like. Many people wanted to go to McDonald's for a hamburger or go to the smart shops to spend the money that was promised to everyone from the East who crossed into the West.

"There had been a steady stream of people crossing since midnight. They all wanted to see the lights and the big shops.

"Guards on duty at all twelve checkpoints were just letting everyone through and handing out bananas and coffee. I joined the line and slowly walked through Checkpoint Charlie. You will have heard of that, I think?" he asked with a question in his voice and Sam and Helen nodded.

"I took a paper cup of coffee from someone and it was the best coffee I had ever tasted. I forgot about work and I forgot about everything for a few hours. I sat in one of the smart cafés. Actually, not far from the hotel where you were staying, Sam. I enjoyed my first taste of real freedom as well as my first taste of real coffee. The cafés stayed open all night, of course, to cope with all the new visitors.

"Of course we East Berliners looked very different to the smart West Berliners. Our clothes were different, our hair cuts were different and our demeanour was different. The Westerners were free and easy and those of us from the East still looked over our shoulders before we spoke." He looked sharply at Eva, "I saw by your face when I met you in the tea room that you thought I looked strange. I think you thought my clothes were peculiar. I think you forgot I was from the East". Eva looked away, because Hans was telling the truth. She had thought he looked odd when she'd first met him. "Go on," she said. "I want to hear the rest." Hans stood up and walked to the door. "I need to use your bathroom," he said and Sam told him where to go.

There was absolute silence while they waited for his return. Eva was slumped in her chair and Sam was nervously tapping his fingers on the table. Helen looked weary and rested her head briefly on her hands, sitting upright when Hans came back in the room. He sat down and started again.

"I walked around the city, breathing in the scents of cigar smoke and perfume coming out of the doors of bars and clubs. People stopped me and smiled and welcomed me. It was so strange but I smiled back.

"I was happy to be there because I felt that now this world could be mine. I knew that first I needed to sort out money and a passport, ready for my visit to England.

"I crossed back into the East a bit reluctantly and returned to my flat. It hadn't changed but I had. I now had a purpose.

"I am a great list maker, Sam. I think I am like most Germans – organised and methodical. I found a pencil and some paper. I made some coffee, which didn't compare with the cup I had enjoyed such a short time ago in the West and I settled down at the table to organise my thoughts.

"I knew I needed a passport, which required a photo and various documents. I searched the drawer in the sideboard till I found what I needed then sat down again.

"I would apply to the telephone company to have a phone installed. I had no idea how long the waiting list for a phone might be so that was a priority. Once I could be called, and didn't have to go to the phone box, I knew I would be able to make arrangements better.

"I had to book an air ticket to London after I'd made an appointment to see Eva. That would be a shock for her, I thought with satisfaction. She would never think I was going to call on her.

"None of this could happen without the money to pay for it and there was no point in trying to hurry the bank up. That might even make it a longer process. I would just have to be patient, hard though it might be. I would keep on going to work until I received that all important letter from the bank, telling me the transfer had gone through.

"The next day after I'd finished work I went to the photographer so I could have a passport picture taken. There were a lot of people waiting. They all had the same idea. Now the Wall was down, it seemed that every East Berliner wanted to travel.

"I didn't mind waiting because I knew that it would be a while before I had enough money to book an air ticket. The photo was just the first step in a long journey.

"I found it difficult to concentrate on work. I spent a lot of time thinking of the meeting I would have with Eva, and the other men started to tease me.

'Thinking of your girl, are you Hans?' they asked and I smiled to myself. They took this as proof there was a woman in my life and I didn't disillusion them. There was a woman in my life but not the sort they meant.

"The day my passport arrived was a real Red Letter Day. You know this expression, Sam? I flicked through the pages, all blank and pristine without any stamps. Soon, that would alter and I would put my feet on British soil. I could see my plans working out. I only needed the money before I could book my ticket.

"There was a sense of anti climax when I realised that the money had been transferred. There was no letter, just a large amount in my account when I went to draw my living expenses out. The cashier winked at me.

'Had a windfall?' he enquired. 'Won the lottery? It's all right for some.'

"I didn't answer. I just took the cash and my receipt and went to a café while I thought out my next move. There was a travel bureau opposite and I crossed the street and pushed the door open.

'What can I do to help?' asked the manager.

"I had never been in such a place before. The Reisebureau controlled all domestic travel for German citizens so I wasn't sure if they would be able to do anything for me. I explained that I wanted to go to London.

'Ah, yes,' said the manager. 'Doesn't everyone. You may not be aware but it will be a very expensive trip.'

'That won't be a problem,' I said firmly. 'I can pay now.'

'That won't be necessary,' he responded. 'We'll need to see what's available. Now, when did you want to go?'

"I think I stammered a little. I hadn't thought this through as well as I should. There was no way I could go to London without making sure Eva was there. I would need to phone her to see when would be an acceptable time to go.

'I'll be back,' I told the manager but I didn't miss the look he exchanged with his colleague. I could see they thought I wouldn't be back at all.

"There was a card in the letterbox when I got home. The telephone company would come tomorrow to connect the phone. That would make it so much easier for me so, instead of going straight home, I called in at Drosselmeyer's for a meal.

"Normally, this would be out of my reach but tonight was special. The restaurant was crowded and I was lucky to get a table. I really felt as if my luck had changed."

CHAPTER 38

"The waiter handed me the menu and asked what I would like to drink.

'Just a beer,' I told him and decided I would have the largest, most expensive steak available.

'A good choice, sir,' the waiter said when I asked for a rib eye. 'May I suggest you have it with our special cream sauce?' I wasn't used to such a fancy place but I enjoyed every mouthful.

"I was floating on air when I walked home. I felt ready for anything and I was looking forward to using my own phone, in my own flat to call Eva."

As Hans described his feelings before he went to London, Sam looked at Eva. She was sitting back in her chair with her eyes closed but, obviously, not asleep. Sam felt she was re-living that first contact and it wasn't a pleasant memory.

Hans looked over at her too.

"I could sense you were frightened of what I could do," he said. "I knew that you wouldn't want the story to come out but I was determined to confront you."

"I know," she said faintly. "And I knew it was something I had to do. That's why I agreed to meet you."

"You were scared weren't you," Hans repeated, "and I knew it. Actually, I had a little bit of admiration for you. You were being so brave about a situation which could have altered your life and Sam's too. And it still can," he added. "I need to see what was in that letter."

"All in good time," said Eva and Sam looked sharply at her. Did she really intend to let Hans see the damning contents of the letter Frau Hoffman had written?

"You haven't said when you arrived in England," Sam prompted, "and where you've been staying."

"I've been here a few weeks," said Hans, "with a little detour back to Berlin, as you know."

Sam shook his head. This whole story was getting more and more bizarre.

"So, let me get this clear. You came to England, then you went back to Berlin and now you're back in England again. Why would you do that?"

Hans turned to Eva.

"She will tell you," he said. "Let Eva tell you."

"I don't think I can," she responded. "You must carry on. Finish what you've started."

They all looked at Eva. She was obviously struggling and Helen went to hug her.

"It's ok, Ma," she said. "Hans will go on." Eva looked gratefully at her daughter-in-law. "Won't you, Hans?" Helen repeated, throwing a firm glance at him.

"Yes, I will go on. If Eva can't tell you the rest, I certainly will."

There was a movement at the door and once again Daniel poked his head round.

"Can we come in?" he asked. "You've been talking for hours and you'll only have to do it all over again. We need to know what's going on just as much as you."

It was obvious that Hans was thinking.

"I don't want an audience," he began. "I'm not giving a lecture…" His voice tailed off. Making his mind up swiftly he said, "Okay, but don't interrupt me. I can't think when I am interrupted."

The two youngsters came in and sat either side of their grandmother. They each put an arm round her and she looked gratefully at them, saying,

"Let Hans continue with his story and your father will fill in the rest of the details later."

Hans started again. "You told me to meet you at Fortnum and Mason's. I had heard of it, of course. The big, special shop where your Queen buys her groceries. But not on her own," he said harshly. "I expect she sends some lackey or other."

He looked at Eva. "Did you think going to such a prestigious shop would intimidate me?"

"No, of course not," replied Eva quickly. "I just wanted us to meet in a public place and I thought it would be easy for you to find."

"Mmm," said Hans. "I'm not sure I believe you. Still," and he scratched his ear, "I suppose it was as good a place as any. I looked around for you when I came in to the tea place. Most of the tables were occupied and there were lots of women sitting together, drinking tea." He grimaced. "Always the tea.

"And then I saw you sitting alone. You were dressed very smartly – a navy suit, if I remember, and you had your bag and gloves on the empty chair beside you.

"There was a look of recognition on your face as I walked across the room. I think it was easy for you to work out that it was me! I look the same as Sam but it was more difficult for me to recognise you.

"I had never seen a photograph of you so I had to hope I wasn't making a mistake when I spoke to you. You asked me to sit down and I looked at you. You looked so ordinary that in a way it was difficult for me to accept that you had stolen my brother."

Eva started to interrupt, then thought better of it and let Hans go on.

"We sat there silently for a while. I could see your chest moving up and down as you tried to control your breathing and I was glad you were scared.

"I wanted you to be frightened. I wanted you to think your whole life might come tumbling down like one of those houses children build out of bricks.

"How scared were you, Eva?" he asked. "Are you still scared? You know I have the power to destroy your life." He looked around the room, and there was a deep malevolence in his voice. "I have the power to destroy all your lives."

He stopped for breath and Esther immediately shouted at him.

"You have no right to come here and frighten my grandmother. Stop it. Stop it now."

"Or what?" sneered Hans. "What will you do? What can you do? Go to the police and tell them some cock and bull story? I don't think so. There is nothing you can do."

Esther subsided back on to the settee and passed her grandmother a tissue. She kept her arm around her and waited for Hans to continue.

"Okay, I go on. You knew who I was, of course, but I was very formal. I introduced myself and waited for you to speak but you didn't. You kept silent, looking at me and trembling, until eventually you asked me what I wanted.

"Why had I got in contact, why had I travelled to England and so on? It was so strange for me. I had to think before I answered because it seemed crazy that you should ask those questions, Eva. Were you really unaware of why I was in England or were you just in denial? I couldn't work it out.

"So I told you briefly that I was in England to find my twin brother who had been stolen at the end of the war and that I thought...no, I knew, that you were the thief.

"Your eyes were wet with tears when you looked at me. You didn't try to deny that you knew what I was talking about.

'I did not steal your brother,' you said. 'But, yes, he is my son. Your mother gave him to me and there is no doubt in my mind that I saved his life. If it wasn't for me, he would have died with the other children.'

"And then you told me all about your wonderful son, and how you had left Germany, etc, etc. It was so boring. I wasn't in the least bit interested in hearing your explanation of why and how you had kept Otto."

Daniel and Esther looked at each other but Eva swiftly motioned to them to be quiet, murmuring,

"Later, later," and they subsided back on to the settee.

"I asked you for the letter and again you told me you didn't have it. I didn't believe you. I knew, of course, you would have put that letter somewhere for safe keeping. Was it possible that you had given it to Otto?

"It crossed my mind that he knew all about his origins and I was desperate to find out. I hadn't travelled all the way from Berlin to find that there was no story at all. I asked if you had given the letter to Sam.

'Let's not bring Sam into this,' you said and I felt then that there was a good chance that Sam was in the dark. And then, you made one very big mistake.

"You told me that Sam was in Berlin."

Helen gasped, and Sam looked bemused. He started to speak and then thought better of it. Hans looked at them all.

"Ironic, wasn't it. Sam was in Berlin and I was in England. Your pride in him got the better of you and you told me he was there as a candidate for the job of Chief Rabbi. I nodded as if I approved. You were so upset and confused that you had no idea I was already planning my next move.

"I thanked you and apologised for disturbing you and then I shook your hand and left you there, drinking your tea and trying to pull yourself together."

"Oh, Ma," said Sam. "Now I understand why you didn't want me to go to Berlin. I thought it was because you had bad memories after the war but it was more than that, wasn't it. You didn't want Hans to find me. Poor Ma. How you have suffered."

Eva's tears fell unchecked and Esther and Daniel tightened their arms about her. All eyes were on Hans.

"It was easy to get the date on my air ticket changed and fly home and it was easy to find out where you were staying, Sam."

Sam looked at Hans with a questioning look on his face.

"Oh, yes," said Hans. "You forget that East Berlin was a police state before the Wall came down. I have many friends who were able to help and so when I got home I called one and asked if he could find out where a certain Rabbi Sam Goldman was staying.

"We don't get many rabbis coming to Berlin even now so you were easy to find. I even found out what flight you were on. I was already in the hotel when you arrived.

"I was sitting in the coffee shop waiting and, once I heard the concierge tell you what room you were in, it was easy for me to take the lift before you and go up to the third floor. Then I pushed the envelope under your door and waited for you to come to the café.

"When I realised you weren't coming, I rang your room. I could hear the hesitancy in your voice but when I said I would come to you, you soon decided to come downstairs. It's amazing what a little threat will do," he added.

"For me, meeting you was a momentous occasion. I knew you were my twin and I watched your face curiously to see if you had any idea who I was. You seemed not to but I had to make sure.

"The only way I could get you interested was to tell you to talk to Eva. I wanted you to know that she is the key to this whole damn puzzle.

"My friend in the hotel told me you had gone out so I was able to ask him to get into your room and search your bags. I told him what I was looking for but he couldn't find anything like the letter from our real mother. Only the details of your appointment with the rabbis."

Sam interrupted.

"I thought someone had been through my things and then I decided I was over reacting. So it was you – or at least you organised it."

Hans went on.

"I followed you out of the hotel and I kept watch over where you went but it was all totally boring. I think you just wanted to be a tourist. Am I right?"

Sam nodded.

"I wasn't sure if I would ever go back to Berlin so a walk around seemed like a good idea."

"You surprised me, Sam. I wasn't expecting you to fly back to England immediately but, thanks to my friend in the hotel, I managed to get a ticket on the same flight. I wanted to see what you were going to do. I didn't have to follow you, as I already had your address…"

"You had my address…?"

"From my friend at the hotel."

"I see," said Sam. "You really do have friends in high places."

"I watched you take a taxi and go home and I could imagine what was going to happen next. Your whole life was about to change."

"So now it's time you gave me the letter. Whoever has it must give it to me, and then we can decide what to do. There is no doubt in my mind that Eva should have made some attempt to find your birth family and there is certainly a problem about how you were raised.

"You might think you are Jewish – you might feel you are Jewish but we all know you are not."

No-one in the room moved. The air hung heavy and it was hard to breathe. Eva broke the spell.

"What are your intentions?" she asked Hans. "Do you want money like the Commandant? Do you want us to buy your silence? What? What?" She dissolved into tears, looking piteously at the man who was a mirror image of Sam. "Or do you want to go to the press and destroy Sam's life?"

"Ah. So many choices," Hans gloated. "So many decisions. Of course, no-one will blame Sam. That is, if they believe he was unaware of what you'd done."

"Of course he was unaware…"

"Well, we only have your word for that," Hans spat. "We don't know for sure."

"But it's true," Eva wailed. "Until I told him, he knew nothing."

"I'm curious, Sam. Did you not feel something when we met in the hotel café?"

"I felt uneasy, that's all, and there was something about you. I couldn't put my finger on it. There was just something about you."

"Well, you certainly made a quick decision to ask your 'mother' after I told you to, so something must have sunk in."

"It was the whole idea that I was in a situation where something might affect my candidacy as Chief Rabbi. In my wildest dreams I couldn't imagine anything like this. In fact, I still can't.

"Do you know something, Hans. Ma has never spoken about her time in the camp or even much about living in Palestine. It took you to make her talk, and for that I thank you."

"What is it with you people," Hans shouted. "I tell you the most awful things about your mother. As a result she re-lives her time in a concentration camp and you thank me."

"Without me, your life would have gone on as before. How can you sit there and thank me? I need to get away from you all. I need to go back to where I'm staying but don't worry. I will call you and we will pick this up where we left off."

He got up swiftly and moved to the door.

"I will find my own way out. You all have much to talk about." He turned to look at Eva. "You have to take the blame for this mess, you know. You are the one who has to think most about what should happen next."

They heard the click of the front door and sat there, stunned. And then they heard a distant crash and a commotion in the street.

CHAPTER 39

Daniel was the first to move.

"Don't come out, Granny," he shouted. "Please stay indoors," but Eva pushed her way through the small crowd that had collected in front of her house.

"I'm a doctor," she said. "Let me see what has happened." The crowd parted to let her through and she saw a body lying in the road. A body wearing the distinctive plaid jacket Hans had been wearing as he left the house. She moved swiftly to where he was lying in the road.

Picking up his wrist, she called out.

"Someone ring for an ambulance, and Esther, could you get my medical bag, please? It's in my bedroom."

Esther turned and ran into the house, emerging a few moments later with Eva's well worn leather bag. A couple of men moved forwards, intending to move Hans but Eva said sharply,

"Please don't move him. I need to assess what the damage is first," and they stood back immediately at the note of authority in her voice.

She ran her hands swiftly over him, noting his shallow breathing and the widening pool of blood appearing from under his skull.

"Where's that ambulance?" she asked worriedly, just as the siren heralded its arrival.

"Do you know his name?" asked one of the ambulance men. "Yes, it's Hans Hoffman. He is a visitor from Germany."

"It's all over now," said the driver, shepherding people back on to the pavement. "You need to get off the road before there's another accident. Are you the driver of the car which hit this man?" he asked.

A young woman was sitting on the kerb and someone had wrapped a blanket around her. She was shivering, but with shock not cold.

"Yes, I er," she stammered. "He came out of nowhere. I wasn't going fast. He just stepped in front of the car. It wasn't my fault. Truly, it wasn't my fault. There was nothing I could do," and she burst into tears.

"Has someone called the police?" a voice from the back called. "Yes, I called it in," said the ambulance driver. "We'll need to get you to hospital, young lady. We'll put you in the ambulance as soon as we've got this young man in." He turned to Eva. "It's Dr Goldman, isn't it? I remember you from your days in the hospital. You may have saved this chap's life by keeping him still. Do you know him? Would you like to come in the ambulance with him?"

Sam stepped forward and immediately took charge of the situation.

"I'll go, Ma. You stay with Daniel and Esther. Helen, you bring the car so I can get home later." He looked at his children.

"Daniel and Esther, you stay here and look after Granny. We'll call from the hospital when we have news."

Eva allowed herself to be led into the house. In truth, she hadn't wanted to go in the ambulance with Hans. She would have the time, now, to tell the story all over again to her grandchildren.

"And so, you see, it really is all my fault," she ended. There had been total silence from the two youngsters, not even a question but when she looked across she could see that Esther was crying and Daniel was trying very hard to subdue tears.

"Poor Granny," said Esther. "What a burden you've carried all your life. How do you feel now?"

"I feel drained. It's been such an awful few days. I thought I might manage to keep this secret to the grave. Now, I don't know what your father will do. I think I have spoiled all his hopes and dreams. There's no way he can become Chief Rabbi now.

"My dears, I am so sorry but you must know that you are safe and secure in your lives. Your parents love you and I'm sure that your father will find a way of resolving the problem. And, whatever happens, you know you are Jewish so no problems there." She smiled weakly and lay back against the soft cushions.

The phone rang, disturbing their thoughts and Esther rushed to answer it.

"So," said Eva, as Esther came back into the room. "How is he?"

"He's alive," said Esther slowly, "but he has a fractured skull and it seems he might have a clot on the brain. Mum and Dad are staying at the hospital until he's out of danger but it's touch and go. They said we should all go to bed and they'll be home when they're home."

Eva stood up.

"You know, I think I could sleep for a week. Will you help me up the stairs, please? I'm still a bit sore from when I fell in the kitchen." They moved together and saw Eva settled.

"I don't know about you but there's no way I could sleep. I need to find something to eat." Daniel grinned.

"Do you never think about anything but your stomach?" replied Esther but she was smiling.

"I'm a growing boy," responded Daniel. "I'll have a look in the fridge."

"Okay, I'm going to put my dressing gown on, then I'll come down," said Esther.

"What do you make of all this?" asked Daniel as Esther came into the kitchen. "Can you believe that Granny kept this a secret all these years?"

"I don't think there's any doubt that Hans was telling the truth," Daniel went on slowly. "It's just hard to take in. There are still so many unanswered questions. And what a chance Granny took, first of all never telling Grandpa and then coming to England as a refugee."

"I expect that was easy enough," said Esther. "It's pretty obvious that a lot of the Jewish refugees that came after the war didn't have proper passports. They probably only had temporary documents. I know that Granny and Grandpa were naturalised pretty soon after they got here."

"When we were kids she did tell us about that. I think she said it cost about ten bob and was the best money she ever spent." They both smiled at the memory. "I should imagine that after that she felt she was safe. She was in a new country, with a new name."

"Mmm," said Esther. "But imagine the strain she was under. I'm surprised she didn't have a nervous breakdown."

"She's made of strong stuff," said Daniel. "I can't imagine her cracking. Not after what happened to her during the war. She keeps a clear head, does our Gran."

There was the sound of a car in the drive and then a key turned in the front door. A weary Sam and Helen came into the sitting room. Daniel and Esther looked at them expectantly.

"We don't know if he's going to pull through. The fracture is severe and they had to operate to remove the clot. He hasn't regained consciousness yet so we were sent home. The hospital will call if there's any change." Sam looked at Esther. "I don't suppose the kettle's on?" he asked.

"No worries, Dad. That's an easy thing to do. You and Mum sit down. You both look exhausted."

"The good thing, though," Helen said, "Is that the young woman who knocked him over isn't going to be charged. One of the neighbours saw what happened and it's obvious that Hans did just step out into the road. It's possible he forgot he was in England and that we drive on the opposite side to the Germans. He was just unlucky that a car came just as he stepped out."

"Right," said Sam. "I'm going to finish this drink and then I'm going to bed. I don't know what's going to happen now but tomorrow is another day."

321

Once in bed, Helen asked Sam,

"What are we going to do?"

"Sleep, I hope," he replied.

"No, I mean, with all this mess."

"What can we do?" asked Sam. "I will have to tell the rabbis what's happened. I'll have to resign my job." He moved restlessly. "Oh, Helen, I don't want to talk about it. Let's leave it till the morning and maybe I'll be able to think straight. At the moment I feel I can't take any more in. I seem to have been saying that over and over but every day there is more for me to try and understand and now... Well, I can't take any more."

Helen wrapped her arms round him and kissed his brow.

"Rest, my darling," she said. "Rest and we'll talk tomorrow," but she was talking to the air, as Sam had slipped straight into a deep sleep, his breathing slow and steady.

She held him for a long time, drawing comfort from his nearness. Eventually, she closed her eyes and lay in the comforting dark while her mind turned over and over the events of the last few days.

She drifted into sleep with her head on Sam's shoulder and it seemed only a few minutes before she was awakened by him saying urgently,

"Wake up. Wake up, Helen. We have to go to the hospital."

"Did they call? What time is it?"

"It's about four o'clock and they didn't call, but I have a strong feeling we should go now."

Helen struggled to process what Sam had said.

"I don't understand. They won't let us in at this time of night."

"Maybe not, and I can't explain it but I have to be with Hans. I need to be there."

Helen threw the covers back and felt for her slippers.

"Give me a minute and I'll be ready," she said. She pulled on the clothes she had flung over the chair the night before and looked for her shoes. They were under the chair and she slipped her feet into them. Sam was already dressed and busy writing a note on a piece of paper.

"I'll leave this next to the kettle," he said, "Then when someone gets up later they'll know where we are."

CHAPTER 40

The early morning air was crisp and clear as they got into the car. Sam set the wipers to clear the condensation and moved off smoothly. The roads were quiet and there was no-one about as they drove towards the hospital.

"Why do you think you have this feeling about getting to the hospital?" asked Helen quietly. "Is it that twin thing I've read about?"

"I don't think so," said Sam, changing gears. "Or maybe it is. I've never had this uneasy feeling before so I don't know why I should have it now."

"Well, you've never had a twin before," said Helen comfortably. "Who knows what kind of feelings that might have brought up."

They were both silent on the rest of the journey and Sam was pleased to see the car park was empty.

"Not many people around, fortunately," he remarked.

The hospital was dimly lit but there were lights shining out of the A & E windows. They pushed their way through the swing doors and went to the counter. The clerk looked up wearily.

"I'm looking for Hans Hoffman," said Sam. "He was admitted yesterday evening after a collision with a car."

"Did the hospital call you?" asked the young woman. "It's the middle of the night, you know. Not exactly visiting time."

"No-one called but I have a feeling that I should be here."

"Are you a relative?" queried the clerk, but before Sam could reply there was a commotion in one of the side wards. She looked towards the source of the noise and then looked again at Sam and Helen.

"Actually, that's the ward Mr Hoffman is in. Something seems to be happening. If you take a seat over there," she pointed to a row of chairs, "I'll let you know what's going on."

They sat, holding hands, until a doctor in a white coat, stethoscope dangling round his neck, came over to them.

He looked carefully at them.

"I'm sorry to be the one who has to tell you this but, sadly, Mr Hoffman passed away a few moments ago." He looked at Sam, taking in the kippah he was wearing. "I think you are a rabbi," he said. "I know things are done differently in the Jewish community so please tell me if there is anything I can do to make things easier for you.

"Will you be organising the funeral? I do know that it should take place as soon as possible," he continued. He looked keenly at Sam. "Or, maybe you are a relative?"

Sam looked at him directly. "You are right that I am a rabbi," he answered, "but Mr Hoffman is not Jewish. He is someone I only met recently," he went on, choosing his words carefully. "As far as I know, he is on his own. He lost his family during the war and his wife died some years ago. He came here from Germany," he paused, thinking how to explain the reason why Hans was in England, and Helen finished the sentence.

"To see us on a business matter," she said succinctly. "We hardly know him."

"How sad," murmured the doctor. "I'm not sure what we do under those circumstances. Someone has to take responsibility." He looked helplessly around. Helen and Sam exchanged glances.

"If it is allowed," Sam began, "we can make the necessary arrangements. Even though his death was an accident, I feel in some way responsible. I should have reminded him that the traffic drives on the other side of the road before he left my home."

"It wasn't your fault. Please don't think it was. Neither was it the fault of the driver of the car. It was an accident, pure and simple. I haven't yet spoken to the coroner but I'm sure he will accept my recommendation on the death certificate that it was, indeed, an accident.

"If he agrees, we will be able to release the body later today. Why don't you go home and get some rest and someone will call you when we have completed the formalities. Will you want to arrange for the body to go back to Germany for burial?"

"At this moment, I don't know but by the time you call I will have clarified what needs to be done. Thank you for everything, Doctor. We appreciate it very much."

Sam shook hands with the doctor and took the bag containing Hans's possessions the nurse handed him. He left the ward, Helen following closely behind.

"We do have a dilemma," she said as they went back out through the swing doors. "How do we arrange to take him back to Germany?"

"I don't know," Sam said wearily. "It's just one thing after another. We have to decide if he needs to go back to Germany. As far as we know there are no relatives but when we get home I'll go through his bag to see if there's any useful information there."

The house was stirring as they went in. Daniel came out to meet them at the door, hair rumpled and face unshaven. He took the bag from Sam and helped Helen to a chair.

"What's happened, Dad? Did Hans get worse?" The look on Sam's face told him all he needed to know. "That somewhat complicates things, doesn't it."

"I suggest we all sit down and work out what to do. I've told the hospital that we'll see to the arrangements. It was a knee jerk response because I haven't thought it through properly. I don't know how to take a body to Germany; I don't know how to organise a funeral in Germany. Actually, I don't know if it's even legal. In fact, there's very little I do know." He looked ruefully around and then added. "Suggestions, please."

"Suggestions for what?" asked Esther, coming into the room. "What's going on?" She listened carefully, as Sam outlined what had happened. "There is one way you could take him back to Germany. If he was cremated, you could take his ashes back."

"Cremation is out of the question," said Sam firmly.

"Why, Dad?" asked Esther. "He wasn't Jewish so we wouldn't be breaking any rules. In fact, we might even be carrying out his wishes."

327

"I don't know," Sam followed through. "It's unlikely that he'll have brought a will with him and even more unlikely that he will have left instructions about what he would like to happen in the event of his death. I need to take some advice on this and the best person to ask is Rabbi Langer."

There was a gasp from Eva. "I can't believe you said that, Sam. You mean you're going to tell him what's been happening?"

"No, Ma. I'm not going to tell him anything about Hans, at least not yet. And you're right, Esther. Cremation would be the best option but I'm a rabbi…I don't know whether I can agree to it or organise it. It's so against all Jewish principles."

"But Hans wasn't Jewish," Daniel reinforced. "If he was cremated, someone could fly back to Berlin with his urn."

"Even so, I'm going to call Rabbi Langer. There are also other things I must sort out with him. Let's have breakfast first, though. I need something inside me before I face the esteemed Rabbi."

They all smiled. Everyone knew that the old rabbi was not a frightening figure in the least. He was Sam's mentor and surrogate uncle. It was unlikely he could refuse his protégée anything.

"Sam, there is one thing I want to tell you. If you decide to do this, I want to come to Berlin with you." Eva brushed tears away from her eyes. "I know I've always said I would never go back to Germany but I am getting older," she raised her hand. "Yes, I am getting older. This accident of Hans has made me realise that whatever happens, he will get a funeral. His father had a funeral. His grandparents are buried somewhere.

"Sadly, my family has no gravestones. There is nowhere I can lay a stone in their memory. The time has come for me to face my demons and put this right. If you can somehow organise this for Hans, I will come with you."

"Are you sure, Ma? Are you really sure? You have always been so adamant you would never go back."

"Some of that was because I thought I might see someone who would recognise me; some, of course, is because of what happened to me and your father." She faced Sam. "And then, again, you have a look of the Commandant about you. I could never have gone back before, just in case." Her voice tailed off. "It seems that now is the right time."

Helen busied herself about the kitchen as Sam went into the hall to telephone Berlin. He could hear the faint sound of her washing the dishes as he waited for the phone to be answered. He was relieved when Rabbi Langer answered the phone himself.

"Ah, Sam, I was wondering when I would hear from you. Have you decided when you will come back for your interview?"

"Not exactly," Sam began. "It's a bit more complicated," and he outlined the problem.

"It's quite clear, Sam," said Rabbi Langer thoughtfully. "You cannot officiate at a non Jewish funeral. You know that, but there is no reason why this man, whoever he is, can't have a burial in the tradition of his own religion. You say he is a Christian?"

"As far as I know. He certainly isn't Jewish, that I do know."

"Well, Sam," responded Rabbi Langer. "If you are sure, or as sure as you can be that he has no relatives, it would be a mitzvah to help this stranger in our land. I think the funeral directors we use for our own burials might be able to do something. You should call them and see what they suggest. There will be a cost, Sam. Are you prepared for this?"

"The cost won't be a problem. I feel strongly I should do something and I thank you for your advice. Sensible and kindly as ever."

"And now, Sam, what about your interview? From what I've worked out, there is something major going on in your life." He paused and took a deep breath before continuing. "Even so, you can't keep on putting it off. I should imagine that this funeral will take a couple of days to organise and then you will come to Berlin?" There was a questioning tone to his voice.

"I will give you one more week, and then I cannot delay this any longer. Do you understand, Sam? I've done as much for you as I can. Don't let me down."

Sam noticed how frail Rabbi Langer's voice was and he hurriedly said,

"Let me get the funeral over first, please, then I'll call you. You have my word that I will be at the interview. I know how important it is and I'm grateful for the postponement." There was a catch in his throat as he repeated, "Don't worry, I will be there."

CHAPTER 41

"While we're waiting for the hospital to call, I think we all need to sit down and talk over what's been happening," Sam began. "I don't know about any of you," he said, looking round the table, "but this is an incredible story and it's difficult to process," he added.

"It's knowing where to start," Esther said gently. "I think we're up to speed with what Hans said, unless you've found out some more, Dad."

"No, I think we got to the end of it before the accident; it's how we move forward, now."

"Let me speak first, then," said Helen. "It seems to me that this could have affected our marriage but I can assure you all that it won't. Dad and I are married, in civil law anyway. We'll need to check about the rest but, as far as I'm concerned, we are still Rabbi & Rebbitzin Goldman." She moved over to put her arms round Eva.

"Whatever happened in the past, happened! It doesn't affect how I feel about you and it certainly doesn't affect how I feel about Sam."

Eva looked at her with watery eyes.

"I think I have spoiled everything but I didn't mean to. Right from the first moment I saw Sam I loved him. I know I should have done something after the war to see if he had any family left but I'd almost forgotten about it. Or maybe I just didn't want to remember." She looked bleakly into the distance.

"I can't deny it's been a shock, Ma," Sam responded, "but when I look back I know I can't have had a better childhood and better parents." Eva wiped her eyes.

"I seem to have done nothing but cry," she said weakly.

"And you're not a cryer," chipped in Daniel. "In fact, I don't think I've ever seen you shed a tear."

"You've always said that what can't be cured must be endured," Esther tried to make her grandmother smile, but this caused Eva to cry even more.

"We'll have to tell Rachel and Ivor...and then your parents, Helen. What will they think of me?" she asked through her tears.

"Ma, they'll think what we do. That you're an incredibly brave woman who did her very best and saved my life. Rachel and Ivor don't get back for another ten days. Let's wait until then before we tell them, and let's wait before we tell your parents, Helen. They don't need to know anything yet."

The phone rang and Helen went to answer it. "It's the hospital for you, Sam," she said, handing the receiver to him.

Sam cleared his throat before he spoke. "Rabbi Goldman here. What news do you have for me?"

The others listened to his replies. "Yes. Yes, I see. Of course. I'll make the call and then I'll get back to you. Thank you. You've been most helpful."

He sat down again.

"At least the formalities have been dealt with. The hospital will release the body as soon as I tell them which funeral director I've contacted. After that, it's out of their hands and we can make whatever arrangements we like.

"The doctor who pronounced Hans dead and issued the death certificate said the coroner is very happy to accept his recommendation that a post mortem is not needed. I think that's unusual but I wasn't going to argue. All that remains now is for me to give Stuart at the funeral home a ring."

Sam spoke briefly and succinctly to Stuart, explaining that he would like to organise a cremation for a German visitor and would pay the bill but, as the deceased wasn't Jewish, he wasn't going to be able to lead the service. He hoped that the funeral home could find a suitable person to do whatever was necessary.

"That's not a problem for them," Sam told his family. "They do organise funerals for people who don't have any particular religion. He was a bit surprised that I was involved though.

"He's used to me officiating at Jewish funerals but he wasn't overly curious. The one advantage is that he can do it the day after tomorrow. He's going to ring the hospital and make arrangements to collect Hans. That will give me time to book flights for you and me to go to Berlin, Ma."

"What do you mean, Dad? Granny's going to Germany? After all she's said about never going back. How is this happening?" Esther looked shocked.

Eva explained. She ended up by saying,

"And so you see, now that Hans and the Commandant are both dead, I don't need to feel frightened any more. I don't think I will ever be happy about going to Germany because it holds a lot of bad memories for me but I won't fear a hand on my shoulder.

"I want to go back to my childhood village. I want to see if there is anyone left there who knew me. I want to see my old home again and I want to put up some kind of memorial to my family. So many Jewish families like mine were wiped out completely and I feel it is my responsibility that the name of Frankenberg is remembered."

"If that's the case, and I agree with you Granny that it would be fitting to do something for your parents and brother and sisters, then I think we should all go. You shouldn't be on your own for this and you do still have a family, just not the one that was murdered during the war."

Daniel saw the handkerchief go back to Eva's eyes.

"Come on, now. No more tears, Granny. You'll make a puddle on the floor."

Reluctantly, Eva smiled. This had been a favourite saying of hers when the children were small.

"So, you would all do this for me. Thank you," she said simply. "It would mean so much to have you there with me."

"We have a lot to do in a very short time. Will the travel agents still be open?" Sam answered himself. "Yes, I think so. Esther will you ring them and book our seats on the first available flight in three days time.

"Daniel, will you go next door please and see if they will have Tess for a few days. You don't have to go into much detail. Just say that we have to make a quick trip abroad but we'll be back as soon as we can.

"Helen, will you take Ma home so she can get a few things together. It would be better if we were all in the same house before we go. We need each other's support, I think."

Eva nodded.

"I would like that. Shall we go now?" She was putting on her coat and pulling on her gloves as she spoke.

The phone rang again and Sam answered it.

"Thanks for getting back so quickly, Stuart. Is everything sorted out? The day after tomorrow at ten in the morning. Good. And who will do the service? Ah, yes, I know him. I think he's the minister at St Oswald's church. Does he understand that we don't know if Hans had any religion? That's fine, then."

He paused, listening to Stuart.

"I don't really know much about him," he said eventually. "He was here to see me on a matter of business. The only thing I knew about him was that he was a construction worker and he was born in 1944. He did tell me he had wanted to be a veterinarian but I don't know if that's useful for the minister. Okay, then. I'll leave it to you. Thanks, Stuart."

Daniel looked across at his father. "You've been very clever giving out the jobs, Dad. What are you going to do?"

"I'm going to go through Hans's things to see if I can find out any more about him. An address in Germany would be useful, as well as the address where he was staying in England."

The family scattered, each doing their allotted task and Sam sat down at the kitchen table. He opened the plastic bag the hospital had given him. Hans's passport was there and he flicked through it. It gave his birth date – not the same as his but then Eva wouldn't know the exact date when the twins were born.

There was a key with a large fob on it. It had a telephone number and a hostel name on it; probably where Hans had been staying in England. There was a small address book, with pitifully few entries and a letter with an address on in Berlin.

Sam opened it and saw it was a bank statement. There was a surprisingly large amount in the account. Good, he thought. That means the address on the envelope is probably his flat.

The hostel answered at the first ring and Sam introduced himself, explaining that Hans had met with a fatal accident and asking when it would be convenient for him to collect his things.

"Any time is okay," said the manager. "We are open twenty-four hours a day. Please remember to bring the key with you, though. We lose a lot of keys when people forget to return them."

Sam asked if anyone would want to come to the funeral and the manager said he thought it was extremely unlikely. Hans hadn't made any friends while he was staying there. The manager said he would try and come but from the tone of his voice, Sam knew that, sadly, it was unlikely.

Helen and Eva came back just as Sam was putting the receiver down.

"We need to collect the rest of Hans's things," he said. "I've had a look through his bag but there's nothing of any interest, except his birth date. Ma, I have to tell you that I am a month older than I thought I was. Oh, it's okay. It just accounts for the grey hairs," and he laughed. Eva smiled wanly.

"You sound as if you've been busy. Is everything done, now?" asked Helen.

"I think so," said Sam. "I'm going over to the hostel to get the rest of Hans's stuff, and Esther's getting the air tickets." He looked up as Esther came into the room. "How did you get on?"

"All done, Dad. I have five seats on the early afternoon flight and I managed to book some rooms at the hotel in Granny's village." She turned to Eva. "I remember you said once that there was a little inn on the mountain. It's still there, Granny, and it has just three rooms so I booked them all. You and I can share, if that's all right with you, and Mum and Dad and Daniel can have the other two."

Eva's hand went to her throat. "Things are happening so fast," she said. "But I suppose they have to. I'm ready to go so let's have a quiet time until the funeral."

Sam turned to her, a little surprised. "Are you really going to the funeral?" he asked. "I didn't think you would want to."

"I think we should all go," Eva said firmly. "Hans has no-one else to be there. No family, nothing. And however troubled he was in life, he needs someone with him on this last journey. We are the best he has."

The morning of the funeral dawned bright. The sun shone and when they arrived at the crematorium, the minister was waiting for them. "I'm sorry to see you under such circumstances," he said. "Did you know Mr Hoffman well?"

"Not exactly," replied Sam. "He was visiting us on a business matter but we know he has no family so we thought this was the least we could do for him. I have to go to Berlin in a couple of days so I'll take his ashes back and put them with his grandparents."

"I see," said the minister thoughtfully. "You've taken a lot upon yourself but I would expect nothing less from you," he added with a smile. "Your kindness is well known in the area."

"I don't like cremations," muttered Eva to Daniel. "But, under the circumstances…" Her voice tailed off.

They were all outside in the fresh air, waiting for the funeral director to talk to them, to give final instructions for the collection of Hans's ashes.

"Under different circumstances, you might have to wait a few days to collect them," he said, "but I understand you are flying to Berlin tomorrow." Sam nodded. "In that case, if you call early in the morning, I will have everything ready for you," and with that he shook everyone's hand and they found themselves out on the street.

The minister came over to them, suggesting some tea or coffee but they all shook their heads. "No," said Helen, "but thank you. We need to get home and get organised for our flight tomorrow."

"And I have to get over to the hostel to collect Hans's things. We need to take them back with us. Thank you for what you have done today. Your words were very moving."

During the drive back home there was a stillness in the car. Each person was lost in their own thoughts. When Sam pulled onto the drive it brought them back to reality.

"I'm going straight over to the hostel," Sam said. "The rest of you make sure you have everything you need for tomorrow. Do you know where your passports are? for example," he said with a smile. "I'll be as quick as I can."

CHAPTER 42

The hostel was a sad place. Set back from a busy road, the paint was peeling from round the window frames and the net curtains looked as if they could do with a good wash. The door was open and there was a small lobby inside. A middle aged man, wearing a plastic name badge pinned onto a tired jumper, sat behind the shabby counter.

Sam introduced himself and the man acknowledged him.

"I have Mr Hoffman's bag here for you," he said, passing Sam a small suitcase. "His bill was paid in advance but I can't refund anything owing as he left without warning. Do you have the hostel key?"

Silently Sam gave it to him and left the building, glad to be out in the open air again, away from the smell of stale cabbage and cheap disinfectant.

There seemed little in the bag; it was no weight at all so Sam assumed it held only a change of clothes. He put it down on the hall floor and went in search of something to eat. Daniel followed him into the kitchen, carrying the bag. "Aren't you curious, Dad? There might be something important or at least interesting inside."

"So, open it. Put it on the table and let's see what's inside."

Esther pulled out clothes; a couple of shirts, some socks and underwear and then, at the very bottom a packet of envelopes and a folder of photographs. Daniel picked one at random.

"Listen to this," he said, and Sam could hear the disgust in his voice.

"Actually, Daniel, I don't want to read any of the letters. I suspect they are full of hatred and it would be better if we didn't know what's in them."

"But, Dad, they were written by the Commandant."

"I don't care if they were written by Adolf Hitler himself. I'm not interested. Put them back."

"What about the photographs, then? They seem to be of the Commandant with children."

"Yes, I'll look at them. Pass them over, please," and he spread them over the table. This was the first time he'd seen any photos of his birth parents and, as he looked at them, he realised that he had no attachment, no feelings for them at all.

His love for Eva and Friedrich was all that mattered to him and he felt comfortable now, knowing that his parents were the best in the world. Despite the accident of his birth, he truly was the son of Eva and Friedrich Goldman.

He sighed as he accepted there was much to do to ratify that but he knew he could do it, however long it would take.

"Do you want to see these, Ma?" he asked, as Eva came over to see what he was doing. She picked up a picture of the two young children.

"This is Dietrich and this Giselle. They were such good children. How could anyone do this to them? How could any parent take the lives of their own child? I don't think I want to see any more. It's too upsetting".

She put the pictures back down on the table and sat down, closing her eyes. Sam slid the pictures back into the wallet and urged Eva to get some rest.

Despite the reason for going to Berlin, Daniel and Esther were excited. They chattered together in the back of the big taxi until Sam, looking at Eva, realised that the noise was affecting her. She was obviously stressed. No wonder; her first visit back to a country and people who had tried to destroy her. Sam asked her gently how she was feeling and she made a face at him.

"It will take strength to go back," she answered, "but the worst bit will be getting there."

"Getting there?" enquired Sam. "I'm not sure what you mean, Ma."

"It's the plane. I've never been on one before and I'm very scared."

Sam groaned.

"Ma, why didn't you tell me before? I never knew you were frightened of flying."

"Why would you? Whenever Pa and I went abroad we took the car. We went on a ferry and then drove to wherever we wanted to be."

Sam smiled, remembering the raucous times he and Rachel had shared as they drove through the French countryside. All those holidays and he'd never once considered why they had always driven.

"I thought you liked to take the car so we could get around easier," he offered.

"To some extent, darling, but also because I like to keep my toes firmly on the ground and not thousands of feet up in the air."

"Don't worry, Granny, getting on a plane is just like getting on a bus." Daniel turned to his sister. "We'll look after you, won't we Essy? You'll be fine."

Eva shuddered and closed her eyes again. She would let them know how she felt about flying when they arrived in Berlin.

It was a fairly slow time in the airport, and for that Sam was grateful. It didn't take long for them to be checked in. They were directed to the waiting area and sat until their flight was called. Eva gave a visible start. Sam helped her up and she was grateful for Helen's hand under her elbow.

Hopefully, there would be plenty of assistance for Eva if the plane had empty seats. Looking around, he could see it was only about half full.

"I'll sit with Ma," he said, "and you three can sit together. Put your seat belt on, Ma." Eva's fingers trembled until Sam took over, buckling her in securely.

The calm voice of the stewardess came over the loudspeaker and Eva clung on to the seat in front of her, listening avidly, as the safety procedure was outlined. Her face was grey with worry and she didn't even relax when the plane was in the air.

The drinks trolley was being pushed down the aisle, and she gratefully accepted a brandy. "There's hardly time for anything to eat. It's a short flight but we should get a snack," Sam said. "I don't think I'll be eating anything," Eva responded. "I don't think I could swallow!"

"Okay, Ma. Tell me about what you want to do when we get to Berlin. I've organised a hire car and it should be waiting for us at the airport. A big car, so we can all be comfortable. Esther's sorted out the hotel so we could drive straight there and settle in. Did I tell you that I've found Hans's address? I also found a receipt in his wallet for his grandmother's funeral so I have the address of the cemetery. You might prefer to go there first so we can scatter his ashes."

"Yes, I think that would be better. Is it much of a detour? because I am getting tired."

"Not too far. If we get that out of the way we'll be able to move on to the hotel quickly."

Once again, Eva held on to Sam's hand tightly as the plane's altitude altered. His knuckles were white by the time they landed and he rubbed his fingers gently.

"You've got a good grip, Ma," he said, but was relieved to see the colour was coming back into Eva's cheeks.

Getting through customs was easy and quick. The car was waiting at the kerb outside the arrivals hall, and a uniformed driver gave Sam the keys.

"You need to sign here, and here, and then you can be on your way. There's a map in the glove compartment if you plan to drive any distance and the tank is full. We expect it full when you return it," he added with a smile. "And don't forget, sir. We drive on the opposite side of the road to you in England."

Sam shuddered. After what had happened to Hans, he didn't think he would forget that piece of advice. He just nodded and loaded the luggage into the boot.

The road stretched ahead. Sam was a good driver so he was soon au fait with the car and he turned out of the airport onto the autobahn, towards the cemetery. It was a sober group who got out of the car and walked to the office to enquire where the Hoffman family grave was. Sam explained that they had an urn containing Hans's ashes and asked if it would be possible to place them on the grave of his grandparents.

"Even better," said the administrator, "I can arrange for them to be buried there. If you would like to do that, you can leave them with me and I will organise it. You may wish to be here…"

"Probably not," said Helen. "We didn't really know Mr Hoffman. He died in an accident in England so we have brought his remains. We'll leave the rest of it to you."

"As you wish, madam. Thank you for your kindness in doing that," and they all trouped back to the car.

"I'm glad that's over," said Esther. "It's a bit strange. We didn't know Hans but we have this connection."

"I know," said Helen, soothingly, "but it's over now. We can get on with the real reason for our visit." She turned her head to address Eva. "Have you any idea what kind of memorial you would like?"

"Not exactly. Maybe a plaque of some description. I think that could be done fairly quickly. A plaque with the family name on and a short message. And I would like kaddish said. You can do this, Sam," she added.

Sam didn't reply. This quandary again. He was a rabbi but he wasn't a Jew. He was the grandson of the deceased but he wasn't. He said nothing, knowing that he would have to call Rabbi Langer once more for advice.

The car ate up the miles and the others nodded off one by one. Sam pulled up in front of the hotel and spoke gently. "Wake up. We're here and it looks lovely. Well done, Esther."

The bellboy had heard the sound of the car engine and he came out almost before the car was at a standstill, pulling behind him a luggage rack. He loaded all the cases on and pushed it into the foyer.

"Good evening, sir." The receptionist greeted him with a smile. "I think you must be the Goldman family. Am I right? Perhaps one of you would sign the register and we'll get your bags up to your rooms. Dinner is at eight pm and I took the liberty of making a reservation for you. I hope that's all right."

"We're all vegetarians," said Sam very quickly. "We don't eat meat. Will that be a problem?"

"Not at all. We always have a vegetarian option on our menu. I think you will be pleasantly surprised."

Helen took charge. "We can all get sorted and then we'll meet in the restaurant at eight pm. How does that sound?" There were nods and smiles all round. There was a moment of confusion as everyone claimed their bags and then they dispersed, each to their own room. All except Sam, who beckoned to the receptionist.

"Would you have the telephone number of an engraver?" he asked her.

"An engraver, sir? For jewellery?"

"Not exactly. Someone who could engrave a metal plaque and do it quickly."

"Ah. You need to talk to Johannes. He has the shoe repair shop in the village but he also makes discs for the dogs. That sort of thing?"

"Perfect. Do you have the number?"

"You don't need the number," the receptionist replied with a smile. "Johannes will still be in his shop. It's just down the main street. Next to the pharmacy."

CHAPTER 43

In the distance, the sun was hovering over the trees as Sam walked down the village street. There were still a few people about and they looked at him with curiosity. It was obvious that there were not usually many visitors so a newcomer was a matter of interest.

The bell rang melodiously as Sam pushed the door open. It sounded like a cowbell and, when he looked up at it, he saw it was indeed a brass cowbell.

The man behind the counter wiped his hands on his leather apron and asked if he could help. Sam was pleased he could understand, even though the local dialect was a little different. There was a smell of tannin and resin in the air and he could see the equipment for shoe mending and engraving in a corner.

"Could you engrave a plaque quickly for me?"

"How quickly?" asked Johannes.

"Tomorrow?" queried Sam.

"It would depend on how big a plaque and what you wanted on it."

"Not too big. Something to go on the wall of a house, maybe," and he passed over a sheet of paper with the words he and Eva had agreed on.

"Yes, I can do this by tomorrow. It is not so much. Are you a part of the Frankenberg family, then? I was only a child when the Nazis were here but I remember when they took the Frankenbergs away. My father was the mayor and he felt very bad about it."

Sam's ears pricked up. Could Johannes's father be the man who had told the Nazis about Eva and the rest of her family?

"Is your father still alive?" asked Sam hardly daring to hope.

"Not my father. He died several years ago but my mother is still alive. She lives with us. She is in a wheelchair now but her mind is as alert as it ever was."

Sam spoke without thinking.

"Would it be possible to see her? I have my family with me. My mother was a Frankenberg and her father was the village doctor."

Johannes paled but answered,

"I will ask my mother. If she is happy to meet, I will tell you when you collect the plaque," and Sam had to be satisfied with that.

He walked back to the Hotel Prinz, looking around at the street. The road still had the original cobbles, and on either side the half timbered houses leaned gracefully towards each other. The shops had the old style Gothic writing above the doors and there were very few cars parked. It was beautiful and Sam thought it would have been a lovely place to spend your childhood.

There was just time for him to make a phone call and shower and change before dinner and he luxuriated under the stream of hot water. The smell of jasmine permeated the small bathroom and he reached his hand over to the towel rail to grab a monogrammed towel.

The bedroom was large, with two dormer windows looking out over the street and a bed with square fluffy pillows and pristine white duvet covers. The blue drapes framing the windows were pulled back and Helen was sitting at the small table, drinking coffee, and looking down on to the street.

"What a lovely place," she said. "How sad that Eva didn't have the chance to live here after the war. I often wondered why she didn't come back but the last few days explains it all. I can understand now why she didn't want any mention made of the war."

"Time for dinner, I think." Sam proffered his arm and Helen, smiling, took it. "My goodness, Sam," she said. "You are getting chivalrous in your old age. You'll be telling me I look nice, next."

"You always look lovely, my darling. Is that a new dress?"

"Oh, Sam. Only you could ask that when I'm wearing something I've had for five years. Come on, then, or we'll be late."

Daniel, Esther and Eva were already seated and the waitress was just unfurling the starched white napkins onto their knees. The menus were standing to attention on the table and Sam leaned over to take one.

"The concierge was right," he said happily. "There's actually a good vegetarian section." He looked at the choices. "Mushroom soup first, I think, then the pasta."

"And Black Forest cherry cake," said Esther. "We can't be in Germany without tasting it."

"Whatever you like, Esther," Sam said indulgently and then, turning to his mother, he asked gently,

"How do you feel, Ma? Are you managing all right?"

"Managing? Yes that's a good word. I don't know if I'm all right but, if we put a plaque on the wall of our old house, I will feel that my family have not been forgotten.

"Then I will be able to draw a line under everything that's happened and just get on with my life in whatever time I have left. Strangely," she looked around at them all, "I feel a sense of relief now everything's out in the open.

"What did you think of the village?" she asked. "I can see that it's changed a little but not much, I think. Did you see my old house? It was on the corner before the road goes further into the mountain. Right at the very end of the street."

"I didn't go as far as that but what I saw of the village I liked very much. Johannes at the cobblers is going to bring the plaque here in the morning and then we can do what we have to do. I expect new people will be living in your old house so I presume they won't mind what we're planning."

A shadow passed across Eva's face.

"Oh my goodness, I never even thought of that. What happens if they don't want the plaque on their wall?"

"Let's wait until tomorrow and then we can ask Johannes what he thinks. He probably knows everyone in the village. There's something I need to tell you all, though, before tomorrow. I called Rabbi Langer before dinner and I asked him if he would join us and say kaddish."

"Say kaddish," Eva spluttered. "No, please, Sam, that's something you must do. You must say kaddish."

"I can't…"

She interrupted him.

"Of course you can. You're a rabbi and a grandson. Who better?"

"No, it's impossible; how can I do this when I'm not Jewish, therefore not a rabbi? I feel it would be wrong. I would be doing it under false pretences. And that's final, Ma."

There was a stunned silence at the table as the significance of what Sam had said filtered through. No-one had thought in depth about how Sam would be affected deep down. His refusal to say kaddish brought home to them all how serious his situation was.

"Have you said anything to Rabbi Langer?" Eva asked.

"Not yet. I'll do that when I go for the interview. It's the least I can do and I will tell them all at the same time. I asked him if he could come and be with us, and I think he will feel it's an honour to say kaddish."

Eva got up from the table, picking up her bag.

"I can't eat any more. I need to go to bed." Turning to Esther she asked her to be quiet when she came into their shared room. "Please don't disturb me. I feel as if I could sleep for a week."

"That was a bit of a bombshell," Daniel muttered. "Maybe not the most tactful way to tell Gran."

"Maybe so but better she knows Rabbi Langer is coming. She would have got more of a shock if I hadn't told her."

"Your father's right," added Helen. "It's going to be a difficult day for her and it would have been worse for her if he had arrived unannounced." She turned to Sam. "Did he say what time he would get here?"

"Mid afternoon, he thought. I'll sort the plaque out with Johannes in the morning and let Ma see it so she can approve it. Heaven help us all if it's not want she wanted."

There were smiles all round and then they all dispersed to their rooms. Sleep came easily. It had been a long day but they all felt now that the loose ends were being tied.

"I'm sorry to disturb you at breakfast," the young waiter said the next morning, "but you have a visitor. Would you like me to bring him in? It's Johannes Kobler with your plaque."

"Yes, please, and could you bring a cup and saucer for him?"

Sam stood up as Johannes came into the room. He was carrying a parcel wrapped in brown paper and tied with twine, which he placed into Sam's outstretched hand. Sam passed it over to Eva and watched as she unwrapped it.

"Won't you join us for breakfast, Herr Kobler?" Sam said. "We've just started and the buffet is magnificent. Please. Sit down and have some coffee," and he passed over a steaming cup.

"Thank you. Maybe just a little," Johannes said, his hand already reaching out for a warm roll. Esther passed him the cherry jam.

"It's perfect," exclaimed Eva. "It's just what I wanted. You are a craftsman, Herr Kobler. Thank you so much. Please tell me how much I owe you."

Johannes paused, a piece of bread halfway to his mouth. "Eva. It is Eva, isn't it? There will be no charge. It is an honour for me to do this for you. Forgive me but I was there the day you and your family were taken away."

Eva flinched. "You must only have been a small boy," she said.

"Yes, I was about ten, I think, but I can still remember what happened. I was hiding upstairs on the landing when the soldiers brought you all in. I couldn't look properly at you because you were all in your nightclothes and I was...I was...verlegen." He paused, searching for the word.

Eva interrupted. "You were embarrassed," she translated.

"Yes, yes, embarrassed. I was but a small boy and to see ladies in nightgowns was not proper, I think. I heard the shouting and I heard Mama crying. The soldiers had locked her in her room and they told my father they would hurt her if he didn't tell them where the Jews were.

"Father had to tell. You must understand. He had no choice." There were tears on his cheeks.

"Can you ever forgive us?" he asked brokenly. "We didn't know what was going to happen to you. We thought maybe..." his voice faded. "No, that's not true. We had heard what was happening to the Jews. Papa just hoped it would not happen to you. Your father was well respected in the village. He did a lot of good, I know."

Eva put her arm round him as he continued to weep.

"It was not your fault," she said. "And I don't blame your father. He was only protecting his family. If he had refused, you would all have been shot and we would still have been captured."

Johannes took her hand and kissed it.

"Thank you for those words," he said. "Until the day he died, my father kept saying over and over again that he should never have told the soldiers where to find you. He thought all your family had been killed and he died a broken man."

"And your mother?" asked Sam. "You said she was in a wheelchair. What happened? Was it the soldiers?"

"Not exactly. When they let her out of her room, she rushed to my father and tripped. She fell down the stairs and her spine was broken. So not exactly the soldiers but, yes, as a result of what happened that night."

The faces round the table showed their sympathy.

"Ach. Before I go. I spoke to the Meiers who live now in your old house. They have no problem with a plaque on the wall of the house but they wish to speak with you. They have lived there since after the war when they lost their own apartment because of the bombing.

"They thought there was no-one of the family Frankenberg left. Now they know that is not true, they want to compensate you. Will you speak with them?"

"Yes, I will speak with them. Thank you for being a good messenger," and Eva smiled at Johannes who hurriedly finished his roll and shook the crumbs off his napkin.

"I will see you later. At the old house. I think four o'clock would be a good time to do this."

Eva looked surprised. "This is a family affair, Johannes."

Johannes replied carefully. "Yes, I know, but I think also it is a village affair. There are many people who wish to speak with you, to shake your hand and to welcome you back– my mother for example. Please agree to this," and he looked at Sam for support.

"Ma, we've come so far. Let's do this and maybe it will give the villagers and you some peace."

Reluctantly, Eva nodded. "Four o'clock this afternoon," she agreed. "I'll see you then."

CHAPTER 44

Esther and Daniel were intrigued by the old village. It seemed as if time had stood still. It had rained during the night but now the sun was shining. The cobbles were still wet and slippery but they decided to go out and have a look around. They had enjoyed their breakfast so some exercise was a good idea.

The town hall was at one side of the square. The entrance was imposing; tall columns flanking a worn staircase. The windows gleamed in the sunlight and there was a steady stream of people going in and out of the large wooden door. They watched as trestle tables were brought out and chairs placed in rows.

They moved on down the main street, past the coffee shop with the old sign swinging in the light breeze. Tree branches swayed and leaves dropped silently onto the ground. There was a stillness in the air as if the village was waiting for something.

Glancing at his watch, Daniel realised it was well after two o'clock. It was time to get back to the hotel and change out of jeans and sweat shirt into something more appropriate for the occasion.

There were comfortable chairs set out on the balcony and as they approached Daniel and Esther saw Sam in deep conversation.

"He's with Rabbi Langer," Esther said, running lightly up the stairs. She dropped a kiss on the old man's brow and he said, 'Pshaw', wiping it off with his hand but smiling nonetheless.

"And how are you? Your father invited me here because your grandmother is placing a memorial plaque on the wall of her old house. Other than that, the whole thing is a mystery." Looking at Sam he shrugged and added, "I expect you'll tell me when you're ready."

"There's something going on at the town hall," said Daniel. "Possibly a fete day or maybe a wedding. Perhaps we can see later. It might be nice to join in."

Shortly before four o'clock they walked through the village as a group, Eva carrying the plaque. It was eerily quiet. There were no old men sitting at the pavement café. No young wives pushing prams. The shops seemed closed. When they reached the corner they could see why.

There was a huge throng of people standing outside the old Frankenberg house. The crowd parted to let them through and escorted them to a row of chairs at the front. An elderly woman in a wheelchair was sitting at the side. Behind her and holding on to the back of the chair was Johannes. There was a small dais and they invited Eva to stand with Rabbi Langer.

The mayor cleared his throat before he started to speak.

"You have to believe us when we say that the day the Jews left our village was the worst day in our history. We have always been a small community. There are not so many families here and during the war we led simple lives. We didn't define people by their religion but by their actions.

"Your father was the doctor here, and delivered our children and healed our sick. He never spoke ill of anyone and even when he was taken away, he forgave Mayor Kobler.

"Many of us here today will be able to remember when the soldiers came and disturbed our peaceful way of living. Even then, we managed for some time to get along with them." He looked at Eva.

"We are glad you are here and we welcome you back home. We want to join you in the memorial prayer for your family, if you will allow it."

The tears that had been brimming in Eva's eyes, spilled over. She looked at her family and saw that they, too, were crying. Rabbi Langer took over.

"Together we can share in the special prayer that Jews all over the world say to remember the dead." His voice strengthened in the calm air and, when he had finished, he beckoned to Sam to say something.

Choosing his words carefully, Sam spoke.

"I never knew the Frankenberg family, other than my mother, of course. Generations of Jews were lost during the Holocaust and every family has been affected. On behalf of my family, I thank you for today."

He sat down abruptly, unable to continue and listened to the swell of applause.

The mayor spoke again.

"We have organised a meal in the town square for everyone. There are so many people who wish to speak with you. Please join us." And he waited anxiously, while Eva exchanged glances with the others until, eventually, she nodded.

"We would be honoured," she said and walked proudly through the mass of people, leading the villagers following behind her.

For the rest of that day, the Goldmans sat at a long table, talking and sharing anecdotes. Eva told everyone who spoke to them about her friend Mina's death in the camp and they were silent again, reliving that awful time.

The Meiers tried to organise some payment for the house they had taken over but Eva wouldn't think of it. She told them she had everything she needed in England and they were welcome to stay.

"There is one thing, though, Frau Meier," she ventured. "I would like one last look around the house. Could we call to see you in the morning, before we set off for Berlin?"

"Of course you can," responded Frau Meier. "I'll have some of my special apfelstrudel waiting for you," and she smiled comfortably.

Finally, as the shadows lengthened and the sun went down, Eva got up stiffly to go back to the hotel. The cool air couldn't remove the warmth of the welcome she had received. In her bag she had many slips of paper with addresses and phone numbers on.

In her heart of hearts, though, she knew that she wouldn't keep in touch with anyone. The village, beautiful though it was, held no attraction for her. It would only be a reminder of a part of her life she had left behind and people she had lost.

There was only one last loose end for her to tidy up. Something she thought would never happen. In the morning she would walk for the last time through the village and spend some time in her old home.

Rabbi Langer came over to the group.

"I am going to Herr Kobler's house now. He has invited me to stay the night as there is no room here. I may not see you in the morning because I need to leave early but, Sam, I expect you at your interview in the afternoon." He looked at the younger rabbi over the top of his glasses.

"I know what you're going to say. You're going to tell me it's too soon, and you're not properly prepared. I have to tell you that tomorrow is your very last chance. The other candidates are already in Berlin and they have coped with the delays well enough, but it's not fair to them. Please be there and please be on time." Daniel waited for the old rabbi to leave the room before speaking.

"Oof," he said. "That's you told, Dad. You'd better get yourself to that interview on time."

They said their goodnights and drifted off to their beds.

The following morning, the family were walking along the main street when Helen asked her mother-in-law why she wanted to go back to the old house.

"From what you said yesterday, I kind of assumed you'd never go back."

"I don't particularly want to go back but there's one thing left for me to do. I told Sam that my father had buried everything that would have identified us as Jews in the garden." Helen nodded wordlessly.

"I need to see if they're still there. If they are, I will take them home with me." She turned and called out to the others,

"Hurry up. I want to get this over."

She took a sharp breath as they approached the corner. The old house hadn't changed since she was a child. Honey coloured stone, with ivy covering the walls. The front door was painted a soft rose colour and was wide open, welcoming her back.

The Meiers came forward to greet her and to invite her in. She allowed herself to be led into the warm kitchen. There was a sharp smell of apple and cinnamon and an aroma of fresh coffee. Thick pottery mugs and plates were waiting. Frau Meier poured, and the steam rose from the coffee pot. She passed around huge wedges of strudel, liberally covered in cream.

"Sit, please sit," she said and pointed to the chairs.

"What can I show you? Would you like to see around the house? It hasn't changed much over the years. New curtains, I think, and some new pieces of furniture. And maybe the kitchen looks better. We have improved it, yes?"

Eva showed her appreciation of the changes and then, looking through the kitchen window, asked if she could see the garden.

"Of course, of course," said the kindly Frau. "We will come with you."

"Do you have a shovel I could borrow?" asked Eva.

Frau Meier paled and looked fearfully at her husband. "A shovel?" she asked tremulously. "Why would you want a shovel?"

"There is one last thing I need to do before I go back to England. Some time before the Nazis came, my father, Doctor Frankenberg, buried some of our belongings in the garden. I think I will be able to find them, if I have your permission to dig up a little of that beautiful lawn."

The colour came back into Frau Meier's cheeks.

"For one moment," she started and then stopped. "Yes, we have a shovel. It's in the cellar so we will get it for you."

They all trooped outside and Eva looked carefully about her, locating the big tree at the far corner of the garden. She made a bee line for it as the others watched, and then she paced out a line directly at right angles.

"Daniel," she called. "I think here might be the right place. Will you take the shovel and start to dig, please."

They gathered around in a semi circle. It was as if they were exhuming a body, as Daniel carefully removed the clods of earth.

"I can feel something," he called excitedly as he felt the shovel hit something metal. Using his hands, he carefully removed the last bit of earth to reveal a tin box and some oilcloth wrapped parcels.

"That's it," Eva cried out. "That's what Papa buried."

Sam helped Daniel to lift out the box. It was fairly heavy and rattled a little. Then they laid the other parcels on the grass.

"Shall we take them into the house?" asked Frau Meier and busied herself with spreading some sheets of newspaper on the kitchen table.

The box wasn't locked and Eva threw back the lid. They all stood back as she carefully removed all the items inside.

She unwrapped the newspaper from the silver candlesticks and the menorah and laid them out.

There was a blue velvet bag and, when Eva saw that, she paused. "It's my father's tallit bag," she said. "And here, look, our prayer books. They have survived well." She unwrapped one of the parcels. "It's our shabbos cloth. See, here's where Mama spilt wine and the stain never came out. She was so cross with herself about that." Eva smiled at the memory.

"This is what's left of our family, Frau Meier. Your generosity in allowing us to retrieve it is much appreciated."

Daniel and Sam carried everything back to the hotel between them, with Eva clutching the precious tallit bag close to her chest. She was breathing deeply and she looked over at Sam.

"I can still smell my father's cigars," she said. "I had forgotten about that but this has brought it all back. I feel as if my father is near me. Can you understand what I mean?" She looked over at Sam, who nodded.

"Whatever happens now, Sam, I thank you for this. Without coming here I would never have been able to get back this part of my life."

Sam hugged Eva and they smiled and laughed a little. Then Eva asked the burning question.

"What are you going to do about the interview?"

Sam looked directly at her. "I'm going, Ma, and we need to get a move on. Once we're in Berlin, I'll drop you at the café near the shul and you can wait there."

Sam was a good driver and the miles flew by. The emotion of the last few days made them all subdued. Sam, especially, was thoughtful as he went over in his mind what he would say to the interview panel. The traffic into the city was light and he was able to park neatly in the car park of the little café. He looked at his watch.

"Nearly time. I'll leave you here and walk the last bit. I don't suppose I'll be too long," he said with a grimace. Helen put her arms around him and kissed him lightly on his cheek. "You'll do whatever is right, I know," she said.

Daniel shook his hand and Esther hugged him. Eva didn't have any words for him but her eyes said it all. She couldn't bring herself to speak.

CHAPTER 45

Sam waited for the traffic to stop and then crossed the street. There was a low sun, and the vestige of warmth in the air.

He saw the old synagogue ahead, the bricks mellowed by age. It was a miracle that the building had survived not just the desecration on Kristallnacht but the subsequent bombing during the war. There was scaffolding against the façade and workmen milling around. It gave Sam a warm feeling.

The Star of David looked down at him and the wooden door shone with years of polishing. There was an old fashioned bell pull, with a printed notice stuck to it. It told him to ring if the door was locked. He turned the handle and the door swung open.

It was obvious that the synagogue wasn't in full use and he stepped carefully over the debris still lying in the corridor. There was a smell of damp plaster in the air and he could taste it on his tongue. He cleared his throat nervously.

He could hear in the distance, the sound of children reciting the Hebrew alphabet. There was a warm smell of kuchen coming from the kitchen and the happy chatter of women's voices drifted towards him.

A man, wearing a black kippah, approached him,

"Can I help?" he asked.

Sam told him he was looking for the interview room.

"Ah," replied the man. "I suspect you are the elusive Rabbi Goldman. I'm Maurice Levy, the synagogue chairman. Welcome, welcome. Follow me and I'll take you to where you want to be. This old building is like a rabbit warren, and most of it is still in a very unstable state. We are only starting the renovations but, as you can see, we have the most important bit done. We have a room for the children and the kitchen is working. Sort of," he added with a smile.

He led Sam along corridors and up a short flight of stairs. He pointed to a door set back into the wall. "They're in there," he told Sam. "They're waiting for you. Good luck."

Sam knocked at the door and a deep voice called,

"Come."

He stood on the threshold of the room. Everything, and nothing, waited for him.

Rabbi Langer smiled encouragingly at him. The other two rabbis watched dispassionately.

Sam closed the door, and took a deep breath.

GLOSSARY

Aliyah	Making aliyah: emigrating to Israel
Bershert	Destiny
Brit Milah	Circumcision of baby boys at eight days
Bubba	Affectionate term for grandmother
Challah	Traditional plaited Shabbat bread
Challah Cloth	Covering for Challah
Chanukah	Eight day Festival of Lights
Chuppah	Marriage canopy, under which bride and groom stand
Chutzpah	Audacity, cheek
Eshet Chayil	Woman of worth
Get	Jewish divorce
Halacha	Jewish religious law
HaMotzei	The blessing over bread
Kaddish	Prayer said at funerals and also religious services
Kichel	Cookie
Kiddush	Prayer said over wine at the end of services

Kippah	Small, traditional Jewish head covering
Kosher	Foods complying with Jewish law
Kvatter	The person who carries the baby to be circumcised
Latkes	Potato pancakes, traditionally eaten at Chanukah
L'Chaim	A toast: 'To Life'.
Mamzer	Bastard
Mao Tzur	Traditional Chanukah song
Meshugah	Crazy, foolish
Mitzvah	A commandment/good deed
Sandek	Person who hands the baby to the person who is circumcising
Semicha	Ordination to become a rabbi
Shidduch	Matchmaking
Shiva	The seven day mourning period
Shul	Synagogue
Torah	First five books of the Old Testament – the Hebrew Bible

Printed in Great Britain
by Amazon

38751140R00208